NIGHTTIME VISITOR

She awoke to find the room darkened and lit only by the fire and a candle that burned on the dresser. Mr. Markham stood over her, a pillow in hand, and she gasped as he grinned down at her.

"Good evening, Miss Farthington," he said, his voice pleasant. "It occurred to me that you might need another pillow." Katherine stared suspiciously up at him through sleep-drugged eyes.

"Am I dreaming?" she demanded.

His smile deepened. "Do you often encounter me in your dreams, Miss Farthington? Your sweetest dreams, perhaps?"

"Nightmares!" Katherine started, then had to pause to cough as he chuckled. She glared up at him. "You, sir, are the stuff nightmares are made of!"

Charter Books by Judith Nelson

PATIENCE IS A VIRTUE
BEAU GUEST

BEAU GUEST

JUDITH NELSON

CHARTER BOOKS, NEW YORK

BEAU GUEST

A Charter Book/published by arrangement with
the author

PRINTING HISTORY
Charter edition/February 1990

ISBN: 1-55773-306-6

Charter Books are published by The Berkley Publishing Group,
200 Madison Avenue, New York, New York 10016.
The name "CHARTER" and the "C" logo
are trademarks belonging to Charter Communications, Inc.

PRINTED IN THE UNITED STATES OF AMERICA

10 9 8 7 6 5 4 3 2 1

For Mom and Dad,
who taught me their love of reading,
and of laughter.

Chapter One

CHLOE FARTHINGTON, ELEVEN, the youngest of the three daughters of the late Robert and Emily Farthington, had been at her reading for nearly an hour. She was struggling as best she might through the book of exceedingly dry sermons the Vicar Woodsley, who came religiously every Wednesday—and any other day he could manage—for tea with her eldest sister, Elizabeth, had given her upon his last visit.

From time to time she raised despairing eyes toward that sister who sat placidly by the fire. Elizabeth's embroidery hoop was in front of her, and the weak November sunlight filtering through the mullioned windows at her back made it appear that a halo shadowed her golden head. Now aware of her younger sister's movement, Elizabeth looked up and said kindly, "Only a half hour more, my love. Then you may go play."

Chloe sniffed. "I don't know why I have to read something so deucedly dry—" She caught herself up guiltily on the second-to-the-last word, her honey-colored head dipping as she flushed under her sister's serious gaze.

"Perhaps we should say another forty-five minutes, Chloe," Elizabeth suggested, her soft voice reproving, "as a reminder to mind your tongue."

"But *Katherine* says it—" Chloe started in self-defense, saw her sister raise an eyebrow, and subsided.

"Katherine has many virtues." Elizabeth's voice was firm.

"But her command of the king's English is not one of them. Especially when she is angry."

Chloe muttered sotto voce that if Elizabeth had to make her way through the book, she would be a little angry, too. Elizabeth shook her head at the child, trying hard not to smile. A fair young woman, she knew there was much truth in Chloe's argument.

"It was very kind of the Reverend Woodsley to bring you one of his books to read," Elizabeth said. "You wouldn't want to hurt his feelings by not having read any of it the next time he comes to call, would you?"

The hopeful look on her sister's face gave answer to that question. Elizabeth, her lips pressed firmly together to prevent the smile once again starting there, returned her attention to her embroidery hoop, merely saying that in half an hour Chloe might go play. She added, with real nobility of character (for Elizabeth had no desire to gainsay the contents of the reverend's book, either), that her sister might read aloud to her if she liked.

With a heavy sigh Chloe began, and both sisters were more than a little relieved five minutes later when Horton, their elderly butler, entered the comfortably furnished if slightly shabby back sitting room with a letter for Miss Elizabeth. Both he and Chloe looked on expectantly as, with one of her gentle smiles, Elizabeth took the letter from Horton's silver salver and turned it over, studying the handwriting on the envelope.

"Why, it's from Uncle Edward," she said, surprised. "I wonder what—"

She started to break the wax seal then stopped, conscious of her highly interested audience. A kind but dismissive "thank you" to Horton sent him toward the door, and Chloe's attention was diverted by the firm suggestion that she go on with her reading—quietly, this time, to herself. Waiting until the butler had left the room and her sister had, with regret, returned to the sermons, Elizabeth started the letter.

A moment later her shocked "Oh, no!" brought Chloe's head up. Seconds after that the sermons tumbled to the floor as the child rushed to Elizabeth's side, alarmed by her pale color.

"Elizabeth, what is it?" Chloe cried, standing anxiously beside her sister's chair, peering down into her face. "Are you all right? What's wrong?"

For several moments a blank-faced Elizabeth stared at her, eyes wide. Then, to Chloe's dismay, large tears welled out of Elizabeth's full lash-rimmed eyelids, and made their way down her cheeks. Aghast, Chloe took to her heels and fled down the manor house hall, calling, "Katherine! Katherine!" at the top of her voice. When she neared the kitchen a laughing voice answered hers, and her second sister's head appeared around the pantry door, followed shortly by that of Mrs. Goodsley, the housekeeper.

"Whatever is it, Chloe?" Katherine asked, amusement lighting her bright brown eyes, so like the child's own. "You'd think the French were attacking, to hear you come! Do you want Elizabeth to hear you, too? Think of the despair she'll feel if she finds she can't make a lady out of you, either!"

"Now, Miss Katherine," Mrs. Goodsley began, shaking her head at the middle Farthington sister.

She was interrupted by a panting Chloe, who gasped, "But Katherine—it *is* Elizabeth—and she is in—in—" memories of the sermons she'd just labored through filled Chloe's mind, and she stuttered "sore distress!" and gazed up at her sister in fright.

"Sore distress?" Katherine's eyes still were laughing as she smiled down at her small sister. "*Whatever* have you been reading?"

"Reverend Woodsley's book of sermons." Chloe's tone was one of disgust, her concern for her eldest sister for a moment overridden by the recent trial she had suffered. Then she recalled her mission. "But Katherine—you must come—Elizabeth is in the small sitting room—"

"And you want me to make her give over on the reading," Katherine guessed, patting her sister's shoulder. "Well, I'll talk with her about it, my dear, after Mrs. Goodsley and I have finished our inventory. For now, though, you'd best do as Elizabeth says. I'm sure she'd be happier if one of us doesn't grow up to be a heathen!"

"Now, Miss Katherine," Mrs. Goodsley chided again as the two older women turned back toward their duties.

In despair Chloe tugged on her sister's gown. "But Katherine!" she wailed. "You don't understand! Elizabeth is all white, and she's—she's—crying!"

Instantly Chloe had all the attention she might want and rather more as Katherine, her concentration now fully focused on the child, grasped Chloe's shoulders and leaned down to peer directly into her eyes. "What, Chloe?" Katherine asked as Mrs. Goodsley also bent forward to hear.

"Elizabeth got a letter, and then she told Horton to leave and me to go back to my reading, and then she said, 'Oh, no!' and I looked up, and she was all white, and then she started to cry, and I came for you. . . ."

Chloe had run out of breath by this time, but it didn't matter. Katherine, her forehead furrowed, already had released her and was hurrying down the corridor, stopping only to call back, "You said the small sitting room, didn't you, Chloe?"

Chloe nodded, then took to her heels to follow the fleet-footed Katherine. It took her some time to edge her way past the puffing bulk of Mrs. Goodsley, who also was hurrying to Miss Elizabeth's aid, and she arrived at the small sitting room several paces behind her sister. Still frightened, Chloe watched Katherine reach Elizabeth's chair and take their eldest sister into her capable arms, smoothing her sister's soft hair as she comforted, "There, there, Elizabeth! What is this? Chloe tells me you've been crying!"

She tilted her sister's head up, and saw that what Chloe said was true. Not only had Elizabeth been crying, she still was, her eyes drenched with tears that rolled steadily down her cheeks and dropped into her lap.

"Oh, Katherine!" Elizabeth gasped. "Thank goodness you are here!"

"Well, of course I'm here, goose!" Katherine gave her sister another hug as she set about coaxing her out of her tears. "Where else would I be?"

The latter was said in a bracing manner, but it had quite the opposite effect. If anything, the words made Elizabeth's tears fall faster, and she moaned, "Where else, indeed?" in a manner that Mrs. Goodsley, talking later to her good friend Mr. Horton, said she fair thought would break her heart.

"Mrs. Goodsley," Katherine said, turning toward the house-keeper with an expressive roll of her eyes that the house-keeper understood immediately, "would you be so good as to bring us some tea? And, perhaps," she added, spying her younger sister's fearful face that looked as if Chloe, too, might burst into sympathetic tears at any moment, "some of your small cakes. Chloe will help you, I'm sure."

Understanding, the housekeeper put her hands on Chloe's shoulders and led her away despite the young girl's expressed desire to stay with her sisters.

"There, there," Katherine heard Mrs. Goodsley say as the door shut behind them, "your sister Elizabeth has Katherine to help her, but who would I have to help me if you don't come?"

Then the middle Miss Farthington, the most—the neighbors said—*unusual* of the Farthington sisters, set herself to discovering the reason for her normally-placid sister's distress.

"Now, Elizabeth," Katherine said, her voice kind after she had patted her sister's back for several minutes and found herself still no closer to knowing the cause of Elizabeth's pain, "what is all this about? You've scared Chloe dreadfully, and I must admit that you've made me a bit nervous myself. Surely nothing can be this bad—"

"But it is," her sister protested, turning her head into the sanctuary of Katherine's shoulder. "Oh, what are we to do? Where are we to go?"

"Well," Katherine was practical in the face of Elizabeth's hysteria, "we haven't the funds to go anywhere, so there is no use thinking about it. But why we should need to go anywhere—at least right now, although I have hopes of London later—I don't know. And, my love, I'm still as much in the dark as ever! What *is* all this about?"

"It is too hideous." Elizabeth's words were muffled as she left the comfort of Katherine's shoulder to bury her face in her handkerchief. "I can't tell you."

"Well, if it's that hideous, you'd better tell me, hadn't you? Or else how can I do anything about it? Now, Elizabeth." Katherine's voice lost its coaxing note, and took on one of authority. "Tell me. What has caused you this upset?"

Elizabeth raised tragic eyes to her sister's face, and uttered two words. "Uncle Edward."

"Oh." Katherine leaned back a moment to survey her in surprise. "Well, my dear, Uncle Edward is hideous, to be sure, but why that fact should suddenly shake you so badly . . ."

"No, no, no!" With each syllable Elizabeth shook her head, her blonde curls bouncing against her cheeks in a most attractive manner of which she was totally unaware, but which Katherine many times had appreciatively watched affect the neighborhood's young gentlemen in a most amusing manner. "You don't understand!"

"But that's what I've been saying—" Katherine started. Elizabeth applied one last touch of her handkerchief to her still flooding eyes before holding out her left hand toward her sister. Katherine, watching in puzzlement, saw that there was a much-crumpled piece of paper in Elizabeth's extended hand and, remembering Chloe's reference to Elizabeth receiving a letter, took it from her sister. Crossing to the small table by the fireplace, Katherine smoothed the piece of paper and bent forward to read by the light of the fire; outside dusk was settling over the estate. The room had not yet had its candles lit and was growing dim.

Elizabeth watched anxiously as Katherine perused the letter. Like her elder sister, Katherine paled when she mastered its contents, but unlike Elizabeth, Katherine did not burst into tears. Instead, her jaw tightened and her eyes snapped as she read the letter again, and then again, before consigning it to the crackling flames.

"Oh, Katherine—" Elizabeth moaned in dismay, half rising before sinking back into her chair as her sister turned toward her. Katherine's small backbone was straight, and her chin jutted out in determination.

"If I were a man," Katherine started, her small fists balling and unballing at her sides as the words emerged through clenched teeth. "If I were a man, I'd show Uncle Edward and his fine friends—although if I were a man, he wouldn't dare!"

In light of the fire in Katherine's eyes, Elizabeth refrained from noting that since her sister was *not* a man, never had been and never would be, what she would do if she were was of no moment. Instead she fidgeted uneasily as she waited for Katherine to continue.

Katherine did. "He thinks he holds all the cards, and we're just weak, silly, powerless females. Well! We'll show *him*!"

"We will?" Elizabeth said the words doubtfully, her foreboding increasing as she watched her sister. She had seen that look before, and could not remember the last time it had not meant trouble.

"We will," Katherine affirmed just as a knock at the door signaled Mrs. Goodsley's arrival with Chloe and the tea.

"But—*how*?" Elizabeth almost wailed the word, so anxious was she to hear her sister's plan. The thought of eating at this disastrous time made Elizabeth so impatient that, had she not been so well-bred, she certainly would have screamed.

"And what—" Already Katherine was helping Mrs. Goodsley and Chloe clear a spot for the tea tray as if nothing else troubled her mind. Elizabeth rose to take her sister's arm, and shook it persistently.

"Katherine," Elizabeth demanded, throwing the most threatening note she could into her voice and stance as she stared down at her second sister from her superior height, "*what* are you planning? Tell me at once, or so help me, I'll—I'll—"

She could not think of a threat bad enough and was still trying when Katherine, her eyes bright with determination and the mischief that her sister knew so well, only shook her head and said, "Why, Elizabeth, don't be dense! Anyone can see that I'm planning to have tea!"

Chapter
Two

ELIZABETH COULD BARELY contain her impatience as Katherine, betraying by no more than the sparkle in her eye that anything untoward had occurred in the past hour, thanked Mrs. Goodsley for the tea. After the faithful housekeeper left the room, Katherine passed Chloe the crumb cakes that were her delight and inquired kindly what her small sister had learned from her perusal of the reverend's book that afternoon.

Chloe gave her head a sad shake in remembrance and took a generous bite of cake before replying, "To be absent whenever the vicar comes to call!"

Katherine laughed, but Elizabeth, after adjuring the child not to talk with her mouth full, shook her head and said that Chloe should not talk that way about someone as worthy as the reverend.

Emboldened by Katherine's laughter, Chloe lifted her small chin in a gesture Elizabeth immediately recognized as their second sister's. "The reverend," Chloe said in positive accents that emphasized how strongly she believed her own words, "is a prosy bore!"

Katherine, biting into a crumb cake herself at that precise moment, was obliged to suffer a coughing spell as she tried to swallow her laughter in the face of her elder sister's apparent disapproval. Elizabeth raised an eyebrow.

"And I imagine I need not inquire further as to where Chloe might have heard that description?" She shook her head at them both, thinking again, as she so often did, that Chloe was just a smaller version of dear Kate, both of them dark-haired, with a sprinkle of freckles across their noses, and deep brown eyes that could flash fire or gently glow from a warmth within. They carried their father's coloring and their mother's size, while she herself had been blessed with her father's height and her mother's fair, good looks.

"Now, Elizabeth," Katherine began. She knew she shouldn't have laughed after the upset Elizabeth had suffered that day. "Chloe didn't mean anything by it. It's just that Woodsley is so—so—"

"So worthy?" her elder sister supplied helpfully.

Katherine shook her head.

"So prosy?" supplied her younger sister with what Katherine considered a great deal of honesty but a deplorable lack of tact. She willed herself not to laugh as she met Elizabeth's eyes and shook her head again.

"So what, then?" asked Chloe, honestly puzzled, her head tipped to one side and crumbs covering the front of her dress.

"So—oh, I don't know!" Katherine shook her head after several moments, giving up the search for the right descriptive word. "So—Woodsley, I suppose."

Elizabeth said he could hardly be blamed for that, and Katherine sighed. "No, I suppose not," she said. "But it's hardly something for which we need praise him, is it?"

Feeling that she *should* argue, Elizabeth found that, under the skeptical gazes of her sisters, she had to admit that the vicar could, at times, be a bit too—too—

"Woodsley," Katherine supplied.

Elizabeth smiled and shrugged her fair shoulders. "But he means well," she added.

Katherine and Chloe, whose interest in the reverend was never strong, and who had grown tired of him as a topic much earlier, agreed to that. Elizabeth, her duty toward the absent vicar discharged, put down her teacup and paced restlessly around the room and back again to her chair. She paused only when a knock at the door brought Horton to supervise the one remaining Farthington Hall footman in the lighting of the room's candles. Watching him, Elizabeth sighed.

When their parents were alive, there had been more footmen, more maids, and a French chef who had made the most incredible pastries. . . .

Her eyes fell on Chloe contentedly munching the cakes prepared by Mrs. Goodsley's sister, who came in days to cook for them, and she sighed again. Chloe did not remember those richer times. She'd been only four when their parents were lost in a channel crossing, on their way home early because their mother missed her children so. Their father, the last letter they'd received from France said, missed them also.

Since then the sisters' guardianship had been in the hands of their Uncle Edward, their father's brother. He'd left the girls in the country, at Farthington Hall, with their servants and their redoubtable governess, Miss Poole, who at the moment was with her ailing sister in Scotland, but who was expected to return as soon as she was able. That thought made Elizabeth sigh yet again.

"I wish Pooley were here with us now," Elizabeth said, her tone wistful as she thought with fondness of the strong, spare-framed woman who had shepherded her and Katherine through their childhood years, and who still shepherded Chloe. "She would know what to do."

"Yes. Well!" Katherine, who had been watching her graceful sister and wishing, as she often did, that she, like Elizabeth, were just six inches taller, decisively dusted her hands of crumbs and stood. Walking forward to put an arm around Elizabeth's waist, Katherine led her to the fireside overstuffed chair that had once been their mother's favorite retreat. "I wish Pooley was here, too, but she isn't. And since I *also* know what to do, you needn't worry, need you?"

The doubtful look on Elizabeth's face did not suggest any great faith in Katherine's knowledge or abilities, and Katherine made a face at her. "You needn't look at me like that, Elizabeth, for I do have a plan, and a good one!"

Chloe, who had been watching them with great interest ever since she was allowed back into the room, interrupted to ask what they needed a plan for. The sisters turned toward her guiltily. Elizabeth started to say, "It's nothing for you to bother your head about, love," but Katherine interrupted with, "She will have to know, if it's to work."

Elizabeth shook her head. "We shouldn't worry her, Kate,"

she protested. Chloe, looking from one to the other of them, said she already was worried. That settled it for Katherine.

"The thing is, Chloe," Katherine said, walking over to the child's chair and perching herself on the chair arm, "you've heard us speak of Uncle Edward."

"The worm," Chloe said, recalling several of Katherine's conversations verbatim. She beamed up at her sister.

"*Chloe!*" The dismayed way Elizabeth said her name made the little girl blush, but Katherine patted her shoulder encouragingly.

"Yes, dear," Katherine said, "that's right. The worm."

"And the gudgeon." Chloe repeated with relish the treasured words her second eldest sister had once let fall, but she herself seldom had the opportunity to say. "Despicable old makebait. . . ."

Katherine, her eyes on Elizabeth's shocked face, and knowing well a lecture was soon to follow, hurried into speech. "That's right, dear." Kate gave Chloe's shoulder a warning pinch. "You have the right man in mind."

"*Katherine!*" Elizabeth breathed.

Kate's inquiring glance was purposefully innocent before she returned her attention to her younger sister.

"The thing is, Chloe," Katherine said before Elizabeth could say more, "Elizabeth received a letter today from Uncle Edward— "

Scowling, her small sister interrupted with the information that she did not like Uncle Edward. At all.

"Chloe!" Elizabeth remonstrated again.

"I do not like anyone who makes you cry," the child said with a dignity that sat oddly upon her small shoulders. Katherine patted her back approvingly.

"Neither do I," Katherine agreed, meeting her elder sister's eyes with challenge.

"Yes, well, that is all very well," Elizabeth said, "for I'm sure that I don't like people who would make you cry, either—not that I can remember that anyone ever could—but you can't be encouraging her to say that she doesn't like her guardian, Kate!"

Chloe, listening with interest, said that she didn't see why not; Kate said it all the time. In fact, she called him a—

"Yes, yes, that's all very well," Katherine interrupted hastily as Elizabeth suggested, with a frown, that Katherine said a great deal too much. Kate's look was one of comic dismay as she told her younger sister that the difference was that she, Kate, didn't say such things in polite company, before people who would be made uncomfortable by them, as Elizabeth was. . . .

Katherine believed it a good explanation and was thinking she'd worked her way out of that faux pas when Chloe proved inclined to argue.

"Yes, but," her little sister said, her forehead wrinkled in acute concentration, "you said it to Tom—"

"Tom is *not* polite company!" Katherine snapped.

Elizabeth's *"Katherine!"* was heard once again. "How can Chloe learn proper manners if you don't practice them yourself?" Elizabeth asked, her voice reproachful as she fixed her sister with a reproving stare.

Chloe, not wanting to attract a lecture on proper manners but puzzled by Kate's last remark, interrupted cautiously to say that she thought Kate *liked* Tom.

Katherine ran a hand through her hair. "Well, of course I like Tom," she said, grinning ruefully at the child. "We *all* like Tom. We've known him forever, haven't we? What I meant was, I can say things to Tom that I can't say to people who aren't family."

"But you and Elizabeth are family." Chloe could always be depended upon to pinpoint the gaps in her sister's logic. "And all I said was that Uncle Edward is a—well—" she eyed her eldest sister consideringly before substituting, "—you know—and then Elizabeth got upset, and—and—"

Kate sighed. "Elizabeth," she said, "this explanation is not working."

Elizabeth agreed. "The thing is, Chloe," she said, "it will probably be most helpful for you to remember this: Never repeat anything you hear your sister Katherine say."

An inarticulate sound of protest rose in Katherine's throat, and Elizabeth fixed her with a questioning gaze. "I'm hardly as bad as all that—" Katherine started, saw her sister's eyebrows rise, and subsided.

"Oh, very well," Kate said, one foot kicking against the

chair leg as she raised her expressive eyes to the ceiling. "Listen to Elizabeth."

Chloe, looking from one to the other of her sisters, found it all very confusing and sighed. Elizabeth, watching her face, suggested that Kate go on with her explanation. Kate did.

"You see, Chloe," she said, "Uncle Edward—" afraid the child might add yet another descriptive phrase of their absent uncle, Kate hastily put a hand over Chloe's starting-to-open mouth, "—wrote Elizabeth a letter saying he is coming here next week with two of his society friends."

Chloe, looking from one to the other of her sisters, knew that was not all, and waited.

"One of his friends, Uncle Edward says, is interested in—in—" Katherine seemed to have trouble finding the words to express herself, and Chloe, who had never witnessed that before, stared at her in puzzlement. Elizabeth tried to help.

"To—" Elizabeth said, "—that is—"

She, too, stumbled badly. Kate, taking a deep breath, resumed.

"Uncle Edward says one of his friends—a duke, no less, which I think is a real hum, because what duke would have anything to do with Uncle Edward—" That reverie was interrupted by the warning message coming from her elder sister's fine eyes and, taking yet another deep breath, Katherine continued. "The thing is, Chloe, Uncle Edward says this duke is thinking of buying a house in the country."

Chloe, seeing nothing wrong with that, waited expectantly. Once again Elizabeth tried to help.

"Not just a house in the country, Chloe," Elizabeth said gently, her eyes meeting Kate's as she spoke to her youngest sister. "But a house in this neighborhood."

"Oh." Feeling something was expected of her, Chloe offered that, and waited.

Kate, still perched on the arm of the chair, sighed. "Not just a house in the neighborhood, Chloe," she said, "but this house."

Chloe blinked at her in surprise. "But, that's silly!" the child protested. "We live here!"

"Yes, but, you see, Chloe," Elizabeth started, rising from her chair by the fire to approach her little sister and comfortingly take Chloe's small hands in her larger ones, "sometimes—things happen—Uncle Edward apparently wants to sell the Hall, for some reason unknown to us—and without consulting us, which I cannot like, although I shouldn't say so—"

She was interrupted by Kate who, looking down at them both, patted Chloe's shoulder again.

"You're right, Chloe," Kate said, her voice even. "We do live here. And we're going to go on living here, too!"

Chloe nodded her agreement, for Katherine's last words were the most sensible ones she'd heard that afternoon. Elizabeth, biting her lip, glanced worriedly at Katherine, and said nothing.

Chapter
Three

"YOU KNOW, KATE," Elizabeth said that night as she sat in the old library watching her sister rummage through first one drawer and then another of the mammoth oak desk that had belonged to their father, "it's all very well for you to tell Chloe that everything will be all right and that we'll go on living in Farthington Hall as long as we like, just as we always have, but *I* am not eleven, and I simply won't accept your assurances unless—"

She paused dramatically, and her sister, stopping her rummaging long enough to look up and raise a quizzical eyebrow in Elizabeth's direction, prompted her. "Unless?"

"Unless you tell me at once what this plan you have is!" Elizabeth said roundly, abandoning her dramatic pose for one more sisterly. "I've been on pins and needles ever since that letter came, and I've asked and asked you what scheme you're concocting. But all you do is smile and play at jackstraws with Chloe, and eat your dinner and talk about the new kittens, and act as if nothing at all is wrong, when here we are, facing the possibility of losing our home!"

"I didn't wish to disturb Chloe." Voice and face were calm as Katherine resumed her rummaging. "And I fail to see how my not eating my dinner might make the situation better. If it would, I assure you I would not eat for many days!"

Elizabeth, finding her sister's logic unanswerable, bit her lip and stared into the fire. She wished she had Katherine's spirit in the face of danger, but ever since they were small children, it had been this way. It was Katherine who climbed the apple tree while Elizabeth remained firmly on the ground, and worried. It was Katherine who took each fence at a neck-or-nothing speed, while Elizabeth rode the established paths, and worried. It was Katherine who—

Her musings were interrupted as Katherine, blowing a stray strand of hair from her forehead, slumped disgustedly back into her chair with a loud, "I wish I could find where Pooley put those letters to Uncle Edward. It is unlike her to be so disorganized!"

That was like Katherine, too, Elizabeth thought, the sense of humor that had deserted her that afternoon returning as she told Kate that it wasn't Pooley who was disorganized, and never had been. In fact, Elizabeth said, she wouldn't be at all surprised to hear that Katherine had put whatever it was she was looking for away herself, in one of her "safe" places that was so safe that things put there were never found again. . . .

Her voice trailed off as Kate, with a "that's it!" snap of her fingers, rose from behind the desk and rushed to the bookshelf. Lifting down a worm-eaten copy of *The Iliad,* she said, "How smart of you, Elizabeth! I can always depend on your calm good sense!"

Flushing at the praise, Elizabeth rose to help her sister who was standing on tiptoe and still finding it difficult to reach to the back of the shelf where she obviously was fishing for something. Without any trouble Elizabeth extended her arm and, feeling the bundle of letters there, brought them out and handed them to Katherine.

"I *wish* I were taller!" Kate said enviously.

"Yes, well, you're not." Elizabeth had heard that wish before. "And as Pooley always tells you, there's no sense wishing your life away! Tell me instead what is in those letters!"

She regarded Katherine expectantly, but her sister, brow furrowed, payed her not the slightest heed. Instead, Kate took the letters back to the desk and spread them out before her, intently reading first one and then another before stuffing them back into their respective envelopes.

Not content to wait for enlightenment, Elizabeth walked to the desk and stood reading over her sister's shoulder. Her own lovely brow furrowed as she studied the words there, for she saw nothing in the letters to generate the enthusiasm Katherine was so obviously feeling.

"What are these, Kate?" Elizabeth asked when the mantel clock had chimed the half hour and still her sister said nothing.

Katherine, recalled from her intense perusal, stared up at Elizabeth for a moment as if she'd forgotten her existence. Kate's, "Oh, Lizzie, I'm sorry!" was genuine as she explained, "These are letters Pooley wrote to Uncle Edward over the years. I thought they might be of use to us now, and reading them again proves I'm right! She always copied over for us—writing it all out again—everything she wrote him, in case such duplicates ever were needed. Bless her for not trusting the old . . ." Her words fell off at her sister's quick frown. Clearing her throat, Kate started again. "She always kept his responses, too—when he cared to respond. The letters tell him of our needs here at Farthington Hall, and they are—" she paused a moment so her words would have the proper dramatic effect, "—they are our *salvation!*"

If Katherine had hoped for a gasp of admiration or thankfulness, she was disappointed. Her sister blinked at her and said, "Whatever are you talking about?" in the voice Elizabeth always used when she thought her sister had taken leave of her senses. Again.

Katherine started to say she was telling her but paused when she noted a hurt look on her sister's face as well. Elizabeth, in a too neutral voice, ran her finger along the desk and said that she thought it rather odd that Pooley discussed the letters with Katherine when she, Elizabeth, was the eldest. . . .

"Yes, well . . ." Hastily Kate searched her mind for a plausible story with which she might fob off her dearly-loved sister. Not finding one, she sighed and said, "But you know, dearest, you have been so busy with—other things—"

"You mean I have no understanding of business," Elizabeth said, her head bent to avoid her sister's eyes. "That I'm not nearly as quick at such things as you and Pooley, and that I depend on you to take care of me—"

"No, no!" Katherine rose to put her arm around her sister's waist. "Not at all, goose!"

When that pet nickname failed to win a return smile, Katherine hugged Elizabeth again. "It's not that you have no head for business, Lizzie," she corrected coaxingly, "it's that you have no interest in it. And Pooley showed me these letters during the time Chloe was sick with the chicken pox, and you were nursing her so carefully. I think Pooley was rather afraid she'd catch the disease herself, for she'd never had it, you must remember. She wanted one of us to know where the letters were, just in case!"

"Really?" Elizabeth was watching her sister carefully.

Katherine nodded. "Really."

"Oh." The fact that she hadn't purposely been left out seemed to lift Elizabeth's spirits; she said that she quite understood before inquiring just how the letters were to be their salvation. Katherine seated herself at the desk again and chortled as she picked up the first of perhaps twenty letters that comprised the pile. She waved it at her sister as she said, "This is the first letter Pooley ever wrote Uncle Edward after Mama and Papa died. It details the need for work on the chimneys—says they are starting to smoke."

Elizabeth's forehead wrinkled in puzzlement as she objected that the chimneys didn't smoke. They had when the girls were children, to be sure, but then Horton and Matthew, the footman, and Johns, the groom, had, between them, solved the problem, and that was years ago. . . .

Yes, Katherine told her triumphantly, but Uncle Edward didn't know that!

"What?"

Katherine picked up another letter, her eyes alight. "This," she said, "is the letter Pooley wrote Uncle Edward when he cut the funds for the staff, and the second footman and two of the maids were let go. She warned him that the house would be too much for the reduced staff to care for. And this—" Katherine's eyes darkened as she picked up a paper Elizabeth could see was written with a heavy hand and heavily underscored, "is Uncle Edward's reply, recommending that we all work together to keep the house as fit as possible."

"Which we did," Elizabeth said.

Yes, Katherine agreed, but Uncle Edward didn't know that!

Her sister's forehead remained puckered, and Katherine picked up yet another letter.

"This," Kate said, grinning in delight, "is the letter Pooley wrote Uncle Edward three years ago saying that the roof in the west wing was leaking badly, and the east wing roof might start at any moment. She requested funds to fix it immediately." Katherine paused, and her eyes grew dark as she reflected upon her uncle's perfidy. "Uncle Edward never even answered that one!"

Yes, but, Elizabeth objected, Pooley and Katherine had gotten the funds somehow, and the roof had been fixed with the help of the groom and two of his nephews. . . .

"We got the money by pinching and scrimping from the small amount Uncle Edward allows us of our inheritance. I've no doubt he lives off the interest and siphons all he can from the estate!" Katherine said. She picked up several more letters. "This one is Pooley's request for a larger clothing allowance and money to take you to London for a season; Uncle Edward recommended you forgo the season and thus save on the clothing costs." Katherine chewed her lip reflectively, settling back into her chair to stare for a moment into the fire. "I really thought that one would break Pooley's and my hearts."

"But, dearest," Elizabeth said, coming around the desk to place a comforting hand on her sister's shoulder. "I never wished for a London season—not really—"

She met her sister's penetrating gaze and, sighing, looked away. "Well, perhaps, when Miss Mannerly went up to London, I couldn't help wish just a bit that—but I got over it, you know, and am quite happy here at Farthington Hall. It was dear of you and Pooley to try, of course. . . ."

She was interrupted by Katherine, who bounced out of the chair declaring that it wasn't fair; Elizabeth was so beautiful, and she *should* have had a season. Katherine *knew* she would have taken the town by storm, "And next year, when you are of age to escape Uncle Edward's guardianship, and the inheritance comes into your hands—then, oh then, Elizabeth, think how grand it will be!''

Elizabeth, who knew without being told that her reaching the age of majority as set forth in their father's will really meant the inheritance would come into Katherine's capable hands, ably aided by their old governess, smiled ruefully.

"Oh, Kate," she said, "what would I do without you?"

Her sister, surprised by the question, said she never really had considered it. But then, she said, she didn't suppose they had to; Elizabeth wasn't without her, hadn't been for nineteen years, and wasn't likely to be. So what was the use of worrying about it?

Elizabeth laughed and asked what all Kate was telling her had to do with her sister's plan to save Farthington Hall from being sold.

Katherine's eyes lit up again. "Don't you see?" she asked. "Over the years Pooley has told Uncle Edward of all the things going wrong with the Hall. However, since he never visited or showed any interest, merely sending funds for our survival as seldom as he possibly could, she never bothered to write him telling how each problem was solved."

"But," Elizabeth protested, "I don't see—"

"Don't you?" Katherine cried, rising to place her hands on her sister's shoulders. "Lizzie, think a minute! Over the years Pooley has painted a picture of a house falling into gross disrepair because of neglect. She has told him there is a roof that leaks, dust settling on furniture as staff cuts are made, poor little nieces with little more than rags to wear, and little to eat—"

"Yes, but," Elizabeth objected, "that's not how we are at all!"

"No," Katherine agreed, "but Uncle Edward doesn't know that! And when he and his fine friends arrive next week, they're not going to find the Farthington Hall we live in today!"

For one wild moment Elizabeth thought Katherine meant to move the estate, and she stared at her sister worriedly. "They're not?" she asked.

"No," Katherine said. "They're not!"

Katherine was regarding her sister in such triumph that

Elizabeth hated to ask, but felt that she must. "Then," she said, her voice cautious, "what *are* they going to find?"

Katherine snatched up the letters and waved them at her sister. "This!" she said. "The Farthington Hall of the letters!"

"But, Katherine," Elizabeth protested, "how can we? And even if we fool Uncle Edward this once, I'm sure we can't do so forever—"

"But we don't have to fool the old—ahem!—forever!" Katherine interjected, dancing a little jig in her delight. "We only have to fool him for six months—until you're of age!"

"Until I'm of age . . ." Elizabeth repeated, faint but pursuing. Katherine threw up her hands in frustration.

"Don't you see, Lizzie?" she demanded. "When you're of age, Uncle Edward will no longer be our guardian. Papa—bless him!—stipulated that in his will. So then Uncle Edward won't be able to sell Farthington Hall because it will be out of his control. Oh, isn't it a wonderful plan?"

Elizabeth, to whom words other than "wonderful" came to mind, suggested that perhaps if they just *told* their uncle that they didn't wish Farthington Hall to be sold, he would take himself and his guests off again. Her sister regarded her in disgust.

"Honestly, Lizzie!" Katherine scolded. "Sometimes you are so dense! Uncle Edward hasn't cared a rap about what we've thought or wanted for eight years, so why would he start now?"

Elizabeth had no ready answer for that so she sat, shaking her head dubiously. Katherine continued, her soft skirts swishing as she moved about the room in her excitement.

"Besides," the second Miss Farthington said shrewdly, "it's my guess that our dear uncle has rolled himself up, and that is why he wants to sell the Hall. Perhaps he even owes this—this duke, if he really is one—and he hopes that if the man likes the Hall, it will help ease our Uncle Edward's debts."

Elizabeth, who had not earlier spared much thought for the two men her uncle said he was bringing to the Hall, now objected. Instituting Katherine's plan would treat the un-known gentlemen who would be guests in their home unkindly. The statement drew a most unladylike snort from her sister.

"Well, if they wish to turn us out of our home, they certainly cannot be gentlemen!" Katherine declared. "And if this duke were to buy the house away from us, that would be most unkind!"

Elizabeth suggested that the gentlemen might not know the Farthington sisters lived at the Hall. Perhaps if they were aware that the sisters had no interest in selling their home, they might go away. She gazed hopefully toward her sister.

Katherine shook her head, saying that if it weren't these two, Uncle Edward would probably bring others if he thought the Hall was fit to sell.

Elizabeth uttered a soft, sad sigh. "It's just that—oh, surely you remember, Kate, when Mama and Papa were alive, and Farthington Hall was such a hospitable place. It seems so—so—shabby to treat visitors in such a way. If only there was something else we might do . . ."

Katherine declared stoutly that if these unknown visitors were friends of Uncle Edward, they were no doubt shabby themselves and quite deserving of such treatment. After slanting a glance at her still unconvinced sister, she added, tone and demeanor pious, that if Elizabeth had a better plan, one she could guarantee, she would certainly like to hear it.

Elizabeth, with no plan of her own to offer, could not see that Kate's idea guaranteed success either, but was much too wise to say so.

Chapter Four

TOM MANNERLING, THE squire's son who lived four miles to the west of Farthington Hall and who had considered it his second home ever since he or any of the Farthington sisters could remember, never had possessed the wisdom exhibited by Elizabeth the night before. When Katherine told *him* her plan when he came to call the next day, he, unlike Elizabeth, had no qualms about sharing his opinion of Katherine's idea.

"You've taken leave of your senses!" he told her. His open face was perturbed as he took a half turn around the library where he'd found her ensconced at the desk, writing busily all that would need to be done—or undone—before her uncle's visit. "Honestly, Kate—this is even more foolish than your plan to enter Thunderer at Newmarket and race him yourself, disguised as a boy!"

"That would have worked!" At once Katherine fired up in defense of an earlier idea. "If you hadn't been so pudding-hearted as to refuse to help me!"

"Pudding-hearted!" Tom told her roundly that what he'd helped her do was avoid social scandal, for she surely would have been discovered—

"Would not!" Katherine interrupted, frowning at him.

"Would too!"

"Not!"

"Too!"

They glared at each other for several moments more, the

brother/sister relationship they'd established in their earliest years evident. Then Katherine sniffed and resumed her place at the desk. In decisive tones she told him that if that was how he felt, he might as well leave because she had work to do and no time to talk with him, which she wouldn't do anyway because she wasn't speaking to him, thank you.

Tom, running a hand through his already disturbed red hair, stared down at her, his young face troubled.

"Now Kate," he began.

She sniffed again and turned away.

"Ah, Kate!" He was starting to grin. Although two years older than Katherine, he never had been a match for her in will, nor had he ever been able to remain angry with her for long.

Elizabeth and Chloe might listen to him; might, on occasion, actually turn to him for guidance. He'd stood as a brother to all the Farthington sisters ever since he could remember, his only-child status having made it seem natural, from his earliest years, to gravitate toward the Hall and the girls who lived there. But Katherine, unlike the others, must always lead.

"All right," he said, capitulating. "I'll do what I can to help—even if it ends us all in the basket, which I've no doubt it will!"

Instantly Katherine's frown disappeared, and she turned a smile-wreathed face his way. "Really, Tom?" she asked.

He nodded, grinning ruefully.

"Oh, I knew I might depend on you!" Catching hold of his hand, she led him to the overstuffed chairs that faced each other by the fireplace. Pushing him gently into one, she inquired kindly if he would care for tea or wine. When he declined, saying he couldn't stay long, she took the chair across from him and leaned forward eagerly.

"Now, when Uncle Edward and his friends come—" Katherine began; Tom interrupted to say she hadn't told him who her Uncle Edward's friends were. Katherine contended that it didn't matter; any friends of Uncle Edward's were not friends of hers. Tom objected that she wasn't really sure the men *were* friends of her uncle's; they might just be acquaint-

ances, two men looking for homes in the country whom her
Uncle Edward knew. . . .

Seeing that this and similar digressions could go on forever
when she had better things to do, Katherine was cross as she
said all right. If he had to know, it was some duke and his
friend her uncle said he was bringing.

"A duke?" Tom sat up straight and emitted a low whistle.
"Well, Kate, you're lost already. No duke is going to come
to this part of the country and stay for a time without being
found out."

"What?"

Tom shook his head at her. "Come now, Kate! Every
hostess in the neighborhood is going to come calling to invite
you and your guests to their houses once they hear it's a
duke. Especially if he's a young one." Tom's face brightened. "Is it a young duke, Katherine? Because if it's one of
the old dukes who already is married and has a dozen children
or so, perhaps no one will care. . . ."

Katherine, who hadn't considered this further complica-
tion, told him stiffly that she did not know if it was a young
duke or an old duke, and she did not care; she didn't want
either coming to buy her home.

"Besides," she said, her anxious eyes coaxing him to
agree, "perhaps word *won't* get out that Uncle Edward and
his guests are here. We shall do our best to keep it quiet!"

A clearly disbelieving Tom asked her the last secret she
could think of that had remained a secret in the country. A
determined Katherine said that this must certainly be one.
After regarding her in awe for several moments, Tom sighed
and said that perhaps it would be best if she showed him her
uncle's letter. He held out his hand in expectation, but Katherine made no move to fill it. Tom frowned at her.

"Well?" he asked.

"Well?" She lifted her chin at him.

His hand worked further havoc in his hair. "Well, really,
Kate!" he said. "If you don't trust me enough to show me
the letter, I certainly don't see how you can trust me to help
you!"

Turning her head away, Katherine said it wasn't a matter of
trust; it was just that she didn't have the letter anymore. . . .

"You don't?" Puzzled, Tom asked why.

Her chin came up again. "I burned it."

"You *what?*" Tom thumped the side of his head several times, certain he'd heard wrong. Then, cautiously, he asked, "You *burned* your uncle's letter?"

"Yes."

"But—*why?*"

Kate looked at the ceiling, the floor, and the door. "I was angry," she said. "I burned the letter because I was angry."

"If that isn't just like you!" Tom had no trouble believing her explanation. "How many times, Katherine, have Pooley and Elizabeth and I told you, look before you leap; think before you do! What if the letter said something you need to know, and you've gone and burned it—"

With a fierce frown, Katherine told him that she knew everything the letter said. "I know it by heart; it burned its way into my mind."

Her childhood friend was openly skeptical. Frowning even more, Kate began, *"My Dear Niece Elizabeth, it is my pleasure to inform you that on Thursday next, I shall be arriving at Farthington Hall with my Two Good Friends, the Duke of Bellingham and His Friend, Mr. Markham, the Duke being interested in purchasing—"*

She could have gone on, word for word, but she was stopped by the extraordinary effect her recital had on her friend. One moment he was listening closely, waiting for her to falter, and the next he was making fish faces at her. He was, in fact, gasping for breath in a way that alarmed her so that she rose and came hastily to his side, asking with grave concern if he might like a glass of water, or—or—something. . . .

Her words trailed off as Thomas continued to regard her incredulously.

"The Duke of—*Bellingham?*" Tom repeated, his awestruck tones causing her forehead to pucker more. "And, *Mr. Markham?*"

His voice rose even further as he repeated the latter name. Katherine, unsure what it all meant, nodded and continued to regard him with great anxiety.

Tom pushed himself up from his chair and took a full turn

around the room, coming back to stare down at her in disbelief as she, still at a loss, gazed doubtfully up at him.

"Katherine," he breathed, "*Bellingham*—and *Markham? Here? At Farthington Hall?*"

He was off around the room again, leaving Katherine to wonder if his voice ever would return to normal. As she wondered, one thought rose uppermost in Tom's mind.

"Oh, Kate, I must order a new coat, at once!" he cried, causing her to stare at him blankly. "Two new coats! If only I had time to go to London for them—"

This unusual and, in her mind, quite uncalled for, interest in his wardrobe, coming as it did in the midst of a morning call, made Katherine regard him more doubtfully still. "Thomas," she said, putting a hand on his forearm, "are you all right?"

He gazed down at her, his eyes those of a man with pressing details cluttering his mind. Slowly enlightenment dawned. "You don't know, do you?" he asked in that same incredulous tone that was beginning to annoy her.

"Know what?" Katherine hoped that by humoring him she might eventually bring him back to the subject at hand.

"Know—what?" He repeated the words, a touch of laughter edging his voice. The touch turned into a chortle, and the chortle into full-blown chuckles as, seeing the disapproval growing on her face, Tom threw himself back into his chair and sat grinning up at her. "When I was in London last year, Katherine—" he started, those familiar words making her brow darken. Ever since the squire had sent his son to London for two months to acquire a bit of town bronze, Tom had held the experience over his friends at Farthington Hall, who had never been farther abroad than York. Long ago Katherine had grown tired of sentences that started, "When I was in London last year . . ."

"You met them?" Katherine guessed, hoping to forestall one of Thomas's long-winded remembrances. "You met this duke and his friend?"

"No!" Such a thought sent the laughter from Tom's voice and made him sit bolt upright, eyes widening. "As if I would! It's not as if they'd have time for the likes of me, my dear! Not at all!"

"Aha!" Katherine's earlier conjectures on the personalities of her uncle's guests were in her mind confirmed. "Top-lofty, are they?"

"Oh, no!" With a quick shake of his head, Tom proved eager to dispel that image. "Not at all! At least, if they are, I wouldn't know it. Quite above my touch, Kate. Really. Although I could almost swear the duke almost smiled at me, once, when we were in a group. And at a cockfight one night, I stepped into Mr. Markham's way—quite by accident, I assure you!—and he waited most civilly for me to remove myself before he proceeded!"

Katherine, who saw nothing particularly memorable or praise-worthy in such actions, and whose practical nature wondered what else Thomas thought the man might do, was annoyed by her friend's obvious admiration for the two men of whom he spoke in such awed tones. She scoffed that he had let London ways go to his head, and London values blind his eyes.

Shocked at her misinterpretation of his words, Tom stared at her open-mouthed before protesting. "Katherine, don't you understand?" he asked. "Your uncle—whom I also saw in London, but never in such exalted company, believe me!—is bringing guests to Farthington Hall who are the leaders—the very top—of the London beaus!"

Tom was so overwhelmed by the idea that Katherine longed to hit him.

"Hmmph!" she said, her full contempt for London beaus in general and these two in particular evident in the sound. "Well, they shouldn't last long here then, a couple of London fops, intent on their comforts and their entertainments, and not used to honest labor or any hardships at all!"

Her eyes glowed at the thought and she felt immeasurably better. Tom, however, could not allow this disparagement of two men of whom he stood so much in awe.

"Not fops, Katherine!" he protested. "The crème de la crème of London society! Their coats, cut to a nicety; their cravats, always miraculously tied; their horses, the best; their manners—at least the duke's—all that is pleasing. And while I never saw the Duke of Bellingham at Jackson's, I know that Markham strips remarkably well in the ring—"

"Boxing!" Katherine was determined to hold to her first

opinion of her despicable uncle's despicable guests. "Well, Thomas, if *you* think that recommends a gentleman—"

Hastily Thomas said that it wasn't that; it was just that both gentlemen seemed alive to every trick—especially Markham. And they weren't likely to be driven off by any plan a green chit from the country might concoct. If she tried to cross swords with them—especially Markham—she was likely to find herself very much worsted. . . .

The latter was a poor choice of words. He recognized it immediately and tried manfully to undo the damage he had done, but it was too late. Katherine, her eyes spitting fire, said, *"We will see!"* in a voice that brooded no good for the coming visitors. Then, her tone frosty, she told him that he might run off home if he was so daunted by the Londoners that he was afraid to help.

Tom, flushing, said it wasn't fear, it was just—just—

Katherine's skepticism was apparent in the way she raised her delicate eyebrows at him, and he stopped. "Dash it, Kate, if you aren't the most high-handed, stubborn female I ever met! Of course I'll help you—said I would, and I will. But if we land in the basket, don't say I didn't warn you!"

Katherine, who had no intention of landing in any basket and certainly did not intend to be bested by two London beaus, said magnanimously that they were both agreed it was on her head. With a darkling look, Tom reminded her that the last time she'd said something was on her head, he was the one who had ended up in bed with a badly sprained ankle.

"When we were children!" Kate cried, stung that he would be so unhandsome as to remember something that occurred *ages* ago.

"Last year!"

"Oh! Well!" Katherine waved the regrettable memory away with one airy hand. Tom, realizing it would do no good to argue further, subsided to hear more of her plan.

Chapter
Five

A WEEK LATER, as Edward Farthington, the Duke of Bellingham and Mr. Markham in tow, made his way toward Farthington Hall, all was in readiness for his visit, in accordance with his niece Katherine's plan.

Although the Farthington groom had, as he confided to the nephew who from time to time helped him with extra work at the Hall, been "fair gormed" by Miss Katherine's instructions, he had, after much head scratching and several objections, climbed the roof of the west wing—where the guests would be housed—and removed the patches he and Matthew, the footman, had labored so hard to install several years earlier.

Upon descending the ladder with the sorry news that the roof would now leak, sure, should any rain or snow fall, and that he had no doubt the wind would howl and whistle in the rooms below all night long, Miss Katherine's face had lit up. Then she had instructed him, with Matthew's help, to remove a few panes of glass from the windows in those rooms as well.

She had further confounded him with the news that Tom, the squire's son, would arrive the next day to collect and take to his father's stables for an indefinite stay all the Farthington horses but the old cob that had long since passed his better days. She added that he, Johns, was to carry all the manure he recently had cleaned from the stables back into the stalls, and do his best to make it appear that no highbred animals had been there for many a day.

"You might even remove a few of the shingles from the stable roof," Katherine suggested, but there Johns drew the line. Never, he told her severely, in all the years he had worked at Farthington Hall, had he allowed his stables to show disrepair or to leak, and he certainly wasn't going to start now. Also, Miss Katherine ought to know better than to ask it of him, if she hadn't so taken leave of her senses, which, bless him—and bless her, too, for she was clearly the one who needed it—it was abundantly (he was sorry to say) clear she had . . .

Tom, who was standing behind Kate at the time, started to chortle, and the sound recalled Johns to his position and his usual self. He blushed bright red, begging Miss Katherine's pardon, he was sure, but feeling bound to do his duty. . . .

Katherine said kindly that she quite understood and that she wouldn't ask him to do anything to compromise his principles. It was just that, for a short time, while they had visitors, she needed the stables to appear as unusable as possible.

The groom looked at her suspiciously. "Now, Miss Katherine," he said in that tone used by servants who have known their masters and mistresses from early childhood, "what might you be about with this queer start?"

Sighing, Katherine told him about her uncle's coming visit, bringing with him two gentlemen, one of whom might like to buy the Hall.

"Buy the Hall?" the groom repeated. "Don't be daft, lass!" Tom chortled again and Johns, beet red, again begged pardon before continuing. "This is Farthington Hall, and so it has been ever since I can remember, and so it was when I came here to work for your father, when he and your lady mother were first wed. Why would you and your sisters be wanting to sell the Hall?"

Katherine assured him that she and her sisters had no wish to sell the Hall. In fact, she told him, they were doing everything possible to see that it *wasn't* sold, which was why she wanted it to seem as uninhabitable as possible.

With the full picture drawn for him, the groom told her that not only would he haul back manure he'd removed from the stable, he'd visit neighbors to see if he might borrow some manure from them as well!

It didn't take Thomas's quick poke in her ribs to make Katherine see that this would not do, and she hastily assured Johns that there was no need for that extra work. When he appeared unconvinced, she confided that they didn't want the neighbors to hear of their actions because then someone might tip Uncle Edward and his guests to the deception.

Nodding wisely, the groom told them that he could well see that. Trotting off to survey his domain, he promised to do all he could to make it appear unlivable. And, he added, if any of the coming gentlemen were to question him about anything at the Hall, he'd play deaf, and they would just see what they'd get out of him, they would!

That taken care of, Katherine turned her attention to the inside of the house. It was there that she met her fiercest opposition.

Mrs. Goodsley's fastidious, housekeeping soul was offended by Miss Katherine's suggestion that grimy sheets be spread over most of the furniture in the west wing, and that dust be spread about as much as possible there and in several east wing rooms as well. The suggestion that Mrs. Goodsley should take herself off to her sister's for a few days while the visitors were there so that it would appear Farthington Hall no longer had a housekeeper, and hadn't had for some time, was not, the good lady said, even to be considered.

"No, Miss Katherine!" the housekeeper said when Kate, followed by Elizabeth, approached her with that plan. "That I cannot and will not do. As if I'd leave my poor lambs while your Uncle Edward and these—these—*Londoners!*—are coming down upon you! What would my good friend Miss Poole say if she was to hear I'd gone off and left you unprotected?"

Katherine pointed out that Horton and Matthew would be with them inside the house, and Johns outside, but Mrs. Goodsley's expression and a "Men!" made it clear what she thought of *their* abilities to protect her poor darlings. Katherine added that their uncle was, after all, their guardian, and surely could be depended upon to keep them from any—er—

untoward advances—the housekeeper seemed to think the "Londoners" capable of.

"Ha!" Mrs. Goodsley sniffed disdainfully. "Edward Farthington has done a fine job of taking care of you so far, hasn't he?"

It was such an unarguable point that Katherine, after exchanging glances with Elizabeth, altered her tactics to suggest that perhaps Mrs. Goodsley could stay if she would just play least in sight.

"Least in sight?" The housekeeper was suspicious of what Katherine meant.

"Yes. You know!" Katherine was thinking out loud. "Keep to your room, but be here when we need you—"

"And we always need you," ever-tactful Elizabeth added when it was apparent the housekeeper was about to demur. "I will feel better knowing you're in the house, as will Katherine, I'm sure!"

Katherine, aware that her sister's words were having a smoothing effect on this latest wrinkle in her plan, agreed.

"But I must tell you," Elizabeth said, as if she, too, were only thinking aloud, "while it would be a comfort to me to know you're in the house, I would hate to think that your presence here might make the gentlemen's stay more comfortable."

Mrs. Goodsley said that was something she didn't want to do, for what these "gentlemen" were proposing—to take her poor lambs' home and leave her darlings without a roof over their heads—well, it wasn't to be borne! Still, it would be such a smear on her reputation if the visitors found a dirty house in which it was known that she was the housekeeper. . . .

Katherine, realizing that that would cause a tremendous blow to the woman's pride, was at a loss. It was Elizabeth who suggested that they simply say that Mrs. Goodsley was confined to her bed with a bad back and had been for several weeks.

"Several weeks?" the housekeeper objected, glancing around the one room in which Katherine had already put her plan into effect. Odd objects were scattered everywhere with a liberal application of dust added. "This room looks as if no one has touched it in years!"

"But that's wonderful!" Katherine crowed. "Don't you see? That's just what we want!"

"But, Miss Katherine!" the housekeeper objected. Elizabeth hurried into speech.

"We'll say that this wing has been shut off for several years," the eldest Miss Farthington suggested, drawing her sister's admiring glance. Mrs. Goodsley, although agreeable in principle, was dubious as to why that would be the case.

"Why?" Elizabeth asked. She pondered deeply and at last had to admit that she didn't really know why. . . .

"Because it's falling into disrepair," Katherine supplied. "Because, as Pooley told Uncle Edward, there's not enough staff to keep it up, and the roof leaks, and because—because—" Suddenly she was inspired. "Because of the ghost!"

"Ghost?" both Elizabeth and Mrs. Goodsley echoed. Katherine beamed at them. Their reaction was not the same as hers.

"Katherine, really!" Elizabeth exclaimed, while Mrs. Goodsley informed her austerely that Farthington Hall didn't have, had never had, a ghost—something she seemed to strongly feel they should be congratulated for.

"No, of course we don't have a ghost," Katherine said. Her tone was regretful, for it occurred to her now that a ghost might be just the thing. "But Uncle Edward doesn't know that!"

"Katherine, really!" Elizabeth repeated, shaking her head at her sister. "You don't truly think that Uncle Edward and his friends would believe in a ghost, do you?"

Katherine muttered that Uncle Edward had never struck *her* as the brightest person among her acquaintances. Frowning, Elizabeth agreed that while that might be true of their uncle, the gentlemen coming with him might be more intelligent.

Katherine's skepticism remained.

"Then *what,*" Kate asked, in the triumphant tone of a person who knows she will have the last word in an argument, "if they are so very bright, are they doing spending time with Uncle Edward?"

After biting her lip in search of a reply, Elizabeth shrugged and said that while she did not know, she would thank Katherine to rein in her imagination far short of a Farthington Hall ghost. Katherine, seeing the determination in both her sister's and their housekeeper's eyes, agreed that she would not call upon the ghost—except in an emergency.

Elizabeth and Mrs. Goodsley, exchanging glances, decided to accept that promise for now. Happily for their peace of mind, they could not know what Kate would consider an emergency.

Katherine was not the first to raise the question of what two gentlemen such as the Duke of Bellingham and his friend Mr. Markham—whom Tom regularly referred to as "out-and-outers," until Katherine told him severely that if she heard that phrase one more time, she would scream—were doing in company with Edward Farthington.

Tom had dwelt upon it at length—again, until Katherine vowed she would scream if he voiced the thought one more time. After that he simply kept the question to himself, worrying over it like a dog with a meaty bone whenever it came to mind.

Now, as the carriage carrying the three gentlemen neared Farthington Hall, the question was much on Mr. Markham's mind, as well.

Never one to suffer fools gladly, the first night out of London Markham had been of a mind to turn around and return to the city; the thought of a fortnight in Farthington's company in the north was enough to exacerbate his never-easy temper.

He had approached his friend Bellingham about returning to the metropolis after they left their host drinking himself senseless in the inn's private parlor, but Bellingham proved difficult to move.

"It would be most impolite, Nicholas," the duke remonstrated as they stepped outside to light a cheroot before retiring for the night.

"But it might save our sanity," Markham suggested. The duke grinned.

"I admit the old boy is more than a bit overbearing," he started.

"Overbearing?" Markham snorted. "He's common, George, and there's no sense trying to wrap it up in clean linen."

"Yes, well . . ." the duke sighed. "I suppose you're right. But he does owe us both money, and I imagine this old hall is the only way he has of paying it off. I wouldn't mind having an estate in the north—not really. . . ." He added the last as his friend snorted again, and Markham regarded him with affection.

"What a soft heart you are, George," Markham said. "You're going all the way north to see an estate you don't really want to try to help out a person you don't really like."

The duke grinned. "You make me sound like an idiot!"

"Well?" The tone was sardonic, but Bellingham was not deceived.

"Oh, go back to London, do," Bellingham said, waving his hand at his friend, another grin touching his lips as he puffed contentedly on his cigar. "If you're going to be in one of your moods, I certainly don't want your company!"

"Moods, George?" Markham, too, was enjoying his cigar. "Whatever do you mean?"

The duke clapped him on the shoulder. "There are people who don't know why I bear with you," he teased and could feel his friend smile in the shadows. "Sometimes I wonder myself."

"Do you, George?" His cigar finished, Markham tossed it into the night, watching the embers glow and then fade. "I figured it out long ago."

"You did?" The duke's cigar followed his friend's.

"Yes." There was a pause. "I make you look so good, George. Next to me, you're an angel."

"Which makes you the—"

"Yes." Markham smiled grimly. "I do believe I've been called that, once or twice."

Bellingham's hand clasped his shoulder again. "Well, I know better."

"Do you, George?" It was said with interest as his friend

turned toward him, and they walked back into the inn, making their way up the stairs and down the hall to their respective rooms. "Why is that?"

"Because," the duke said, stopping outside his door to give his friend one of his singularly sweet smiles, "here you are, going all the way north with someone you detest to keep me company and to protect me from my better self."

Markham raised his eyes in apparent disgust. "Somebody has to." The duke grinned, and Markham again urged that they return to London and cut their losses. The duke's smile disappeared.

"Really, Nicholas," he said, "go back to London if you want. I just prefer not to be there right now. You understand."

Markham did, and his own hand dropped heavily on his friend's shoulder in support. "You're not letting her break your heart, are you?" he asked.

The duke shook his head. "No, no," he said before a rueful smile turned up the corner of his lips. "Although she might have bent it a little."

"Under that beautiful exterior beat a heart of pure stone," Markham told him. "You're lucky you escaped with your life—to say nothing of your fortune!"

The duke sighed. "I know that—now. But still, I'd prefer not to be there for the engagement parties and all. . . . You do understand, don't you, old boy?"

Grimly his friend said that he did, and the duke smiled.

"Besides," the duke confided, "my grandmother, your esteemed Godmama, somehow got wind of it all and is, rumor has it, on her way to London to—er—straighten me, and my life, out."

"The dowager duchess?" Markham said. Despite his best efforts, his voice held a touch of nervousness. Bellingham's smile grew even as he nodded.

"You understand my leaving the city," the duke said.

"I certainly do!"

"But you," Bellingham continued, "you feel free to go on back. I'll understand."

Markham shook his head. "And have my esteemed Godmother straighten out *my* life? While all the time ringing a peal over me for not taking better care of *you*? No, I thank you, no! I think I've had enough of London myself, for a while. It gets so deucedly—flat, doesn't it? Perhaps this trip north is just what I need to dispel that feeling of ennui that falls over me each time another vacuous young miss raises melting eyes to mine, or yet another hostess introduces me to her favorite daughter or niece or cousin or friend. I'd hate to have the dowager duchess taking a hand in such introductions herself.''

"You're a cynic, Nicholas," Bellingham told him, shaking his head. "Someday you're going to meet an extraordinary woman, and if you're not careful, you won't even know it."

Markham's eyes were amused as he regarded the duke quizzically. "Do you think so, George? Well, let's hope that won't be soon! You know how eager I am to enter the wedded state."

In spite of himself, the duke grinned; marriage was usually the *farthest* thing from Mr. Markham's mind—and Mr. Markham was usually the *farthest* thing from marriage.

"In the meantime—if you're so set on it, maybe this trip north will be good for us both," Markham said. "Just exactly what we need!"

"For self-rejuvenation or self-preservation?" the duke questioned. Markham was glad to see the twinkle that had of late disappeared from his friend's eyes.

"A little of both, I think," Markham told him. "A little of both."

On that hopeful note, Markham had left his friend for the night. Now, as the third day of their journey drew to an end, he was not feeling at all hopeful. He *was* feeling that if he had to endure another day in prosy old Farthington's company, he'd strangle the fellow. He marveled at Bellingham's ability to keep his good manners in the face of their host's evident foolishness.

As Farthington babbled on about how they were going to enjoy their time in the country, he let drop the information that his three little nieces lived at the Hall where the men would be making their stay. Markham raised an eyebrow at the duke, noting that even Bellingham's good manners couldn't keep the dismay he felt at that remark from showing.

"Children!" Markham thought grimly, settling himself into the corner of the carriage and closing his eyes in a vain attempt to shut out his host's voice. "It needed only that!"

He was grateful when he fell asleep and was spared more of Farthington's aimless wanderings until the carriage drew up just as dusk fell over Farthington Hall.

Chapter
Six

MARKHAM'S AND BELLINGHAM'S first impressions of Farthington Hall were not favorable as they stepped down from the carriage that cold November eve. To their left a loose shutter banged forlornly in the chill wind. It was an artistic touch Katherine had ordered only that morning, and was ably attended to by the enthusiastic footman, Matthew, who considered Miss Katherine's plan the most exciting thing to come his way in his twenty-nine years of life.

No welcoming lights shone at the windows, and the weathered stone of the Hall, which on some days gleamed like silver in the sun, this night reflected the sorry gray of the clouds and gathering night.

Markham, his eyes narrowing as he gazed toward the sky, realized smoke escaped from only one of the many chimneys dotting the roof. He pointed that fact out to the duke as their host banged repeatedly on the door, trying to gainsay admittance.

"I don't know what it is, gentlemen, I assure you," Edward Farthington blustered for the third time as his knock went unanswered. "I wrote my niece that we were coming and why we are all forced to endure this delay—"

His mutterings ended as at last the door swung open, and a small face peered timidly out at them in the night. A child's doubtful eyes looked from one to the other and back again.

"Ah, here we are, and about time!" Farthington said,

relieved at last to see the door open. His voice took on the hearty note of those not accustomed to dealing with children. "And you must be—Elizabeth? No, Elizabeth is the one with the yellow hair! You must be Katherine! I'm your Uncle Edward, come to visit. Step aside now, and let us in! We're freezing in this cold!"

The gentlemen stepped forward but were stopped by the fact that the child did not step back. Instead, she stared solemnly up at her uncle and, the door still only half open, said, "No, sir, and begging your pardon, I'm Chloe."

"Chloe?" Farthington, who had motioned his guests to go before him and now stood in the rear, shrugged himself forward until he stood in front of Bellingham, frowning down at the little girl. "Don't be ridiculous! Chloe is only a baby." He turned toward the other men, the jocular smile on his face not quite reaching his eyes. "Katherine was always the scamp. I remember hearing my brother and sister-in-law say so time and time again." He turned back to the child, the smile disappearing when his back was to the gentlemen. "Move aside now, Katherine, and let us in."

"But I'm Chloe!" Her protest was indignant even as she was forced to give way before her uncle's considerable girth. He, not waiting for her to move, shouldered his way through the door, and Chloe, thrown off balance, slipped and bumped her head against the wall. She was blinking up at all three gentlemen as the fair one, with a "For heaven's sake, Farthington!" came quickly to her aid, picking her up and dusting her off as he said with his most attractive smile and an offering of his hand, "How do you do, Chloe? My name is Bellingham."

Farthington, reading the censure in the duke's tone and the disdain in the eyes of Mr. Markham, shrugged petulantly. "I keep telling you, her name is Katherine. Chloe is—oh, I don't know—four or five years old."

Chloe looked at him in amazement. "I was once, Uncle Edward, but that was seven years ago. I tell you, I'm Chloe!"

Farthington, who did not like children in general and who particularly was not fond of children who argued with him and stared at him with such wide eyes as if they, like most of society, thought him an idiot, sniffed in distaste. "Well,

we'll soon get to the bottom of this,'' he said. "Where's that
butler of yours—what's his name—Horton? Where's Horton?''

Horton, Chloe informed them in very serious tones, was
trying to get the fire started in the sitting room. Elizabeth had
thought the gentlemen might like to take a hand of cards there
after supper and, perhaps, a glass of wine.

"A glass of wine!'' Remembering his brother's cellars
fondly, Farthington rubbed his hands together. "The very
thing! But why—'' His train of thought was never keen, but
as he and his guests stood, still wrapped in their greatcoats
and in need of someone to take those coats away, it did occur
to Farthington that something was amiss. "Why is your
butler starting fires? Why not one of the other servants?''

Chloe gazed at him in puzzlement; for an instant Markham,
watching the child with detached interest, thought he detected
a suppressed spark of excitement behind the innocence in her
eyes. Moving himself to the right for a better look, he decided that it was only a flicker of the shadows falling in the
hall that had made it appear she was more than the innocent
child who turned her wide-eyed gaze his way as he moved.
She smiled and he smiled back without thinking before she
returned her attention to her uncle. "What other servants
would those be, Uncle Edward?'' she asked.

Farthington stared at her in surprise. "Why—why—'' he
blustered, but was interrupted by a disturbance to the right as
three people emerged from what Markham, after a moment of
rapid deduction, could only suppose was the sitting room.
The three, coughing and covered with soot, were followed
into the hallway by a billow of smoke. The tallest of the trio
was an elderly man who, even with soot on his bald spot,
shoulders, and knees, retained the air of a butler of the first
order.

His companions, both young, consisted of a willowy blond
woman who, her face smudged and her hair and clothes
darkened by smoke, still was quite lovely, and a shorter
woman who was the dirtiest of them all. The latter's face and
gown were so blackened that the only features Markham
could easily distinguish were a pair of fine eyes that met his,
widened slightly, and quickly looked away as she coughed
and waved her hand in front of her face. Chloe, glad of

reinforcements, called out, "Elizabeth! Katherine! Uncle Edward has arrived!"

All three of the Farthington Hall inhabitants looked toward the small, huddled group in surprise; then the young blond woman moved forward, her hand extended as she said, "Uncle Edward! What a mess you have found us in! We did so want to make you and your friends welcome here, but as you can see—" She had taken his hand and was now passing it to the shorter woman who followed close at her heels, her own hand outstretched in welcome, "—we have a bit of a problem!"

Farthington, staring from one of the young women to the other, could only stutter, "Who—what—" in a disjointed manner that made the smaller woman pat him kindly on the shoulder. Horton, remembering his duties, hurried to relieve the gentlemen of their coats. Markham noted that the butler managed, with the dark young woman's help, to smear a liberal amount of soot on them as he went about his task.

Feeling that something was in the wind, but not sure what, Markham stepped back into the shadows to watch as the young woman who had helped Horton with the coats returned to patting her uncle's shoulder. Ruefully surveying the door from which she, her sister, and the butler had emerged, she said that it appeared they were quite found out.

"Found out?" her uncle repeated, still staring in bemusement from Katherine to Elizabeth and back again. Katherine turned her rueful smile upon Bellingham, who responded, and upon Markham, who stayed in the shadows. Remembering Tom's warning that the duke's friend was up to every trick, her smile dimmed slightly, but she determinedly held out her hand to the duke.

"And you, sir?" Katherine asked.

"Bellingham," George returned promptly, taking her soot-covered hand in his own and lifting it to his lips as if he did so every day. "At your service, Miss Farthington."

Katherine smiled graciously at him. "I'm Katherine Farthington," she said, pulling her sister forward with her free hand. "And this is my sister, Elizabeth."

The duke made another graceful salute over Elizabeth's hand, lingering there perhaps a moment longer than he had over

Katherine's. He looked up into Elizabeth's blushing face and wondered why soot was not worn by everyone in society.

Katherine, seeing his warm regard for her sister, asked hastily who his friend might be.

"Oh!" Realizing that Edward Farthington was beyond making introductions, Bellingham pulled Markham out of the shadows and presented him to the ladies. Katherine held out her hand imperiously and he took it briefly, inclining his head and forgoing the polite bow of his friend.

"Mr. Markham." Katherine's eyes were frosty.

"Miss Farthington," he returned, his own expression enigmatic.

Kate decided to ignore him as she turned back toward her uncle and the duke.

"I am afraid you have found out one of the little secrets of Farthington Hall," she began, heard the man behind murmur "*One* of the little secrets?" and frowned darkly as she hurried on. "The chimneys smoke."

"What?" her uncle demanded. He gazed from her to his guests, and his color mounted as his eyes returned to his niece. "What do you mean, the chimneys smoke?"

Katherine was a wide-eyed picture of reason as she said she believed that was quite plain.

"You can't mean all the chimneys!" Farthington was uneasily watching the duke, who was watching Elizabeth, who was blushing. Katherine called her to task with, "Elizabeth, Uncle Edward wishes to know if all the chimneys smoke."

"Oh. No!" Elizabeth came forward with a soft smile for their guests. "Not all of them, Uncle. Only those we light!"

Behind her, Katherine heard something that sounded suspiciously like a smothered laugh, and she turned to scrutinize Markham. He had stepped back into the shadows and was standing with his shoulders leaning against the wall. His powerful forearms were folded across his chest as he surveyed them.

"Was there something, sir?" Katherine challenged, disliking his manner.

"Nothing at all, Miss Farthington." Words and voice were smooth. "Although now that you ask, it occurs to me that I'd better go see to George's and my horses. And you might want to send your rented cattle on, Farthington. It won't do to leave them standing in this wind.''

Katherine, glad to see him go, said that that would be an excellent idea. She directed him to the stables with the instructions that when he found them, he should shout—loudly— for the groom who had charge of that domain.

"Loudly, Miss Farthington?" Markham asked.

Katherine nodded.

"Would you like me to show you where the stables are?" A small voice came unexpectedly from his right, and Markham looked down to see Chloe staring wistfully up at the tall man who had the coloring of the painting of her father that hung in the library. Disliking the idea of her confiding little sister alone with this sharp-eyed stranger, Katherine said that there was no need. The gentleman had only to walk around the side of the house and follow his nose to find his destination.

Markham, meeting her eyes, raised his eyebrows slightly as he said that he would be happy of the company. A moment later Chloe was skipping happily off in search of her cloak, Elizabeth having told her she must wrap up warmly if she was venturing outside at this hour.

Shrugging himself into his own coat that the old family retainer retrieved for him with great dignity, Markham was, without thinking, brushing at the streak of soot on the coat's sleeve when he glanced up to find a look of great amusement in Katherine Farthington's eyes. Quickly she lowered her lashes and turned to her uncle and the duke.

"Yes," Markham overheard her say as he and Chloe started out the door, "it is a great sadness to us. But of course you know about the chimneys, Uncle Edward. Pooley wrote you about them—oh, years ago!"

"One or two chimneys," her uncle returned angrily. "She didn't say anything about the whole house! And speaking of that Poole woman—where is she, anyway?"

Chloe, preceding Markham out the door, turned to say, "Gone."

Markham had perforce to stop as Edward stared at the child.

"Gone?" he repeated.

Chloe, who missed her mentor mightily, nodded. A single

tear slid down her cheek and without thinking Markham put his hand on the child's shoulder. Edward continued to stare at her.

"You don't mean—*dead?*" their uncle demanded, seeing the tear. The startled sisters exchanged glances, and Katherine gave an imperceptible shrug. Lowering their eyes, all three nodded.

"But how—when—" Farthington sputtered.

"Last month—" started Chloe as Elizabeth said, "Last year—"

All eyes turned toward Katherine, who rescued the situation. "A year ago last month," she said. Chloe and Elizabeth heaved muted sighs of relief.

Edward regarded his nieces with suspicion. "Impossible!" he said. "Why wasn't I informed? Besides, it can't be. I know it can't. Seems to me I had a letter from the blasted woman not six months ago—"

Katherine and Elizabeth exchanged glances and Elizabeth flushed. "Uncle Edward," Elizabeth started.

Katherine cut her off. "See, Lizzie," Katherine said, her voice lowering until it echoed oddly in the wide hall. She glanced over her shoulder, and unconsciously, Edward, Elizabeth, Horton, Bellingham, and Chloe looked around, too. Markham stared straight at Katherine.

"I told you."

Elizabeth, game but unsure what she was next to say, repeated, "You—told me?"

Katherine nodded and gazed over her shoulder again. "I told you Pooley was still here, looking after us." She gave a delicious shudder. "I can feel her presence."

Elizabeth shuddered, too, a premonition of what was coming in mind. "You—can?"

Angrily Edward demanded to know what his niece was talking about. Katherine fixed her wide eyes upon him.

"Earlier this year, Uncle Edward," she said, her words so low that everyone had to lean forward to hear her, "I arose one night with the strangest feeling; something was calling me, it seemed, down to the library. When I came down the stairs I saw a thin stream of light under the door there—"

She pointed to a door at the back of the house, and

Markham, his hand still on Chloe's shoulder, could feel the little girl tense, "—just as I'd seen it so many nights when Pooley was among us and I'd sought her out, only to find her still working at the big desk where she kept her accounts and things. I didn't know what to think; Elizabeth and Chloe were abed, and Horton would not be there at that hour! Slowly I approached the door, and when, my heart pounding, I opened it, the candle—for there was a candle burning on the desk, just as I'd seen so many times before—was blown out. I was left standing in the darkness with only the smell of hot wax and wick. I looked all around but could see no one, and it was only when I turned to go that I heard—positively I heard, although I've told no one but Elizabeth until now—the *scritch, scritch* sound made by pen on paper. The sound I'd heard so many times before when Pooley was busy at her letters!"

She paused, her large eyes taking in the open mouths of her sisters, the puzzled expression of the duke, and the clear disbelief of Markham. She frowned at the last, who made her a slight bow.

"Shall we go, Chloe?" Markham said. Katherine's younger sister, clearly hating to be torn away from this entertaining tale, sighed her reluctant agreement as the door closed behind them.

That action seemed the cue for her uncle to open and shut his mouth several times before he said, with all the bluster he could muster, "Are you trying to tell me, Katherine, that I received a letter from a—from a—" he glanced around in spite of himself, "—a *ghost?*"

Elizabeth shut her eyes, sighing, and shook her head. Katherine, strictly honest, said that she would tell him no such thing. "All I can tell you, Uncle, is what I heard," she said. "And that I am sure—yes, very, very sure—that wherever Pooley is, we are in her thoughts, and all her good wishes are with us!"

Behind them a door banged heavily as it slipped from Mrs. Goodsley's grasp, for the housekeeper had come up from the kitchen to see the guests for herself, without their knowing it. "Miss Katherine!" she was thinking, her head moving from side to side. A moment later Katherine put her presence to good use; in spite of themselves, the duke and Edward, as well as Elizabeth, jumped at the sound of the door. Katherine, not looking behind her, said, "Yes, I know that Pooley continues to watch over us." She was moving toward the stairs where she turned, one foot upon the first step, to smile sweetly at her uncle. "And I know that she will do everything possible to continue to protect us from those who might do us ill. Just as she always has."

Leaving a moment for that to sink in and watching with satisfaction as Edward peered uneasily around again, she asked Horton to show the gentlemen to the rooms readied for them, while she and her sister changed their clothes and prepared for supper.

Chapter
Seven

"YOUR SISTER IS quite a storyteller," Markham said to the small figure skipping along beside him as they made their way to the stables. Bellingham's hired carriage with the duke's and Markham's riding horses tied behind followed them.

Chloe looked up, and even in the near darkness he could see that her eyes glowed. "Katherine is wonderful!" she said. He smiled.

"Does she often tell you ghost stories?" he asked.

Chloe's small head bounced up and down for emphasis. "The most wonderful ones, and then sometimes Pooley tells us of the Scottish ghoulies and ghosties—"

The little girl caught herself up on the words and conscientiously corrected, "That is, she used to . . ."

By now they had reached the stables, and Markham, after a curious glance at her, stepped inside to hail the groom. He had to shout several times for Johns had decided that he would play his role of near deafness to the hilt. That way, he told Miss Katherine, if any of the gentlemen should try to question him on something he didn't care to be questioned on, he would simply pretend he couldn't hear them.

Katherine suggested he add muteness to his role as well, but after much head scratching, the groom decided he could not do that because there might be something he wanted to say, and then what?

Seeing that he was decided, Katherine had reluctantly agreed. She did, however, tell him that he might pretend to be as deaf as he liked; in fact, the deafer, the better. Now came Johns's moment, and he made the most of it.

After letting Markham shout perhaps a dozen times, Johns slowly made his way down from the snug little loft that was his home. He came forward holding a lantern and using the light of that to survey them curiously. Seeing a face he recognized, he mumbled, "Miss Chloe," and stood, waiting. Chloe smiled sunnily up at him.

"Johns," she said, "this is Mr. Markham."

"Eh?" Johns put his hand to his ear.

"Markham," Markham repeated.

"Eh?" Johns tilted his head forward, the hand still cupped behind his ear.

"MARKHAM!" Markham shouted.

Johns looked from one to the other of them.

"Mark who?"

"MARKHAM!" Markham shouted again. "MY NAME IS MARKHAM!"

"Oh." Johns stared at him.

"AND I HAVE TWO HORSES THAT NEED STABLING!"

"Eh?" Johns said.

Helpfully, Chloe took the old retainer's hand and led him out to the stableyard. "HORSES, JOHNS," she cried, enjoying the game. "LOOK!"

Johns stared toward the two horses pulling the carriage and the two tied at the back. He took a few steps forward, swinging his lantern from one end of the carriage to the other, illuminating the driver on the box. "Horses," Johns said. "Prime 'uns, in the back!" He looked disparagingly toward the team pulling the hired chaise. "Job cattle up front."

The driver on the box grumbled at the disparagement of his team, but Markham, who agreed with the groom's assessment, silenced him before trying again.

"YOU NEED TO STABLE THE HORSES, MAN!" he shouted.

Johns looked at him. "Eh?"

"STABLE THE HORSES, JOHNS!" Chloe crowed.

Johns moved his lantern to her face. "Eh? Oh." At last he

seemed to understand, and he moved toward the team, as if to unhook it. The driver shouted at him as Markham grabbed his arm.

"NOT THOSE HORSES!" Markham shouted.

Johns stared into his face. "Eh?" he said.

Markham rolled his eyes heavenward and guided the man around to the back of the carriage where his and the duke's riding horses still stood. "THESE HORSES!" he said.

Johns nodded appreciatively. "Real goers," he agreed.

Markham untied the horses and handed the groom the reins. Johns stared down at his hand as if he had no idea what to do with what he held there.

"STABLE THE HORSES, JOHNS," Chloe shouted. He looked doubtfully at her.

"COME, I'LL HELP YOU," she said, shouting still. She reached for the reins and Markham's tall roan took instant exception. The gentleman, a chill running down his spine, hastily grabbed the reins and said that he would see to the horses himself.

Chloe looked at him in doubt.

"Do you know how?" she asked.

He grinned. "I think I can manage."

"But Katherine says London beaus—" the little girl started, thinking aloud. She caught herself up guiltily on the words as Markham regarded her with interest.

"What does Katherine say about London beaus?" he asked as he led the horses into the stable, the little girl walking at his side while the groom shuffled ahead, swinging his lantern.

"Oh, nothing . . ." Chloe did not meet his eyes. He put a hand under her chin and tilted her head up toward him.

"But Katherine did talk about us before we arrived?" he asked with one of his most disarming smiles.

Johns, watching, interrupted to ask loudly if there was anything he could do to help with the horses.

"You could pick out your two best stalls," Markham said, still watching the little girl.

"Eh?"

Markham rolled his eyes and turned to the groom. "WHICH ARE YOUR TWO BEST STALLS?"

"How tall?" Johns wore a look of complete puzzlement. "How tall is what?"

In irritation, Markham took the groom's lantern and surveyed the stable himself. He was disgusted to find there were no "best" stalls, other than the one in which a sway-backed old cob stood regarding them with rheumy eyes. About to turn from the unattractive beast, he noted in surprise the cleanness of its stall, and its well-cared-for appearance. His eyes narrowed thoughtfully as he turned again to survey the rest of the stable. At last he decided on two stalls near the door, but said disparagingly that they'd have to be cleaned before he'd put the horses in them.

"DO YOU HAVE A WHEELBARROW?" he asked the groom.

Johns shook his head. "NO," he shouted back, "THEY'RE NOT TOO NARROW. THEY'LL FIT THE HORSES FINE."

Markham regarded him in amazement and Chloe touched their guest's hand. "There's a wheelbarrow over there," she offered softly, pointing, and Markham, after another bemused glance toward the groom, went to retrieve it. Taking off both his driving and his other coat, Markham rolled up his sleeves and asked for a pitchfork.

"No," Johns replied, thoroughly enjoying himself. "We don't have a rich cork. Never heard of such a thing. Don't have a poor cork, either." The last statement seemed to strike him as hilarious and he bent over, slapping his knee. Chloe, her lips twitching, told Markham that there was a pitchfork two stalls down. The gentleman stalked off in search of it and soon was busy cleaning the stall while Johns looked on with interest. Glaring up at the groom, Markham asked Chloe in some exasperation if she thought she might convince the fellow to do similar work in the stall across the way.

The little girl, who in her entire life had not had as many playmates or entertainments as the next two weeks promised to bring, smiled. Taking the groom by the hand, she panto-mimed what Markham wished him to do. When Johns at last decided to understand, he turned with a shrug and shuffled off to find a fork of his own. Soon he, too, was pitching old straw out and new in. Markham, looking up from his labors, noticed that there was a competence in the groom's actions that had not heretofore been seen. His eyes grew thoughtful and he paused, leaning on the fork to watch the groom. It was a moment before he realized Chloe was regarding him carefully.

"Are you tired, Mr. Markham?" she inquired politely.

He grinned. "No, Chloe." His eyes returning to the groom who, absorbed by the task, grew more industrious by the moment. "Just thinking."

Chloe's eyes also turned toward Johns, and she said loudly, "About what?"

Markham could see the groom slow to listen, and he returned to his work. "Oh, nothing," he said cheerfully.

Chloe surveyed him through the same clear eyes he'd seen elsewhere that night, and he grinned at her. "You're very like your sister Katherine, you know."

Obviously the little girl was pleased; she bobbed her head and informed him that while Elizabeth resembled their mother, she and Katherine took after their father—at least, that was what everyone said . . .

Her voice trailed off, and she traced patterns in the straw before looking up to ask if Mr. Markham had known her father. Surprised, he paused to find the groom now obviously listening to their conversation, staring hard at Markham as he gently said no, he didn't believe he'd ever had that pleasure. Her father would have been older than he, she had to understand . . .

Chloe sighed. "He was a wonderful man."

The old straw removed from the stall, Markham was busy spreading new straw, but he stopped at her tone. "I'm sure he was," he said with a respect that made Johns, satisfied, turn to his work again.

"Everyone says so."

His task completed, Markham led his horse into the stall and began brushing him down. Cheerfully he said that everyone couldn't be wrong.

Chloe sighed again. "It's just that—I don't remember him very well . . ."

Markham paused in the brushing to say he was sorry. Chloe smiled gratefully at him.

"You look like him," she offered. Markham, startled, almost dropped his brush.

"I do?"

The child nodded. "There's a painting in the library. He wasn't as tall as you. And his lips didn't curl up the way yours did tonight, when you were watching Katherine—" She looked inquiringly at the gentleman who had made a half-protest before, lips firmly compressed, he returned to his work. "—and perhaps he was slighter, and his eyes were blue, but . . ."

Chloe chewed her lip reflectively. "Maybe you don't look so much alike, after all," she amended. "Although he *did* have hair the color of yours, and, oh, I don't know—just that kind of—*good* look . . ."

"Chloe!" From behind her Chloe heard Katherine's voice, and she turned to see Kate coming toward her, a shawl wrapped closely around her shoulders and on her face a look of real concern. "My dear, you've been out here forever! You must be near frozen to death!"

Before Chloe could protest, Katherine had grasped her hands and proclaimed them like ice. At once Markham was contrite. He said he shouldn't have kept the child out so long; he hadn't realized . . .

Katherine, about to agree sharply that he should not have, turned toward the sound of his voice. She stopped at the sight of him, for his fine boots and trousers, liberally splashed with manure, and the wisps of straw clinging to his shirt and hair made it apparent how he had been spending his time. In spite of herself her lips turned up, and she greeted him with, "Why, Mr. Markham! What a versatile man you are, to be sure!"

Her grin made him conscious of his appearance, and he gazed ruefully down at his stained clothing.

"Yes, Kate, he is," Chloe seconded, beaming up at her sister on behalf of her new friend. "And he's not at all foppish, as you expected him to be, and perhaps being a beau is as good as Tom says it is—" A sudden thought occurred to her, and she looked doubtfully up at Markham. "That is, sir, if you *are* a beau?"

It was clearly a question, and Markham raised a quizzing eyebrow as Katherine Farthington appeared discomfited by her sister's innocent question.

"Well, Chloe," Markham's voice was kind, "I believe that would depend on to whom you are speaking. I, personally, would never categorize myself as a beau."

"Oh." Chloe accepted that as fact, but her head tilted to the side as another thought occurred to her. "Then please, sir, if you will—what would you call yourself?"

"Yes," Katherine seconded quickly, enjoying the arrested and then embarrassed look that crossed his face. "What, Mr. Markham, would you call yourself?"

He paused for a moment in the steady brushing he was giving his horse and turned fully to face her, his eyes reading the challenge in her own and responding to it.

"I, Miss Farthington," he began; then, bowing teasingly to Chloe, corrected himself with, "no, I mean the Misses Farthingtons" —to the little girl's evident pleasure— "would call myself—" his eyes returned to Katherine's, and there was much meaning there, "a man with an inquiring mind."

"Oh!"

He had not before realized how much consternation could fit into such a small word, and he watched with interest as Katherine, a frown replacing the smile that moments before had graced her face, hurried her sister back toward the house. She promised Chloe a hot mug of cider as soon as she reached her room.

Chloe, walking placidly along, called a soft if absent-minded "Good night, Johns," to the groom who replied, also without thinking, "Good night, Miss Chloe," as he continued his work.

Markham, his lips twitching, returned to brushing his horse. It seemed Johns's hearing had effected a remarkable recovery!

Chapter
Eight

WHEN MARKHAM RETURNED to the Hall a short time later, the door was opened for him by Horton. The butler had changed his patched, soot-covered coat for one that, although also patched, was immaculate. Assessing their guest's appearance, Horton sniffed and said that supper would be served in one hour.

Markham nodded. "If you would be so good as to show me to my room," he said, "and send up the man who is to serve me—"

The old butler's forehead furrowed. "The man who is to serve you, sir?" he asked, the tilt of his nose inviting the guest to consider the dejected appearance of the house and to contemplate what that state said about the abundance of servants in the Hall.

"I see." Markham's lips compressed, and he said no more. He followed the man up the stairs and down several corridors, each of which grew progressively chillier, until they reached the west wing. Quick glances through several partially opened doors revealed the eerie shapes of sheet-covered sofas and dressers. Markham suggested, a slight quirk to his brow, that it would appear they had not done much entertaining lately.

The butler, who by that time had stopped at a door on the right of the hall, sniffed. "Is that a jest, sir?" he inquired.

Markham assured him it was.

"Very funny, sir."

Horton opened the door for the guest, then slipped by him to light the several candles that strove to turn back the darkness in the room. One of them, located near a window where the heavy curtain swung ominously, was promptly extinguished again.

"Bit of a breeze," Markham offered, watching the curtain. Horton bowed.

"I'll be lighting the fire for you now, sir, if you like," he said, moving with stately grace toward the fireplace. Mr. Markham said that he would like that very much, and Horton, bowing again, knelt to fumble for several moments before a small flame ignited in the large stone fireplace, bringing with it the first puff of smoke.

"This fireplace smokes, too, I see," Markham said, walking to it and making a show of warming his hands on the pitiful flame.

The old butler shook his head mournfully. "All the chimneys at Farthington Hall smoke—" he began, but Mr. Markham interrupted to say that yes, he believed he'd heard that somewhere before. Horton, eyeing him carefully, decided there was no hidden meaning behind the statement, and told him kindly that perhaps it wouldn't be too bad, the wind being from the west that evening. "Of course, if it turns to the north . . ." He let the words trail off as another gust rattled the west windows and set the heavy curtain hung there rustling again.

"I see." Markham gazed around the room with distaste; the few candles and the small fire burning on the grate cast long, distorted shadows over the heavy mahogany furniture, and he thought it a very good thing he was not given to imaginative starts.

"Well, then, I'm sure I'll be very comfortable here—"

"You will, sir?" Horton was obviously surprised.

Markham worked not to grin. "Of course," he said. "Very comfortable. If you'd just have a bath sent up—"

"A bath?" Horton's surprise increased, and Markham did smile at him this time.

"Certainly, a bath," he said. "I don't wish to sit down with the Misses Farthington or their uncle or my friend Bellingham smelling of the stables!"

Horton sniffed again. "No, sir." His long nose was in the air, making it apparent that he had been too polite to mention the obvious odor Markham emitted. "Of course not." He moved to the door and offered one more of his elaborate bows before withdrawing. "I shall see to it at once. A bath."

As soon as the butler left the room, Markham crossed to the fireplace and energetically applied the poker to the small flame burning sluggishly there. He was rewarded by another puff of smoke and was sneezing violently when a soft tap at his door was followed a moment later by the face of his friend, the duke.

"Oh, I say, Nicholas—" Bellingham started, then stopped. He shook his head sympathetically. "Yours smokes, too, does it?"

Markham turned from the fireplace to regard his friend. "I have reason to believe," he said solemnly, "that every chimney at the Hall smokes. At least—" he turned speculatively toward the fireplace, "every chimney we will see lit."

Bellingham, who by now had entered the room and closed the door, was curious as he stared at his friend. "What do you mean?" he asked, fastidiously taking a handkerchief from his pocket and dusting it across a large leather armchair before settling comfortably there.

Markham grinned. "Only that I believe—" He was interrupted by a knocking at the door. He opened it to find a man he hadn't seen before standing there with hipbath in hand.

"Who the devil are you?" Markham asked, surveying the young man with interest. A vacant stare met his own; Matthew, the footman, once had traveled all the way down to London and actually had *seen* a play. He believed that made him more of an actor than any of the Farthington Hall inhabitants, and he was determined to play the role of dim-witted serving man with aplomb. He paid no attention to his friend Johns's assertion that the role was not too far removed from real life.

Now Matthew, finding his place in the sun, held out the tub as he muttered, "I be Matthew, sir."

"Oh." Markham grinned at him. "Be Matthew or be

anyone you like, my good man! As long as you have my bath there, I'm delighted to see you!''

Matthew maintained his pose as he shuffled in and placed the tub in the draftiest part of the room—a feat Markham watched appreciatively—before shuffling out to say he'd be back with the water.

Bellingham grinned at his friend as Markham went to move the tub closer to the small fire.

''A bath!'' the duke said appreciatively. ''How good of you, dear boy! I didn't want to say anything, but—'' He applied his handkerchief delicately to his nostrils, and his friend grinned.

''You'd be the same if you'd been down cleaning out the stables!''

The duke stared at him in amazement. ''Cleaning out the stables, Nicholas? You do take some queer starts now and then, but really! Whatever for?''

Markham, starting to strip off his shirt and coat, made it clear that his recent task had not been a ''start,'' but a necessity. ''I tell you, George,'' he said, ''we have either wandered into Bedlam or—''

He was interrupted as another knock at the door signified Matthew had returned with the water. Markham told him to empty it into the tub as he went on with his undressing. The servant nodded and, his task completed, was almost out the door when Markham stepped unconcernedly into the bath.

''*Eeeeeeyiiii!*'' said the visitor, stepping hastily out again.

Bellingham, jumping up, asked what was wrong as Matthew, his vacant stare at its best, also turned toward Nicholas Markham.

''You idiot!'' the Londoner shouted, glaring at the servant. ''That water is stone cold!''

Matthew, eyes wide, gazed at him reflectively. ''Yes,'' he said. Then paused. Finally, head tilted to the side, he ventured, ''And was you wanting it warm, sir?''

Markham, who could see nothing funny about the question, was incensed when Bellingham started to laugh.

''Oh, yes, it's all very well for you to laugh, George,'' Mr. Markham told his friend a short time later as, his ablutions hastily completed in the icy water, he briskly dried himself with the rough towel the servant had left him, "but I tell you, something untoward is going on here—"

"Nonsense!" the duke said cheerfully, watching with appreciation as Markham rapidly surveyed the contents of his trunk and selected a claret-colored coat.

"And that's another thing!" Markham objected, rummaging for the rest of his attire. "Here we are, having to wait on ourselves because that fellow Farthington didn't want to hire a coach to carry our valets, and saying that there would be plenty of servants to help us at Farthington Hall, and now—"

The duke objected that they couldn't be sure it was a scaly attempt to avoid paying for another carriage that had made Farthington suggest none of them bring their valets.

Markham frowned at him. "Really, George?" he asked. "What reason do you think he had?"

The duke, after contemplating the question for several moments, sighed. "Perhaps you're right," he conceded.

"Of course I'm right."

The duke's eyes lit with gentle humor. "Are you ever not, Nicholas?"

A reluctant smile appeared on his friend's face. "Do you suppose we might send for our men?" he asked, returning to their original topic. "I tell you, I'd give much to see Swaley's expression if he could see this room!" Another gust of the persistent west wind sent the curtain rustling, and a candle burning on a high mahogany chest flickered, bent in the breeze, and gave up the battle.

"And there's another thing!" Markham said, approaching the window and pulling aside the curtain to survey with disapprobation the hole in the window there. "Are we really expected to sleep in a place where—" He bent forward to peer more closely at the hole. "Where—"

Bellingham, used to hearing his friend run on like this, was puzzled when he stopped. "Where?" he prompted.

Markham straightened to glance at him before returning his attention to the window again. "George, come here," he said.

Obligingly the duke rose to join him.

"Look at that," Markham said, pointing toward the hole in the window. The duke looked.

"Yes?" he said.

Markham shook his head. "What do you see, George?"

The duke looked again. "A hole."

His friend loosed his breath in a long, drawn-out sigh. "Yes, a hole," he agreed, "but look at it carefully. Doesn't anything strike you as, shall we say, peculiar, about that hole?"

The duke bent down to gaze more closely at it. "It's square," he pronounced at last. "A very neat hole."

His friend nodded. "Exactly."

"Exactly?" Again the duke's forehead was wrinkled.

"How many very neat holes do you usually see, George?" Markham demanded.

Bellingham's forehead wrinkled further. He really couldn't say, he said; he supposed he hadn't thought about it . . .

Markham regarded him with disgust. "It is a square hole, George," he said, each word slow so that his friend might follow, "because there was in that square space—and, unless I miss my guess, up until very recently—a pane of glass where a pane of glass should be. And also, unless I miss my guess, a pane of glass will be there again. In—oh, shall we say—a little more than a fortnight?"

Bellingham continued to regard him in amazement. "But—why?"

"Because somebody, or perhaps three somebodies, and a number of accomplices, don't want us here, George! Because they are doing everything in their power to see that our stay is so uncomfortable we'll go away! Because—"

"Nonsense!" The duke's tone was bracing. "There's a hole in the window of my room, too. You don't see me making a tempest in a teapot over it! I'm sure there's a rational explanation!"

"I've been telling you the explanation—" Markham started. Stung by another "nonsense" from his friend, he said, "Well, let's go see!"

"What?" the duke asked.

"Let's go see the hole in the window in your room."

"Oh, well," the duke shrugged, "if you really want to . . ."

"I do."

It seemed an odd request to Bellingham, but Nicholas was an old and dear friend, and if he enjoyed looking at holes in windows . . .

Shrugging again, the duke led the way out of Markham's room and down two doors to his own. Markham, sparing not a second glance for a room in disrepair similar to that exhibited in his own, crossed purposefully to the window and flung aside the heavy velvet curtain hanging there.

"Aha!" he said, pointing to the hole.

"Aha, dear boy?" Bellingham surveyed him doubtfully. "Don't you think that's rather—dramatic?"

Markham, spying a second hole up farther toward the top of the window, pointed to it and said "Aha!" again.

The duke, moving forward to survey his friend's find, gazed dutifully from one to the other before saying, as solemnly as possible, "Yes, indeed. They certainly are holes."

"Square holes," his friend interjected, watching him.

The duke nodded. "Square holes."

Markham shook his head in disgust. "You still don't see, do you?"

The duke was soothing as he assured him that he did, indeed, see holes.

Markham rolled his eyes. "It isn't just that there are holes, George," he said. "It's that they're square holes."

Yes, George said, yes, Nicholas was right; they certainly were. Holes, and square.

Resisting an urge to take his friend by the lapels of his elegant gold coat, Markham eyed him forbiddingly and said, "Can you think of anything that makes square holes, George?"

George, his head tilted to one side, said that no, no, he could not, but he would certainly think about it . . .

About to say more, Markham was interrupted by an "Ahem!" Both men, starting guiltily as they turned toward the door, found Horton standing there with the civil information that Miss Elizabeth and Miss Katherine, thinking they might not be able to find their way through the Farthington

Hall corridors that first night—for, he could not help adding reproachfully, the gentlemen were already twenty minutes late for dinner—had sent him to fetch them.

"Ah, Miss Elizabeth!" the duke beamed, hurrying forward. "So thoughtful!"

Ah, Miss Katherine, thought Markham, his eyes narrowed as he gazed once more toward the gaps in the many-paned windows before flicking the curtain back over them. Quite another thing.

Chapter
Nine

THE GENTLEMEN FOLLOWED Horton down the corridors they'd come up earlier; corridors that, as the temperature outside fell, seemed colder still. Markham, catching the duke's eye, grimaced. Bellingham, too, rolled his eyes and inquired, in the kindest voice possible, if the cold didn't now and again bother the butler's old bones?

Horton, never breaking his majestic stride, said that if his grace thought this was cold, he should visit the Hall in January.

Without thinking, the duke said he could do without that, thank you. The remark made the old man smile, although the action was quickly hid. Markham, his mystification growing, tucked that little observation away in his mind and said nothing.

"The Duke of Bellingham and Mr. Markham," Horton announced as he threw open the doors to the sitting room. His stentorian tones made the room's inhabitants look up quickly, and it was apparent, although Edward Farthington came hurrying toward his guests with a smile, that that gentleman had been in heated discussion with the middle of his nieces.

"Gentlemen!" he said, grasping both by the hands. "Do come in! I trust you found everything satisfactory in your rooms this evening—"

Markham, about to make an acid reply, happened to catch the grin that passed between Miss Katherine Farthington and that dolt, Matthew, who now was carrying in a tray containing a bottle of burgundy. He heard the duke murmuring all that was polite and waited as an eager Edward Farthington turned toward his second guest. "And you, Markham?" Farthington asked.

Katherine Farthington raised her head and looked straight at him. There was a challenge and—yes! laughter—in her eyes, as if she could not wait for his answer.

"Markham?" Uppermost in Farthington's mind was his own hideous room (which, if the duke and Markham could only have known, was infinitely worse than their own), and his tone was a bit more doubtful.

Recalled by his name, Mr. Markham turned toward his host and bowed slightly. "Brisk," he said.

Edward gaped at him.

"I find my room—brisk," Markham repeated, turning his head slightly and meeting the challenge in Katherine's eyes. The smile on her face dimmed as Edward asked just what that meant; if, he threatened, with a hasty glance at the two elder Misses Farthington, anything had been done to make his guests uncomfortable . . .

Markham, who hadn't yet noticed anything done to make them *comfortable,* decided that whatever the game might be, their host was not in on it. Since he did not like the prosy old fool, he didn't want him in on the solution to it, either. No, Mr. Markham, who hadn't felt this interested in life for years now, fully intended to get to the bottom of Miss Farthington's game himself. So he turned to his host and said in the blandest tone possible, "Most delightful, Farthington, I assure you. Can't think of when I've had a more unusual room." His comment drew Miss Elizabeth Farthington's grateful gaze, Miss Katherine Farthington's speculative one, and a look of pure surprise from Bellingham.

Since Markham was smiling that odd little smile that Farthington never understood, he decided that the word "unusual" must connote pleasure among such town beaus as Mr. Markham. Eagerly he seized upon it, asking if he didn't find the Dresden figurines that sat upon the mantelpiece (and which Edward always had admired although the Misses Farthington thought them hideous) unusual, as well.

Markham, strolling forward to survey the pieces through his quizzing glass, murmured, "Most," in a voice that made Miss Katherine Farthington choke and look hastily away. He turned toward her and smiled.

"And you, Miss Farthington," he said with a small bow, "are the most unusual of all your home's treasures."

Katherine, who believed that "unusual" meant among the *ton* what it meant at Farthington Hall, understood his meaning and frowned at him. Edward, his forehead wrinkled, said that no, no, Markham had the wrong sister.

"It's Elizabeth here who would take the shine out of all the London beauties," Farthington said in his loud voice, stepping behind the eldest Miss Farthington and pointing to her in a manner reminiscent of an auctioneer. "You're fair and far off with Katherine! You must need another quizzing glass, Markham! Look again!"

He was honest in his urgings, and Mr. Markham had all he could do not to burst out laughing at the look of indignation that crossed Miss Katherine Farthington's face. The duke, observing the scene with grave censure, came hurrying forward to make a bow to both ladies as he said, in a tone that brooked no contention, that each was lovely in her own right. His kindness earned him a grateful smile from a blushing Elizabeth, and one of clear disbelief from Katherine.

"But—don't you think Elizabeth would be the belle of all balls in London, Bellingham?" Farthington pursued, puzzled.

"No doubt!" the duke seconded the statement with a sincerity that returned the flush of embarrassment to Elizabeth's cheeks. Bellingham asked her kindly if she had ever been to London.

"Oh, no," Elizabeth started.

"There was never any money for that, was there, Uncle Edward?" Katherine interrupted. "Just as there was never any money for chimneys or roofs or broken glass panes, or—"

"There, there," Edward interrupted as Markham said "Oho!" and Bellingham regarded him with disapproval. "No need to air the family linen in public! We'll talk later!"

"We certainly will!" Katherine promised.

Horton, standing in the doorway, announced with dignity, "Dinner is served."

As she accepted Mr. Markham's arm into dinner, Katherine turned a suspicious gaze upon him. "Oho what, sir?" she asked. Her small chin rose in challenge as she surveyed him.

Markham opened his eyes very wide at her. "I beg your pardon?"

"In the sitting room," Katherine said, "just now—you said, 'Oho!' I wish to know what you meant by that."

Markham shook his head, his innocent air making her more distrustful than ever. "You are mistaken, Miss Farthington."

Katherine told him that she was not; she had excellent hearing. At that, the guest smiled.

"Then perhaps what you heard, Miss Farthington, was the wind, whistling through the west wing. Or, better still—" He was laughing inwardly at a private joke, she could tell, and her frown increased. Katherine did not like to be laughed at, especially by someone who might yet spoil her scheme. "—your favorite ghost!"

Katherine gave a small gasp as he pulled out her chair for her and seated himself to her right. She gave him her shoulder as she told the other gentlemen seated at the table that she hoped they would enjoy their meal.

Bellingham, always an easy guest, said that he was sure they would—words he was to eat later and, as he told his friend, find more appetizing than the food set before them— and inquired if the youngest Farthington sister was to join them.

"Oh, no," Katherine said, smiling up at Matthew as he placed a bowl of soup in front of each of the guests. Markham noted the footman managed to spill at each of the gentlemen's places, but maintained remarkable composure when serving the ladies. "Chloe already has eaten and is tucked up in her bed with a hot brick at her feet! Someone—" She shrugged but did not look in his direction, and Markham grinned. "—kept her out in the cold far too long this evening, and Elizabeth and I thought it best that she go straight to bed."

Edward, saying that he wouldn't mind a hot brick for his bed, either, took a noisy slurp of soup and, a moment later, reached hastily for his wine goblet, downing half the glass as his eyes started to run. Markham and Bellingham, about to embark on their meal also, exchanged glances and, spoons halfway to their lips, checked.

Katherine and Elizabeth, eyes on their plates, quietly spooned soup into their mouths.

"*What the devil*—" Edward gasped when he could speak. He was called sharply to task for his language by the duke, and begged everyone's pardon even as he stared in disgust at his plate and then, in suspicion, at his nieces. Both Elizabeth and Katherine raised innocent eyes to his own.

"Is there something wrong, Uncle Edward?" Katherine asked.

He shook his spoon at her. "But of course there is something wrong!" he sputtered. "This—this—" His hand indicated his plate, and Katherine's head tilted to one side.

"Yes, Uncle?" she asked politely.

Markham, at her right, sniffed his spoonful of soup as inconspicuously as possible. The duke took a small sip before dropping his spoon and hastily reaching for his goblet as well. That decided Markham, who put his spoon down and waited.

"What is this?" Edward Farthington demanded, waving toward his plate again. Katherine smiled brightly at him.

"Oh, this is a great favorite of ours, Uncle!" she said. "It's pepper soup!"

"Pepper—" Markham started, then stopped.

"Pepper soup?" repeated her uncle, regarding her with dislike. "There's no such thing as pepper soup! No one makes soup with this much pepper!"

Katherine continued to regard him with her calm wide eyes. "One does when pepper is all one has, Uncle," she said. "And besides—Elizabeth, wasn't there a carrot tonight, and didn't cook toss that into the soup?"

Elizabeth, who seemed to be having trouble controlling her lips, nodded and spooned a sliver of carrot out of her own bowl, to illustrate. Edward Farthington glared at both his nieces.

"This is ridiculous!" he snapped. "I bring my friends here and you try to poison us—"

"Oh, no, Uncle," Elizabeth protested as Katherine said it

was no such thing; they were simply trying to fill the guests up as best they might.

Bellingham, trying as he always did to move as gracefully as possible through any social scene, said that he didn't find the soup so bad and took another valiant sip. A moment later Elizabeth was patting him gently on the back as she handed him his wine goblet; he drained it, eyes watering.

"Perhaps, Uncle, you would like to go on to the next course," Elizabeth suggested, her eyes holding a certain note of reproach for her sister. Katherine was grinning mightily before she became aware of Markham's regard, as well as her sister's, and lowered her eyes.

"Yes," Edward said, snapping his fingers at Matthew, who ignored him until Horton moved forward to direct the other man. "Take it away and bring us something else!"

The five sat in silence as the soup bowls were removed and another course delivered to the table by the shuffling Matthew, who again managed to drop something—this time a turnip—into Edward Farthington's lap. A slight shake of Miss Elizabeth's head seemed to spare the duke, Markham, who was watching keenly, noticed. Markham himself managed to avoid a fate similar to Farthington's by a sharp change of position just as a turnip started to roll off Matthew's serving plate. There was something about Markham's movement, however, that redirected the vegetable into his table partner's lap, and it was a surprised Katherine Farthington who stared down at the white blob staining her skirt.

"Oh, Miss Katherine—" Matthew started, shaken out of his role as dolt by this unexpected turn of events. Feeling Markham's eyes upon them both, Katherine hastily assured the footman that it was of no matter, and that he must go back for the rest of the meal. Recalled to his duty, Matthew, knowing Horton's stern eye was upon him, flushed and nodded. He returned a short time later with an over-browned chicken that Markham could not help but feel had seen better days.

"What the—" Farthington began after his first bite into the stringy creature. In the face of the duke's evident displeasure he stopped himself in time, and swallowed.

"Elizabeth," Farthington said, staring hard at his eldest niece, "this chicken is stringy."

"Yes, Uncle," Elizabeth said, chewing valiantly on a tiny bite of the meat.

"And overdone."

"Yes, Uncle."

Edward Farthington frowned at her. "When your father and mother were alive, this house served the most hospitable table in the country!"

This time Elizabeth stopped chewing, and a look of great sadness descended upon her. "Yes, Uncle," she sighed. "I remember."

"Then what the dev—er, deuce—" he substituted, catching Bellingham's eye in time, "*happened?!*" The question seemed to work mightily on him as, recalling the meals he had eaten there years ago, he added, "You even had a French chef!"

"Yes," Katherine entered the conversation, for her sister seemed inclined to be embarrassed by the meal put before their guests. "But if you will recall, Uncle Edward, you wrote Pooley that children did not need an expensive French chef to cook for them, and the fellow was let go."

"Eh?" Edward had forgotten that, but he did not care to be reminded of it in front of his London guests. He frowned at his second niece. "Well—I daresay—children, you know!" Another thought occurred to him, and his displeasure deepened. "This governess of yours seems to have been awfully free with the information of what passed between us!"

Quietly Katherine said that Pooley felt they had a right to know, since it was their lives that were affected. Farthington cast her a look of dislike before saying that that was all very well, but even without a French chef, they ought to be able to serve guests better than what they were dishing out tonight!

Elizabeth raised pained eyes to her sister. She still, despite what Katherine termed her quite profound acting abilities, found it difficult to treat guests so shabbily even if, as Kate constantly reminded her, they had every reason to do so. The duke, misreading the embarrassment on Elizabeth's face, said hastily that he had always rather liked his meat tough. "It is

good for the teeth, I'm sure," he said. "And it adds a special
tang . . ."

His words trailed off as all eyes turned toward him in
various stages of astonishment and—in his friend Markham's
case, amusement—and he ended lamely, "Besides, a man
eats so much during the season, I'm sure it's good for one
now and then to—kind of—fast—"

In irritation, Farthington said that he had not invited his
guests to the north to fast—and, it was apparent, he hadn't
come north for that purpose himself—and he saw no reason
why—why—

Katherine, growing tired of his sputtering, asked sweetly if
he would care for another turnip.

Chapter
Ten

THE LADIES EXCUSED themselves and left the gentlemen to their port—and a very bad port it was—after a runny meringue completed an infinitely forgettable meal. Markham, who ate little, confounded his host and the duke when he rose after one sip of the wine and said he felt a little ride was in order to settle his stomach.

Farthington protested that it was dark outside and cold, but Markham, who remembered passing a snug little inn perhaps three miles from Farthington Hall that afternoon when they'd arrived, said that he did not mind the cold. That remark made the duke, who'd heard his bitter animadversions on the breezes blowing through his bedroom window, regard him in amazement.

"A word with you, Bellingham," Markham said when he reached the door of the dining room, signifying by the simple jerking of his head that he wished the word to be outside. The duke, excusing himself with a smile, told his host he would return shortly and joined his friend.

As soon as the door was closed securely behind them, the duke said worriedly that he rather thought Nicholas had lost his mind, planning a ride on a night like this in country unknown to him. Markham merely smiled and said, "Unless I miss my guess, George, there's a snug little supper to be had in that inn we passed on our way here this afternoon, and I intend to find out."

Bellingham sighed. "It *was* a rather dismal meal, wasn't

it? And to think those poor young ladies eat that way every night; in fact, they probably eat worse, because you know they'd put their best forward for company. . . ."

Markham clapped a friendly hand on the duke's shoulder and said that he was convinced the young ladies were putting something forward, to be sure, but he hardly thought it their best. His mild blue eyes reflecting his puzzlement, the duke asked what he meant.

Nicholas was almost tempted to tell him; but no, he decided even as he opened his mouth, he'd play this hand out alone and tell George, who definitely did not have a poker face, later, when Markham was sure just what scheme was afoot. Instead, he recommended that his friend join him on his moonlit ride.

George shook his head wistfully. "It isn't that I wouldn't like to, Nicholas," he said. He lowered his voice even though no one was seen in the hallway, and the Farthington Hall walls were thick, "But think how impolite, to go off and leave Farthington sitting there by himself; and then, too, think how Miss Elizabeth—I mean, the Farthington ladies—would feel if they discovered we'd both found the meal so inedible that we'd gone in search of victuals elsewhere! No, such an insult to a hostess would be inexcusable! I cannot!"

Markham gazed at his friend in admiration. "What a good heart you are, George," he said. "Now myself, I think the Farthington ladies—or, perhaps, more specifically, Miss Katherine Farthington—would be delighted to know she'd driven us elsewhere to eat!"

George stared at him in amazement. "I don't understand—" he began, and his friend smiled at him again.

"There are too few people like you in the world, George," Markham said, preparing to go to his room to trade his evening clothes for his riding habit. "Don't ever change."

Watching him go with a small furrow creasing his forehead, the duke wondered aloud what Nicholas could mean by that. He decided after several moments of perplexed cogitation that it didn't matter, because at the moment he couldn't think of anything he'd change if he could, and he probably couldn't, so what was the use of worrying about it, anyway? Then, with a slight squaring of his shoulders—for Belling-

ham's distaste of Edward Farthington's company, while not
as apparent as his friend's, was almost as keen—he opened
the door to the dining room and went back in to find his host,
already foxed, topping off his glass.

In a moment the duke, making a slight face while Farthington
babbled on about the hunting there was to be found in the
area, discovered one thing he'd change, if he could. The port.

In less than an hour the duke made his excuses to his host
and, with mighty yawns that signified how tired he was, left
the room with the excuse that it had been a long day, and he
planned to seek his hostess to bid her goodnight.

Farthington, staring at him through eyes that had a great
deal of trouble focusing, said, "Eh? Oh. Of course!" His
expression left Bellingham doubtful he'd understood a word,
but by that time he didn't care. In fact, he almost wished he'd
gone with Nicholas to that snug little inn down the road. He
was standing outside the dining room door, debating with
himself whether it was too late to do so, when he heard the
faint strains of Beethoven coming from a room far down the
hall. Intrigued, he followed the sound. For a moment he
stood hesitating before the closed door, then opened it a crack
and peered in, prepared to shut it again quickly, with his
apologies, if he were intruding. So entranced was he by the
sound, and the sight of the eldest Miss Farthington within,
sitting with her back toward him as she swayed with the
music, her golden head held back on her long neck as she let
the music flow through her, that it took him several moments
to realize that this room was very different from any other
he'd seen since coming to the Hall.

Although it was lit only by the candelabra that sat on the
piano and a small fire that burned cheerily on the hearth, as
he stepped inside and closed the door behind him, he could
see that the dainty rosewood furniture was highly polished,
and the rose damask curtains cast a warmth that suited the
room's occupant to perfection. He stood by the door until
Miss Farthington had finished the piece, then burst into enthusiastic applause, startling her so that she rose quickly and
almost knocked over the candelabra.

"My lord!" Elizabeth gasped as he hastened forward to help with the lighting.

"Miss Farthington!" he beamed at her, taking the candelabra from her shaking hand and replaced it gently on the piano. "You were wonderful!"

"Oh no—" A warm flush colored Elizabeth's cheeks most attractively, and in the candlelight he thought a thousand fires glowed in her eyes. "Please—you are too kind! But you shouldn't be here—"

She looked around the room in dismay. He begged her pardon and said that he'd been drawn by the sound of her playing even as he cajoled her to let him stay and listen further.

"Oh, no," Elizabeth said, trying to be firm. "You can't! That is—"

She was interrupted by the entrance of her sister who, carrying a tea tray, was not even looking at the people in the room as she fumbled with the door and said, turning the key in the lock behind her, "Lizzie, you forgot to lock the door. You must be more careful, my love, for what if someone else were to find the music room looking so—"

Katherine turned and stopped in mid-sentence as she encountered the duke's mild questioning gaze. She stood for a moment as if turned to stone, her mouth forming a perfect "O" before she closed it and gulped.

Her sister came to her rescue. Moving forward to take the tray, Elizabeth, through a series of grimaces and jerks of her head toward the duke, said, "Someone else did, Kate."

Kate stared from her to the duke and back again. "I see."

The duke smiled deprecatingly and took the tray from Elizabeth, carrying it to a charming little cherrywood table before the seagreen satin sofa. "I'm sorry," he said, looking from one sister to the other. "I don't wish to intrude. But music is one of my loves, and when I heard Beethoven being played with such beauty and passion, I was drawn to the sound. . . ."

His words trailed off as the sisters continued to stare at him as if he had two heads. Discreetly he glanced down to see if he'd spilled port all over himself or if something else was amiss with his dress. Convinced that was not the case, he smiled at them again.

"Please, Miss Farthington!" he begged. "Won't you play one more piece? Believe me, it would be the highlight of my evening!"

The last sentence was said with so much more feeling than tact that Katherine grinned. Elizabeth, her kind heart touched and her conscience still smarting from the way the sisters were deceiving what seemed to be two very nice guests (although personally, she was a little afraid of that Markham man, who had a sharp eye and a sharper tongue), consented.

After handing the duke a cup of tea—which Katherine recommended he drink up, implying that it would soon be time for him to go, Elizabeth seated herself at the piano again and began to play. This time her fingers brought forth one of the old folk songs her mother used to play, which she herself so dearly loved. When she finished the duke's applause was loud and prolonged.

"Miss Farthington!" he exclaimed, rising and setting down his untouched cup of tea (to Katherine's disgust). "What a talent you have! My dear, it is wonderful!"

Unused to such praise, for her family had grown up with her music and expected her to play well, and few others ever heard her, Elizabeth blushed again, stuttering that he was too kind.

"But no!" Bellingham assured her. "I don't believe I've ever heard better playing in my life—not even in London!"

Elizabeth blushed again and said that he must not say so. Katherine, who loved to hear her sister praised, began to look more kindly on the duke as she told Lizzie not to be silly; if he wanted to say it, he could, and she had no doubt it was true.

For a moment Bellingham had forgotten the younger sister's presence, and he turned almost in surprise to blink at her as she seconded his sentiments.

"When you come to London, Miss Farthington," the duke told Elizabeth, his voice grave, "you will have every hostess in the city begging you to play for her guests whenever possible. Believe me!"

He'd meant it for the compliment it was, but the words

erased the soft smile and gentle glow in Elizabeth's face as she said that, well, it was very good of him to say so, of course; but she would not be going to London, so there was no use talking about it. . . .

"But you must!" the duke cried, stung at the injustice of such a beautiful, talented young woman buried in the wilds. "You would like it very much, I know!"

"Oh, yes!" The glow was back on Elizabeth's face. "I know that I would! My friend, Miss Mannerly, went for one season, and she hasn't stopped talking about it—"

"Even though it was five years ago!" Katherine finished for her, with just the slightest hint of disgust. Unlike Elizabeth, Katherine quickly grew tired of Franny Mannerly's, "Oh, my dear, you should have seen," and, "Then he said this to me, and I said, 'La, sir!' " titterings.

"Mannerly?" The duke's forehead wrinkled. "Mannerly? I don't believe I ever met . . . five years ago . . ." He raised admiring eyes to Elizabeth's face. "But she was much older than you, of course!"

Once again the glow faded. "No," Elizabeth said, busying herself with the tea tray, "we are the same age, Franny and I."

Bellingham, glancing up at Katherine, knew that if he weren't already kicking himself for that faux pas, she would very much like to do it for him, and tried to reclaim the situation. "I think," he said, gazing toward the fire and raising his now tepid cup of tea to his lips, "that young ladies often come to the metropolis before they are ready. No doubt being a little older has its advantages."

Katherine, nodding hopefully, looked toward her sister. Elizabeth sighed.

"Don't you mean being on the shelf, your grace?" Elizabeth asked, raising her violet eyes to his.

The duke drew his breath in sharply and leaned toward her. Katherine's timely clearing of her throat was all that kept him from taking Elizabeth's hand. "Miss Farthington," he told her, and it was apparent he meant every word, "no one in his right mind would ever believe you are on the shelf!"

Katherine beamed. Elizabeth, reading the admiration in his

eyes, blushed even as she said again that he was much, much too kind.

Katherine, who wanted him out of the room before he had the opportunity to turn his thoughts to more than her beautiful sister, suggested hopefully that perhaps he was rather tired as well.

Smiling into Elizabeth's eyes, Bellingham found his brain took several seconds to process the younger Miss Farthington's message. When it did he blinked at her twice, and with an "Oh! Of course! Didn't mean to keep you ladies!" he regretfully rose and set his cup down with a grace that Elizabeth would later call elegant, causing her sister to roll her eyes.

At the door he made them the bow he was known for throughout London. Then, thinking it criminal that such a lovely creature as Elizabeth Farthington had never been allowed her chance to shine in the London sun, he considerably shocked both sisters by saying that he would speak to their uncle about furnishing them with a visit to London.

When he left the music room, his thoughts were fixed on Edward Farthington, and they were not kind at all.

Chapter
Eleven

A QUARTER MOON chased dark clouds across the sky as Markham, astride his huge gelding, made his way toward the small inn he'd seen that afternoon on the way to Farthington Hall. The rhythmic pounding of the horse's hooves was the only sound in the night, and he was glad for the time the ride afforded him to be alone and to think.

Something obviously was taking place at Farthington Hall, and Miss Katherine Farthington was just as obviously behind it. The question that perplexed him most was—why?

He could understand the Farthington sisters wanting to rid themselves of their guardian's presence as soon as possible; Markham thought that a just Providence would have done that years ago.

But he himself and Bellingham were not used to being scorned as guests; in fact, the two of them each year received many more invitations than they possibly could accept. Of those many, there were only a few they really cared for. Of course, he told himself, Miss Katherine Farthington, living retired in the country, would not know that.

For some reason it irked Markham—and it irked him that it irked him—that this country miss should so easily dismiss the honor done her and her sisters by having their home graced by two such leaders of the *ton*. Not that Markham, himself, cared for such things, of course; but he had, over the years, come to accept—and expect—that his considerable fortune and high standing in society would confer certain rights. . . .

That line of thought drew him up sharply, and for a moment he wondered if he was becoming one of those fellows he most despised, always prosing on about their wealth and families and what was due them. He had never thought it possible he would act that way, but now that one small country miss chose not to flatter him the way society did, he was perverse enough to resent her actions, just as he resented being toadeaten.

Patting his horse's neck, his smile was wry as he thought that perhaps this trip north would be better for him than he had first expected. If not, it certainly promised to be—unusual.

Giving himself a shake, he was pleased when the lights of the inn came into view, and he could turn his horse over to an ostler he didn't have to shout at. He hurried inside in search of supper. Too much thinking could, after all, be hazardous to a man's comfort. . . .

Markham's expectations of the bill of fare available at the inn were not disappointed, and it was as he was contentedly finishing a rare sirloin that his attention was attracted by a newcomer to the small public room. He'd chosen to take his supper there so he could observe the local citizens.

The fresh-faced young man was apparently well known to the innkeeper who greeted him with both respect and liking and asked just what he was doing out this night? The young man grinned.

"The Reverend Woodsley came to call," he said. "I thought of something I needed to check on in the stables and kept going!"

The innkeeper grinned. "And what are your mama and papa going to think of that?" he asked.

The young man grinned again. "My mother," he said, giving his head a shake, "is going to think it most improper. My father—" He cocked his head, considering, and the grin grew. "My father is probably fifteen minutes behind me!"

The innkeeper laughed and went off to procure the ale the young man asked for. Tom, his most pressing need taken care

of, idly surveyed the room to see if any of his compatriots
might be about that night. His eyes had passed the lone
farmer seated near the door and gone on to the room's only
other occupant, sitting in the shadows near the fire, when he
straightened rapidly, his jaw dropping slightly.

"Sir!" he said, before he could stop himself.

Markham, who had watched the young man with detached
interest, realized the boy was speaking to him, and rose. He
stepped forward, a doubtful smile on his face as he said, his
voice friendlier than Tom would ever, in his wildest dreams,
have believed possible, "Have we met? If so, I'm sorry—my
dreadful memory—"

Stuttering, Tom hurried forward to take the hand held out
to him and say disjointedly that no, they hadn't met; it was
just that Tom had seen him in London and knew who he
was—way above Tom's league, of course—

Markham stopped the stutterings with a casually held up
hand and said that if Tom would just tell him who he was, he
was pleased to make his acquaintance. Tom stared at him in
disbelief.

"You are?" the young man breathed. Markham bit back
the smile forming on his lips and wished Miss Katherine
Farthington were there to see that someone, at least, held
him in high regard.

"I am," Markham assured him. He invited Tom to join
him at his table, causing that young man's cup to runneth
over—literally, for at the invitation Tom spilled a good part
of the ale the innkeeper had just so thoughtfully handed him.
Rolling his eyes, the innkeeper went off in search of a rag to
wipe the floor, and another tankard of ale.

Once they were seated, Tom continued to stare at his
companion in such awe that Markham, amused, asked him if
he'd grown a third eye or another nose. Instantly Tom blushed
and begged pardon.

"It's just that I can't believe you're here!" he blurted.
"Kate said you were coming, but I must admit, I thought it
was all a hum—"

He caught himself up on the words as Markham leaned
forward, obviously interested, and asked why it would be a
hum.

"Well," Tom shrugged, looking around. "You—here. And coming with Edward Farthington . . ." Too late he realized how that would sound, and he begged pardon, saying hastily that he didn't really know Farthington, of course, and he was sure that if he was a friend of Markham's, he was no doubt a jolly good fellow—although he hid it well . . .

As his words trailed off, Markham assured him that Edward Farthington was no friend of his. Relieved, Tom said he hadn't believed a word of it, and the admiration redoubled in his eyes, to Markham's amusement and slight discomfiture.

"You know, Thomas," Markham said when the young man had sat staring at him for several more moments without speaking, "you do look vaguely familiar . . ."

Proudly Tom explained that their paths had once crossed at a cockfight; Markham smiled his most pleasant smile. "Well then, that practically makes us old friends, doesn't it?"

Encouraged by the smile, Tom was emboldened to confide that ever since that night, he'd done his best to tie his cravat in the Markham style. His idol, looking at the young man's cravat, closed his eyes. If that was the Markham style, he didn't want to know.

A disappointed Tom looked down and sighed. "Of course, I haven't quite got the hang of it, yet. . . ."

Markham's eyes opened, and he smiled again. "Well, don't give up, Thomas," he advised. "I didn't have the hang of it the first eighteen years of my life, either!"

Tom sighed again and said that he was twenty-one. Markham, watching him, hid another smile as he said that since the young man knew who he was and that he was coming, he must be a friend of the Misses Farthington. Tom, who had faithfully promised Kate he would consult with her before encountering the gentlemen she said were coming, gulped and said that, well, yes, they were acquainted . . .

The innkeeper, hearing the Farthington name as he brought a new mug of ale for young Tom and another for Mr. Markham, asked the young gentleman if that was Miss Katherine Farthington's Thunderer he'd seen Tom riding just that morning.

Markham's attention grew, and Tom said hastily that no, Farley must be mistaken; everyone knew the Farthington

ladies only had an old cob in their stables. Tom's series of
grimaces and winks were ignored as the proprietor clapped
him on the shoulder good-naturedly.

"Now, young sir, if that isn't just like you!" the landlord
beamed. "Always joking! As if Miss Katherine would give
up her Thunderer! Or any of those other high-bred good 'uns
she has!"

The continued facial contortions, winks, and head-wavings
meant to send him away made the innkeeper stare. After
several moments he took himself off with the warning that
Tom had better watch himself, because he seemed to be
coming down with something, and it might prove serious.
Tom closed his eyes and sighed, remembering Katherine's
blithe promise that it was she who would end up in the basket
if her plans went awry, not he . . .

When he opened his eyes again, Markham was observing
him closely.

"I was in Miss Farthington's stables tonight," Markham
said, watching the effect of his words on his companion,
"and there was only one horse there." Tom waited. "An old
cob."

Tom breathed a sigh of relief and said well, that just went
to show; Farley was well enough, but a bit thick-headed, and
you couldn't believe what he said. . . .

His words trailed off as what he thought was a welcome
diversion entered the room in the form of his father, who,
after calling for an ale of his own, came forward with,
"Thomas, that's Kate's Thunderer you have out there, and
you'd best be careful with him, for if anything happens to the
horse, you know she'll have your hide—"

By now the squire had perceived that someone else was
seated with his son, and he stopped at their table, waiting
expectantly as Markham rose. Thomas, wishing he'd stayed
to hear Reverend Woodsley, made introductions. The squire,
a bluff, good-natured man, shook Markham's hand and asked
whom in the neighborhood he was visiting. Thomas sighed
and Markham, after a quizzical glance in his direction, said it
was the Farthington ladies.

"Eh?" The squire had half turned to say something to
Farley, but at that he turned back, and gave Mr. Markham his

close regard. "Up at Farthington Hall, are you?" Another keen glance took in Markham top to toe and back again. "Got your lady with you, do you?"

Thomas uttered a strangled sound of embarrassment as Markham said smoothly that no, he and his friend, the Duke of Bellingham, were there with the Farthington sisters' guardian.

By now the squire had seated himself, but at that he half rose and glared down at Mr. Markham. "Edward Farthington?" he said. "Well, give me leave to tell you, sir, that he may be a friend of yours, but he is no friend of mine!"

Hastily Tom interrupted to say that Edward Farthington was no friend of Mr. Markham's either. The squire, after considering that for a moment, said that it didn't make sense; if they weren't friends, why would he accompany a man he didn't like to the north in November, for goodness sakes?

Markham, who had been asking himself that same question on the way to the inn that evening, hedged that he and his friend had—business—with Farthington. The squire continued to regard him broodingly as he pondered the question. At last he thought he had it, and his loud "Aha!" made his son, nervously sipping his ale, spill again.

"So that's it, is it?" the squire said, waving a finger in his son's face as Thomas looked at him in trepidation, trying at the same time to keep one eye on Markham. "I never did believe that faradiddle about Kate sending her horses over to our stables because she was having some work done on her own! There aren't better kept stables in the country than those at Farthington Hall!"

Markham, thinking of the stables that had greeted his eyes that evening, raised his eyebrows inquiringly, and Tom gulped.

"Father, please—" Tom started, pulling on the squire's jacket. His father smiled at him.

"No, no," the squire promised. "Mum's the word." His attention returned to Mr. Markham. "And I will tell you, sir, that if Edward Farthington brought you up here by telling you he has some of the best horseflesh in the country for sale, it is a lie. Those horses belong to Katherine; her father left them directly to her, for even when she was a very tiny girl, he saw his own love of a good animal in her. And if you tell Farthington where they are, it would be very scaly of you.

And what's more, I'll help the children hide them again. That I will!''

Shaking his head for emphasis, the squire downed half his tankard in one gulp, his thirst having increased dramatically after what was, for him, a long speech. Tom closed his eyes and sighed. Gravely Markham assured the squire that he had no intention of trying to buy Miss Farthington's horses.

"Good!" the squire said, pleased that his speech had been so effective. Tom, his eyes still closed, sighed again.

Chapter
Twelve

THE GENTLEMEN LEFT the inn a short time later in great accord. After the squire connected Markham's name with the London beau that Thomas was forever going on about, he was even moved to say, "Perhaps some of you London dandies have some sense, after all!"

Thomas, who looked ready to sink at the remark, could only give Markham his stammered thanks after the squire, with a cheerful good-night and an invitation to visit them anytime Markham might like, walked off toward the stables. Markham had to ask just what the young man was thanking him for, and Thomas, flushing, said it was for not setting his father down dreadfully.

Markham's gaze was quizzing. "Is that what you believe I would normally do, Thomas?" he asked. "Set down someone as worthy as your father?"

Well, no, Tom said; it was just that someone so used to being regarded as Mr. Markham was in his world might take umbrage at the remarks of a country squire . . .

Markham smiled at him, that attractive smile that made Tom feel taller in the world's eyes. "Your father is not just a country squire, Thomas," Markham said gently. "He is a man of good sense and conviction. You are very lucky."

Tom's nod was serious, and he would have said more on this comparatively safe subject. Unfortunately Markham turned the conversation in the direction Tom was dreading by asking abruptly, "Now, young man, I will thank you for telling me just what is going on at Farthington Hall."

Thomas tried to assume the innocent expression that worked so well for Katherine and failed miserably. "Going on, sir?" he countered.

Markham grinned. "Why are Miss Farthington's horses in your stables?"

Manfully Thomas repeated the story about the Farthington stables needing work. Markham said that he might very well believe that, but it was clear Thomas's father didn't. Tom bit his lip and said loyally that Mr. Markham would have to ask Katherine.

Markham regarded him with curiosity. "In love with her, are you, Thomas?" he asked.

Tom's eyes widened, and the way he hooted quickly disabused Markham's mind of that notion. For some reason Markham felt his own spirits rise in light of the young man's evident disbelief.

"In *love?*" Tom repeated. "With *Katherine?* You must be joking!"

Markham begged pardon and then asked why the young man was so obviously involved in whatever it was Miss Farthington was doing. Tom objected that Mr. Markham didn't know Katherine very well if he thought it possible to be around her long and remain uninvolved.

"The thing is, sir," Tom said confidentially as the squire emerged from the inn's stable leading his own and his son's horses, followed closely by the ostler with Markham's animal, "Kate's like a sister to me. All the girls are. I have to help them when I can. You see that, don't you?"

Markham said that he did, but he still didn't know what Tom was helping them with. The younger man was more than a little relieved when his father interrupted the conversation to say that Markham rode a horse he wouldn't disdain owning himself.

Markham smiled. "Thank you," he said, "but he's not for sale."

The squire said frankly that he hadn't thought the animal would be, but it never hurt to ask, and the three took leaves of each other without giving Markham any further opportu-

nity to question Tom. For that the younger man was deeply
thankful. As it was, the Misses Farthington's guest still had
more than enough to think about on his ride back to Farthington
Hall.

In the Farthington Hall stable Markham made as much noise
as he could bedding his horse down, but no groom appeared.
He had the feeling that Johns was peering at him from his
loft, making sure no damage was done to the stables or the
old horse left in the groom's care, but Markham could not
catch the man at it. So, after pitching some hay into his
animal and rubbing the roan's neck as the horse nuzzled his
pocket in search of a carrot, Markham walked up to the Hall,
whistling as he gazed at the stars that had made their way into
the night sky.

At the house he let himself in by the side door through
which he'd departed. He was making his way quietly toward
the stairs when the suspicion of a giggle off to his left made
him stop and listen carefully in the darkness. Just as he had
convinced himself he'd heard nothing and was stepping forward, the sound came again. Curiosity got the best of him,
and he made his way toward it, walking stealthily to avoid
making any noise.

As he drew nearer to the sound, he saw a narrow beam of
light escaping a small room that had its door almost closed,
and he sniffed appreciatively at the aroma emanating from the
room. When he was close enough, he cautiously peered
inside and a sardonic smile lit his eyes. Katherine and
Elizabeth Farthington, Horton, Matthew, and an older woman
he did not know were gathered around a table on which
sat the remnants of a ham, a much better baked chicken
than the one he had been served earlier in the Farthington
dining room, and cherry tarts that made his nostrils twitch
appreciatively.

"Mrs. Goodsley," Markham heard Katherine say, "I could
have hugged you when you slammed that door just after I'd
told Uncle Edward about Pooley's ghost writing letters! You
should have seen his face! I know he thought the ghost was
going to get him, then and there!"

Katherine chortled merrily even as the now-identified Mrs.
Goodsley shook her head at her.

"Such a story, Miss Katherine!" the older woman said. "I
could feel my palpitations coming on, sure! And I didn't
slam the door on purpose—it slipped out of my grasp; you
shocked me that much, you did! You always were a one with
stories, even when you were a tiny girl, but . . . ."

Seeing that such remonstrations might lead to other remembrances of past behaviors Katherine would just as soon not
have brought up, she hastily changed the subject.

"And the soup, Mrs. Goodsley!" Katherine said. "The
soup was wonderful! If only you could have seen Uncle
Edward's face when he took that first big gulp—"

Markham's own lips turned up in sympathy as those in the
room burst into laughter. He'd enjoyed that sight himself.

"I thought he was going to spit it out," Matthew so far
forgot himself as to say, drawing Horton's and Mrs. Goodsley's
frowns. He subsided even as Katherine agreed with him.

"And then poor Bellingham, trying to gloss everything
over by saying he didn't think it was too bad—" Katherine
started. She was stopped by her sister, who said reproachfully
that while she perfectly understood why they must trick their
uncle, and she certainly thought he deserved it, she could not
like the fact that they also were playing the same trick on the
duke and his friend. She added that Katherine should not
make fun of a person whose excellent manners and kind heart
had made him try to help them as much as he could.

Katherine, willing to concede that the duke might—just
might—deserve better than he was getting, was wont to argue
when Elizabeth included Bellingham's friend Markham as a
candidate for sympathy.

"Personally," she said, her small nose in the air, "I think
Mr. Markham is every bit as deserving of pepper soup as
Uncle Edward—"

"Oh, Katherine!" her sister's voice was reproachful, and
the middle Miss Farthington sniffed again.

"Well, he is!" she insisted. "The way he looks down his
nose at us, so—" Here Markham was treated to a performance of how he looked down his nose; a performance that
made him want to laugh and figuratively box a certain young

lady's ears simultaneously. "—and the things he says, as if he knows something untoward is going on—"

"But what if he does?" Elizabeth interrupted nervously. "You know that Tom said he is alive to every trick—"

"Tom!" Katherine repeated scornfully in a tone that would not have done that young man's ego any good. "He's so taken with the fact that these two London beaus, as he calls them, are here, and the idea that he might get to come within two miles of them—" Markham grinned and wished he could see Miss Farthington's face when young Thomas told her they'd been much closer than two miles.

Elizabeth objected that that was unfair; she shouldn't speak of Tom so and, after all, Mr. Markham had been quite kind to Chloe. Katherine frowned as she considered that statement; after several moments she allowed that it was true, but she herself thought he was probably just hoping to get information from the child. She added that it sounded, from what Chloe and Johns said, as if his plan hadn't worked.

Markham's brows snapped together, and he was angry not because Miss Farthington was wrong, but because she was completely right. He *had* thought to gain information from the child, and he had gained a little, but he hadn't been long in the little girl's company before he realized, to his surprise, that he was enjoying himself. He'd been amused by the way her forehead wrinkled in concentration when she was puzzling something out and the way she surveyed him with those big brown eyes, so like her middle sister's, when she was listening to what he had to say.

Recalling what his grandmother used to say about people who listen at doors never hearing any good about themselves, Markham stepped back. Inadvertently he brushed against a small table to his left, and the vase that sat there wobbled loudly on the wood before he was able to catch it and right it again. Instantly those within the small breakfast nook—for such Markham had determined it to be—grew silent.

"What was that?" he heard the voice that belonged to the woman identified as Mrs. Goodsley ask.

"Probably Chloe's cat," Katherine said, trying for nonchalance even as she gazed worriedly toward the door.

"Or maybe," Elizabeth cleared her throat, trying to jest,

"it's that ghost you keep trying to bring to the Hall, Katherine dear."

Everyone laughed dutifully as Horton, rising with dignity, said that he would just go see. Markham, his eyes searching frantically for a place to hide, felt his way down the wall until he encountered a suit of armor that no doubt had belonged to an earlier Farthington. Hastily he slipped into the armor's shadow, taking care not to touch the metal and send it clanking toward the butler, who by that time was peering down the hall. At last, satisfied that it had been nothing threatening, Horton turned back into the room, seconding Miss Katherine's opinion that it must have been Miss Chloe's cat as he firmly shut the door behind him.

Markham, thanking his lucky stars, backed away from the armor, gave it a snappy salute, and made his way up to bed. He lay awake there for some time, considering all he had heard and seen that day and watching the curtain blow in the wind.

Chapter
Thirteen

MARKHAM NEXT ENCOUNTERED Katherine and Elizabeth Farthington at the breakfast table. It was early morning, and the
surprise on their faces as he entered the room almost made
him laugh. Instead, he bowed smoothly and took his place
beside Miss Katherine Farthington. She surveyed him with
disfavor.

"Mr. Markham, what a surprise!" she said, her voice
making it apparent it was not a happy one. "I did not believe
Londoners were early risers!"

"Ah, but we are not in London, are we, Miss Farthington?"
he replied pleasantly, which made her frown more.

"Nooooo," Katherine said. She cocked her head to one
side as he had seen Chloe do last night, and her dark eyelashes
fell as she watched him carefully through her half-hid eyes.
"But I imagine you would like to be."

"Not at all," Markham said politely, helping himself from
the plate of cold eggs Matthew was holding out to him. He
noted that steam still rose from the eggs on the sisters' plates
but made no comment.

"I imagine you will be returning to London soon," Katherine continued on hopefully.

Markham cocked his head much as she had, and considered. "I believe," he said, "that your uncle invited us to stay
a fortnight."

"But you won't!" Katherine half rose, throwing down her

napkin in disbelief, as her sister tried frantically to catch her eye. Markham raised an eyebrow in surprise but allowed himself to be distracted as Elizabeth asked desperately if he had passed a good night.

Markham nodded. "Quite good."

"And you were warm enough?" The hope was back in Katherine's voice, and he had to hide a smile as her sister signaled her again with an expressive rolling of her violet eyes.

"Quite."

Katherine gaped at him. "You were?"

"Yes." Markham smiled in remembrance as he sipped the tea Matthew had just poured him, ignoring its cold temperature in a way that made Katherine and the footman exchange looks of great puzzlement. "In fact, I had the most pleasant dream."

He had turned toward Elizabeth with his last statement and she, ever courteous, murmured, "You did?" as she took a small bite of toast.

"Yes," Markham affirmed. "I dreamed I was in a room—oh, very much like this one, actually—and there was the most delicious smell—of ham, and baked chicken, and cherry tarts—"

Elizabeth started to choke on a toast crumb caught in her throat. Markham, his face concerned, rose to pat her on the back. "My dear Miss Farthington," he said, "are you all right?"

Now it was Elizabeth's turn to gape at him.

Katherine, trying to turn the conversation, said she believed his friend had said he'd gone for a ride last night after supper.

Markham returned to his place at the table and picked up his napkin again, forking cold eggs and ham into his mouth as if they were delicious. Katherine and Elizabeth exchanged glances and waited. "Yes," Markham said, wiping his lips on a much-patched napkin, "I did."

He took another bite of egg and washed it down with the cold tea. Katherine, impatient, prompted him. "And where did you go?"

He appeared surprised at her interest and said vaguely that

he'd been here and there. His answer seemed to relieve her, and she'd settled back into her chair and bitten into her own egg when he added, almost as an afterthought, "And, oh yes, I met two of your neighbors last night at the Small Swan Inn."

Now it was Katherine's turn to choke on her breakfast, but she recovered hastily, waving him away as he made to rise and pound her on the back, too.

"My goodness," Mr. Markham said, "something in this morning's breakfast must certainly stick in you ladies' throats!"

Katherine's fine eyes made it apparent just what was sticking in *her* throat, and Elizabeth intervened in haste to ask why he had gone to the Small Swan.

Markham smiled gently. "They serve an excellent rare sirloin, Miss Farthington," he said, surprised when the remark made her color to the roots of her hair. She started to say something when her sister, with a loud "Ahem!" cut her off. Markham turned toward Katherine inquiringly.

"You said you encountered two of our neighbors, Mr. Markham?"

He nodded.

Katherine lifted her teacup and surveyed him over it, her lashes falling forward over her eyes again as she strove for nonchalance. "Which two?"

Markham picked up his own teacup and sipped its contents. "Your Squire—Mannerling, I believe the name was—and his son, Thomas."

"Thomas!" the sisters repeated.

"Yes. A very nice young man."

"Oh, no!" Katherine moaned. Willfully Markham misunderstood her.

"He's not?" he questioned.

Surprised, Katherine cocked her head. "Not?"

"Not a nice young man?"

Elizabeth intervened to say that yes, Thomas was all that was agreeable; in fact, he'd been like a brother to them since—well, since they could any of them remember . . .

Her voice trailed off and Markham, listening considerately, said, "Well, yes, that would explain it," as he again applied his napkin to his lips.

Katherine and Elizabeth exchanged glances and waited. When they had waited what Katherine felt was more than long enough, she eyed him frostily and said, "Explain what?"

Mr. Markham's look was innocent. "Why both the squire and the innkeeper thought that young Thomas was riding a horse that belonged to you. I suppose he lets you ride it a great deal—" He watched with enjoyment as his words sunk in, and indignation grew on the middle Miss Farthington's face.

"He was riding *Thunderer?*" she exclaimed.

Markham nodded. "Yes. I believe that was the horse's name. Beautiful black animal. Grand hocks—"

"At *night?*" Katherine's voice was rising.

Markham nodded again.

"He took out *my* Thunderer—at *night*—without even a by-your-leave—" Katherine stuttered. Mr. Markham raised an inquiring eyebrow, and Elizabeth, trying once again to catch her sister's attention, explained as best she might that Kate so often rode the horse that she had come to think of it quite as her own—

"I certainly do!" Katherine said, a martial light in her eye.

Markham, enjoying himself immensely, said that it was very nice of young Mannerling to loan her the horse.

"Loan—me—the horse—" Katherine choked. Hastily Elizabeth said that it was indeed nice of Thomas.

"In fact, I liked the animal so much that I'm thinking of asking Thomas if he'd sell it," Markham said.

"In a pig's eye!" Katherine was standing now, glaring down at him, as a frantic Elizabeth said that what dear Katherine meant was that Thomas was very unlikely to sell, because Thunderer was such a—special—horse . . . She was floundering badly and cast an appealing glance at her sister. Katherine, recalled to her place, resumed her seat and said gruffly that Thunderer was not Thomas's to sell.

"Oh." Markham thought for a moment. "You mean I should go to the squire—"

"I mean you should go to—" Katherine snapped, her last word swallowed as Chloe tripped into the room, smiling expectantly at all of them.

"Good morning, Chloe." Elizabeth's tone was over-bright,

her usual fond smile for her sister even fonder today as the child offered hope of getting them out of this sticky situation.

"Good morning, Elizabeth," Chloe said, offering her sister a quick kiss on the cheek. "Good morning, Katherine." There was a kiss for her second sister, too, and Markham noted that some of the temper went out of the middle Miss Farthington's eyes as she smiled at her younger sister.

"Good morning, sweetings," Katherine said as Chloe slipped into the chair on her right and smiled around her older sister at Markham.

"Good morning, sir," Chloe said shyly, her apparent liking for the gentleman showing what Katherine considered a woeful lack of judgment.

"Good morning, Chloe," Markham said, noting without comment that a plate of hot food miraculously appeared for the youngest Miss Farthington. "I trust you slept well?"

Chloe, already attacking her breakfast, nodded.

"No sleep troubled by ghosts?" he teased.

Katherine frowned at him as Chloe giggled.

"Ahh," Katherine said, her gaze speculative. "So you have heard about our ghost, Mr. Markham."

He smiled at her. "But of course, Miss Farthington. I was there last night when you told of your dear departed governess."

Katherine, who had thought he'd been gone when she spun that tale, frowned again and shushed her younger sister, who said with a sigh that she wished Pooley would come back again.

"And you don't believe me, sir?" Katherine asked, ignoring Elizabeth's anguished "Katherine, please!" as the middle Miss Farthington lifted her chin and stared challengingly into their guest's eyes.

Markham smiled. "Let us just say, Miss Farthington, that I am skeptical."

"You do not believe in ghosts, then?" The look of speculation was growing, and he was intrigued as he watched her expressive face and countered that he had never met one.

Katherine's challenge grew. "Perhaps it is just the Farthington Hall ghost you don't believe in, Mr. Markham?"

He shrugged. "I have not yet encountered that ghost, either, Miss Farthington."

Elizabeth, reading her sister's eyes correctly, said with real authority that it was certainly to be hoped that he never would, either. Katherine raised her eyebrows, and Elizabeth repeated her statement. Markham laughed.

"I'm sure you are right, Miss Farthington," he said to Elizabeth, even as he rose to leave. "For I'm not sure it would be the wisest ghost who chose to cross swords with me. And now, if you ladies will excuse me—" He made a slight bow toward all three. "I believe I will take a ride through some of this area. I find it interesting. In fact—" He paused until he was sure he had everyone's attention, for Katherine had been sitting as if her mind were far away for the last several moments, and he guessed that a new plot was in her weavings. "—if my friend Bellingham doesn't buy this place, I may even be persuaded to do so myself!"

He watched Katherine's eyes grow wide with disbelief before he bowed himself from the room and made his way down the hall, smiling in satisfaction.

Chapter
Fourteen

"OH, KATHERINE, WHAT are we to do?" Elizabeth wailed as soon as the door was latched behind Markham.

Katherine, already deep in thought, waved her into silence. Chloe, watching them both, said she was sure that if they'd just tell Mr. Markham that they didn't want to sell their house, he would go away, because he seemed like a very nice man. Katherine regarded her with sorrow.

"Ah, Chloe," Kate said, reaching out to tousle her sister's hair, "you're so very young."

Chloe thought about that as Elizabeth once again asked what they were to do. This time Katherine answered her.

"Do?" the middle Miss Farthington said, her eyes alight. "I'll tell you what we're going to do! We're going to redouble our efforts and send those Londoners flying back to the metropolis before—before—" She spotted Chloe's calico cat sitting contentedly in its mistress's lap, eating as many pieces of the girl's breakfast as she could slip it. "—before Calico can lick her ear!"

Just then the cat undertook a vigorous washing, running one paw over the ear in question. Chloe laughed. "That quick, Katherine?" she questioned.

Her sister smiled. "Almost," she promised. "Almost."

Elizabeth, watching worriedly, said nothing.

It was an anxious Tom Mannerling who waited for Katherine in the spinney at 10 A.M. He wanted to warn her about his encounter with Markham, and his father's disastrous disclosure that Katherine had any number of good horses stabled at the squire's. Like the Farthington sisters, his own belief was that a London beau—and a beau who had to wait upon himself, at that, for when he'd stopped by the Farthington stables that morning, Johns gleefully had told him about how the gentlemen were doing without *their* gentlemen—would not leave his room until well past noon. He was considerably startled, therefore, when Katherine's first words upon spying him were, "How dare you, Tom Mannerling?"

He stared at her.

"How *dare* you ride Thunderer at night, you big ox? What if he'd stepped in a hole? What if he'd bolted with you? What if—"

She got no farther. Tom, revolted by her second suggestion, argued spiritedly that there was no danger of Thunderer —or any other horse, he'd thank her to know—bolting with him. They glared at each other for several moments before Tom, realizing what they were arguing about, said feebly, "Oh. He told you then, did he?"

Katherine nodded.

"I'm sorry, Kate. I tried my best to stop my father from telling him. . . ."

"He's talking about buying Thunderer—" Katherine began.

Tom shook his head at her. "At least my father told him the horse wasn't for sale," he offered. "He said you'd never sell him or any of the others . . ."

Now it was Katherine's turn to shake her head, and she did. "What?" she questioned, as if she'd heard wrong.

Obligingly Tom repeated his statement.

"But—" Katherine was staring at him with an odd expression, and he waited patiently. He'd seen that look before. "Are you saying—"

Still Tom waited.

"Are you saying he knows Thunderer is my horse?" Her surprise was evident. It was mirrored by Tom's.

Tom nodded. "Of course," he said. "I told you. My father let the cat out of the bag. Said he figured you were hiding your horses in our stables because your uncle brought

Markham and the duke here to buy them, and you didn't want to sell. And he said I shouldn't be riding Thunderer at night—''

Too late Tom realized he'd brought up a topic he'd just as soon have forgotten as Kate fired up that his father was right. Hastily Tom continued, saying his father had made it quite apparent the horse was Katherine's.

"Then why—'' she started, her brow puzzled. Absently she broke a branch off one of the trees and switched it against her skirt as she thought.

"Why what?'' Tom asked. Katherine stared at him.

"This morning Markham acted as if he thought Thunderer was your horse—I mean, your father's—and he said he was going to try to buy him. Now why—'' She was pondering the question deeply, but Tom didn't have to think about it long before he had an answer.

"He probably was giving you back a bit of your own,'' Tom offered, with more wisdom than tact.

Katherine frowned at him. "But that would mean he knows—''

Tom's nod contained a certain gloomy satisfaction. "Told you he was a downy one.''

Katherine's frown grew. "He can't know!''

Tom, willing to stretch the point, said that perhaps Markham just suspected. Katherine's frown continued.

"But he can't!'' she repeated. "He could spoil everything!''

Tom agreed that that could be the case. Without thinking he added that after all, he'd told her so. . . . Katherine snapped the stick she was holding and threw the pieces away.

"Desperate times call for desperate measures,'' she said.

"Now Kate.'' Tom shifted uneasily.

She smiled as if he'd been quite sage. "You're quite right, Tom,'' she approved. "Now!''

Katherine was still deep in thought as she made her way back to the house and slipped into the library. It was apparent she needed to rid the Hall of these Londoners, and quickly. Not only were they a threat to her beloved home, but one of them was proving a decided threat to her equilibrium as well. Although she would not admit it even to Elizabeth, she, like Elizabeth, found their guests attractive, although she was surprised that Elizabeth could prefer the duke's blond charm to Markham's dark good looks. Such attraction, Kate told herself severely, would not do, and she was smart enough to know that the sooner the gentlemen returned to their world, the sooner serenity would return to hers.

And if she would miss the spice to life that at least one of the guests seemed to have brought with him—well, what did she need with this flustered feeling that occurred when what was really a remarkably rude and disturbing man was near? And what did she need with this continual clashing of wills? Although if he thought he could get the better of her . . . The words about crossing swords with him had almost been a warning, and immediately Katherine had determined that should any such sword crossing occur, she *would* win. Who did he think he was, anyway? Coming here to turn her world upside down. And coming with her odious uncle, which just went to prove that he had no taste. . . .

The thought of taste made her think of pepper soup, and she was smiling as she slipped through the library door, her cheeks still flushed from her walk in the November air, several wisps of her dark hair escaping their pins and clinging to her cheeks. The smile vanished abruptly as she found that this, her favorite room in the house, already was occupied.

Markham, looking up at the remarkably pretty picture she presented, could not but be sorry when the smile disappeared, to be replaced by a scowl he felt was reserved for him alone. He sighed.

"You!" Katherine said.

Markham rose, carefully keeping his finger in his place in the book he'd been enjoying by the fire. "Miss Farthington."

"What are *you* doing here?"

He glanced down at the book in his hand and up again as he said, smiling faintly, "I am quite found out. I was reading."

"You *read?*" The look was one of disbelief, and he felt his laughter rising.

"It was part of my education, yes," he murmured. Almost she colored.

"I just meant—that is—"

Understanding dawned, and his smile grew stronger. "Yes,

Miss Farthington, it is true, but I beg you won't tell anyone. The sorry fact is, even London beaus read."

This time she did flush as she looked away, then back again.

"You said you were going riding." It was almost an accusation, and he nodded.

"I was. But then I chanced to encounter Horton coming out of this room as I was passing by, and I must admit, I was intrigued by the size of your library." He held up the book he'd been reading. "This volume, for instance, is quite rare."

Katherine said that her father had been a great reader, and his father before him, and *his* father before *him*. Markham nodded.

"There are also some quite new volumes on your shelves," he said. Katherine gazed into the corner as she said stiffly that she read now and then herself.

Markham nodded again. "It must be difficult—" he said. "As impoverished as you are—"

That brought Katherine's eyes back to his face, and she regarded him suspiciously. He met her look with one of great innocence, and she said at last that well, yes, it *was* difficult, but their governess often bought books—

"Your late governess, you mean," Markham interrupted. Katherine frowned at him again.

"Of course."

They stood for several moments in silence before Markham remarked politely that it was a most comfortable room. Katherine nodded.

"The chimney doesn't smoke."

She started, and her cheeks reddened as she said that he was lucky; it was just the day; the wind might turn at any moment. . . . Her words trailed off in the face of his evident disbelief, and she said ungraciously that if he meant to continue in the room, she would busy herself elsewhere. Markham smiled his most attractive smile as he told her she was welcome to stay.

"I can't—" Katherine began, saw his eyebrow raise, and stuttered, "—what I mean is—there are other things I must do—"

"If I did not know you to be an intrepid young lady, Miss

Farthington, I would almost believe you are afraid to be in the room with me!''

''That's foolish!'' Katherine said, her eyes sparkling as her chin rose in the motion he was coming to know well. ''I'm not afraid of you or anyone else.''

Markham gazed at the ceiling as he said it was a foolish person who feared no one. Katherine's chin rose farther.

''Are you saying I *should* be afraid of you, Mr. Markham?''

''No.'' She had his full attention now, and it was a bit more than she wanted. There was a look in his eye that she did not understand, and did not care to. ''No, Miss Farthington, you should not.'' She looked away, but her eyes were brought back by his next words. ''But you should be honest with me. I demand that—in all my relationships.''

Katherine meant to say that they had no relationship, but the words faltered in her throat. His gaze held hers, and for a moment she could do no more than look at him. Then she gave herself a visible shake. ''I don't know what you mean, sir,'' she said, pleased that her voice could sound so calm when inside she felt so quavery.

''Don't you, Miss Farthington?'' His voice was soft even as his gaze grew more remote. He shrugged. ''Perhaps. But I wonder.''

Katherine, determined not to understand what he meant, left the room, closing the door behind her with a smart snap. She was not at all pleased when, through the thick door, she was sure she heard a soft laugh.

Chapter
Fifteen

"I'LL SHOW *him*!" Katherine thought as she hurried through the halls, carried along by her anger. "How *dare* he laugh at me? And talk about relationships! As if I'd have a—a—a—relationship!—with a man who is forever baiting me and crossing my will!"

Her last statement brought her up abruptly, and she could hear Pooley admonishing her that to be unable to bear having one's will crossed was a dangerous thing. She felt guilty, before deciding that Mr. Markham could stand to have his own will foiled now and then, too. *He* certainly wasn't a person used to it, that she could tell. And it would give her such pleasure to teach him a lesson. But how to do it? There he sat, comfortably ensconced in her favorite room, while she was forced to go elsewhere. . . .

Her steps slowed as she thought about that, and a slow smile began to play across her lips. Encountering Horton, she asked where Matthew was and was disappointed to hear that he'd been sent into the village on an errand for Mrs. Goodsley. An inquiry for Johns elicited the information that he'd gone over to the squire's to make sure that the horses normally in his care were receiving the proper attention. Katherine smiled as she thought of how happy that would make Tom's groom. Horton, after a moment's hestitation, asked if there was something he might do for her.

Katherine shook her head regretfully as she surveyed the

white-haired butler and said no, she would do it herself; it
was of no moment. Then, one foot on the stairway, she
asked, almost as an afterthought, where Johns had put the
ladder. Horton, about to enter the morning room, stopped and
peered at her in some concern.

"Now, Miss Katherine," he asked, "what would you be
wanting with a ladder?"

Katherine opened her eyes wide and said that he had
misunderstood; she didn't want the ladder now; she just wanted
to know where it was so that she could find it if she needed it
in the future.

Horton stood for several moments, studying her, before he
said that he believed Johns had left it at the back of the Hall.
Katherine thanked him and proceeded slowly up the steps as
if the information was already forgotten. Once around the
bend in the stairway, however, her pace quickened, and
she was almost running as she reached her room. Inside she
crossed quickly to the old trunk that stood at the bottom of
her bed and rummaged there for several moments. She pulled
out the old pair of pantaloons and the shirt she'd cajoled from
Tom before he convinced her that her plan to ride Thunderer
at Haymarket really would *not* work, no matter *what* she said.
Changing into them, she grinned at herself in the mirror
before she picked up a pillow from her bed and crossed to the
door, opening it cautiously to see if anyone was in sight
before she let herself into the hall and made for the back
stairway.

Once outside it took her some moments to find the ladder,
for Johns had leaned it against the wall on the far side, and it
was half-hidden by shrubbery. Hugging her too-big shirt more
closely about her, she noticed that the wind had come up and
tried to hurry her task. The ladder, however, proved unwieldy,
and it took her longer than she'd expected to carry it around
to the west side of the house where the library was located.
Sneaking a quick glance in the window, all she could see of
Markham was his boots as he sat reading by the fire; the rest
of him was hidden from her view by the large chair in which
he sat.

By now she was shivering so in the cold air that she almost
considered giving up her plan. But she had come this far and

so, positioning the ladder so that it extended as near the library chimney as she could get, she clutched the pillow to her and started her upward climb, warming herself with the thought that Mr. Markham soon would find that the library chimney smoked, too! She practically chuckled out loud, but a particularly strong gust of wind swayed the ladder at just that moment, effectively stilling her laughter as she clung to the swaying wood. It was with relief that she reached the roof, and she *did* laugh as she stuffed the pillow into the chimney. She'd see how Mr. Markham liked *that!*

She was still grinning as she turned to scramble down and into the warm house. She was just in time to see the ladder disappear from sight.

"Oh, no!" she wailed, her words carried away on the wind as she made her way to the edge of the roof. Almost slipping on the worn tiles, she was reduced to crawling the last few feet on her hands and knees. When she peered over the side of the roof, the ladder lay on the ground, and she regarded it in frustration for several moments.

Really, Katherine thought, this had been the most trying day. She hugged her arms more closely about her and was wondering what to do next when Tom came into sight. Too glad to see him to wonder what he was doing there, she called "Pssst!" and was provoked when he did not at first hear her. Wondering crossly what held his attention so closely, for he was looking back, she had just said "Tom!" more loudly when the object of her childhood friend's attention also came around the corner. Too late Katherine tried to shrink back as Tom, with a disbelieving "Kate?" directed both his own and his companion's gazes upward. Katherine was left staring into the quizzical eyes of Nicholas Markham.

"Oh, no!" she groaned, even as Tom demanded to know what she was doing up there.

"Well, what are you doing down there?" she countered, exasperated to find her plans once again so far awry. "And—" she frowned heavily at the squire's son, "with *him?*"

Then another thought struck her. "And if you aren't in the library," she demanded of Markham, "who—"

That question was answered almost immediately as the duke came around the house, coughing. At sight of the other two gentlemen he said that the wind must have changed, because the library fireplace had started to smoke alarmingly. Katherine saw enlightenment dawn on Markham's face and sighed.

"Well, well!" Mr. Markham said, staring up at her.

"Well?" Tom repeated, staring at him.

"Well?" the duke asked, looking at both of them before glancing up to see what held Markham's attention. At sight of Katherine he gasped.

"Miss Farthington!" Bellingham said. Kate smiled weakly. "What are you doing up there?"

"Yes, Miss Farthington, what are you doing up there?" Markham almost purred the words, and Kate longed to hit him even as she said, through chattering teeth, that the ladder had fallen. . . .

Since it was in front of the three of them she thought that should have been apparent, but all three stared at the ladder as if they'd never seen one before. No one moved to pick it up, so she suggested, as politely as she could, that that might be a very good thing.

Hastily Tom and Bellingham moved to do as she asked, but Markham held out a detaining hand as he stood, craning up at her. "Perhaps, Miss Farthington," he said, "while you're up there, you might like to check the library chimney, to see if it's blocked."

She glared down at him as Bellingham protested that she could not tell. Markham gazed enigmatically at his friend. "Oh, I think she could," he said. He craned his neck again to look at Katherine. "Couldn't you, Miss Farthington?"

Kate ignored Markham as she asked Tom and the duke to raise the ladder. They did at once, both gazing in reproach at the third gentleman who, ignoring them, started to climb as soon as the ladder was in place.

"What are you doing?" all three demanded as Markham went up. Kate added a plaintive, "I want to come down!"

He grinned as he looked up at her, and said as he reached her side, "But of course you do, Miss Farthington. And here I am, to help you!"

Despite her chattering teeth, Kate's tone was dry. "I r-r-rather d-d-doubt th-th-that," she said. He laughed as he pulled her to her feet, then paused, one eyebrow raised as he surveyed her clothing.

"Katherine!" came from a scandalized Tom, standing at the foot of the ladder. Looking down, she saw that the duke was regarding her in amazement before he glanced away. She knew the color was rising in her cheeks and felt a ridiculous urge to burst into tears as she stood, her hands still clasped firmly in Markham's. She tried to snatch them away, but he held on, saying, "Not until your hands are warmed, my dear. You wouldn't want to lose your grasp and fall now, would you?"

"What?" she gasped.

He continued to chafe her hands, not looking at her as he said he'd once seen someone try to climb down a tree with cold hands, and the loss of feeling had made that person fall. Impatiently she shook her head.

"No, not th-th-that," she stuttered.

That did make him look up, and he was puzzled for a moment before a slow smile slipped across his face. "Yes, Miss Farthington?" he asked.

She frowned at him and this time did succeed in snatching her hands away. "You, sir, are a—a—a—" She could not think of the right word, and he continued to smile at her in that infuriating way until, with an "Oh!" she put her foot on the first rung and prepared to descend the ladder. At that moment it was shaken by a burst of wind, and she found herself clutched—and clinging—to a wide male chest.

"Oh!" Katherine said again, staring up at him.

"Good thing you caught her, Nick, or she was bound to fall," the duke called from the ground where he and Tom were watching anxiously.

"Yes," Markham said, that odd smile on his lips. "A good thing."

"You can let me go now," Katherine told him, again preparing to descend. Markham made no move to do so.

"Mr. Markham!"

"Yes?" He smiled at her.

"You can let me go!"

"Yes." He held on to her until her feet were established firmly on the ladder and watched as she scrambled down to

the ground. Tom put a protective arm around her shoulders
as he and the duke prepared to hold the ladder for Markham's descent.

"Are you ready, Nicholas?" the duke called as Markham,
with a wave, said he'd be right back. Katherine watched with
a sinking heart as he appeared several moments later clutch-
ing the charred remains of Katherine's pillow.

"What have you got there, Nick?" Bellingham asked in
interest as Tom gave Katherine a reproachful shake.

"Kate!" Tom said, and she looked away.

"It would seem," Markham answered his friend, "that
something has been—nesting—in the chimney."

"Oh." Bellingham looked knowledgeably toward his companions. "Birds, you know."

Tom shook his head grimly and said that he did indeed
know. A few moments later, when Markham had joined them
on the ground, the duke regarded the charred pillow with
interest.

"I say!" he exclaimed. "Must have been a very large bird
to carry a pillow way up there!"

Markham grinned. "I'd say so, too. What about you,
Tom?"

"Yes," Tom said, "that's what I'd say. And you, Kate?"

Kate said, "Achoo!"

Chapter
Sixteen

"ACHOO!"

Another violent sneeze, and Katherine found herself wrapped in Mr. Markham's coat. She was swept up into his arms, and he carried her hurriedly around the side of the house to the front door. "P—p—put m—m—me d—d—down!" she stuttered, gasping up at him in surprise and wondering how he had managed to get his coat off so quickly, let alone wrap it around her in that masterful manner. Markham ignored her as Thomas pounded on the door and a startled Horton, unused to such an imperative summons, opened it for them. The sight of his young mistress clasped tightly to a man's chest (for she had started squirming virgorously by now, and Markham was determined not to drop her) struck the butler silent. He gazed open-mouthed as Markham strode past him and up the stairs, Katherine protesting his behavior all the way. Tom and Bellingham trailed after them, the latter protesting mildly, "I say, Nicholas—if the young lady really wants to be put down—perhaps you ought—"

Markham cast him a glance that made the duke think better of the rest of his sentence and kept walking. Encountering Chloe in the hall, he asked the startled child which was her sister's room. He had to ask her again before she seemed to hear, but upon his second questioning, accompanied as it was by his kindest smile (which, Katherine couldn't help notice, was in direct contrast to the grim manner in which he carried *her*), the little girl scurried down the hall to a room on the left and turned the heavy knob, opening the door just before her questioner reached it. Markham did not break his stride as he glanced quickly around, noticed with satisfaction that a small fire already burned in the grate, and dropped his armful of angry young femininity on the bed. Then he crossed to the fireplace to further stoke the flames glowing there.

"I say, Nicholas," came the duke's mild voice from the door. "Perhaps you'd better not, old boy; I mean—the smoke, you know . . ." His voice trailed off under his friend's sardonic gaze, and Markham looked toward Katherine before returning his attention to the fire again.

"Oh, I don't imagine there will be any trouble with smoke from this chimney, do you, Miss Farthington?" Markham asked pleasantly, causing her to frown at him even as she sneezed again. Chloe patted her knee consolingly.

"Do you have a cold, Kate?" the little girl asked sympathetically, before realizing that the knee she'd just patted was not garbed in its usual gown. Her eyes grew large and she gazed enviously at her sister. "Oh, Katherine!" she breathed. "May I have some, too?"

"No, you may not," said an authoritative voice behind her. Katherine glared at Markham, who had answered the child, as she bit her lip in the vain effort to keep her teeth from chattering so. "And your sister is going to burn those the minute she takes them off."

"I—a-a-am n-n-not!" Katherine snapped, trying to rise. Markham, with an exasperated roll of his eyes, pushed her back down on the bed and pulled a quilt up over her.

"Don't be a child, Katherine," he ordered. "Do you want to take your death from this chilling?"

"I am not—not—not a child," the lady in question ground out through still chattering teeth. "And what bus—bus—business is it of yours if I t—t—t—take my d—d—death, anyway?"

His only answer was an enigmatic stare, but she was deterred from questioning him further by a small sob that erupted from her little sister. "Wh—why, Ch-Ch-Chloe," she began, as Markham gathered the child up in his arms and

sat with her at the foot of Katherine's bed—to Katherine's
great dismay.

"Now what is this?" the gentleman asked with a gentle-
ness Katherine had never before seen him exhibit, but one
that she found—or would find, in another man, she corrected
herself—vastly attractive. Chloe's gaze was woeful as she
stared up at him, allowing him to wipe the first tear that had
slid over her eyelid as a second followed it.

"Please don't let Katherine die," the little girl pleaded.
Markham promised solemnly that he would not. Katherine,
heartily ashamed of herself for frightening the child so, murmured soothingly if a bit hoarsely that of course she wasn't
going to die; Mr. Markham had just been exaggerating. . . .

Her explanation ended as Elizabeth and Mrs. Goodsley
entered the room, the former open-mouthed, the latter armed
with a broom and bristling with indignation.

"Katherine!" Elizabeth gasped, hurrying forward to kneel
beside her sister's bed. "When Horton said—we could hardly
believe—Katherine, what has happened? And what—"

She got no farther, for a question of its own loomed in
Mrs. Goodsley's mind, and found its way out her mouth in
forceful syllables. *"And what,"* the housekeeper picked up
on the last of Elizabeth's questions as she held the broom in
front of her like a sword, *"are these gentlemen—if they
pretend to such title—doing in your bedroom?!"*

Had she not by this time felt so heartily sick, Katherine
would have laughed at the sight of the three male faces
before her. Color crept up to the roots of Bellingham's and
Thomas's hair, and even Markham looked like a little boy
with his hand caught snitching tarts.

"You see—" Gamely Tom tried to explain, but Mrs.
Goodsley was having none of it as she waved her broom at
him.

"Mr. Thomas!" she said, reducing him to the age of seven
with one sorry shake of her head. "As if I ever thought I'd
live to see the day! What would your mother say?"

It occurred to Thomas that that was a question he really did
not care to hear the answer to, and with, "Well, I'll just be
running along then, Kate," he disappeared out the door. The
duke followed a second later with, "I'll see the young man

off,'' and that left only Markham. Mrs. Goodsley advanced upon him, a militant gleam in her eye, but he was made of stronger stuff than his compatriots. Markham stood his ground, looking down at her bristling five feet from his considerable height.

"And you, sir?" Mrs. Goodsley challenged.

Markham smiled and threw the brave woman off balance with a slight bow. "How do you do?" he said, voice and face pleasant. "Although I can't be sure, I would assume that you are the housekeeper."

Eyeing him suspiciously, Mrs. Goodsley said that she was. Ever polite, Elizabeth made introductions, and Markham smiled again.

"Well, Mrs. Goodsley," he said, ignoring the voice from the bed that advised the housekeeper to hit him with the broom, and hit him again, "I am glad to see that you are here, for I know that I safely can leave you in charge of Miss Farthington."

Still suspicious but thawing slightly, the housekeeper said that he could.

"She has taken a chill," he said, "from her sojourn on the roof."

"The *roof?*" Mrs. Goodsley and Elizabeth gasped, turning their attention from the gentlemen to the middle Miss Farthington, who closed her eyes and groaned.

Markham nodded.

"But, Katherine," Elizabeth started, "whatever were you doing on the—"

Her sister moaned and rolled over, causing the quilt to shift slightly. At sight of her in the pantaloons, both Elizabeth and Mrs. Goodsley turned red.

"Miss Katherine!" The housekeeper's tone was shocked, and Kate turned toward them, one eye opened questioningly. She followed their line of vision and groaned again, hastily whipping the quilt back over her legs.

"I trust," Markham said, with what Katherine could only describe as an odious smile, "that when you have Miss Farthington tucked up for the night, you will burn her attire."

Nodding vigorously, Mrs. Goodsley assured him it would be done.

"I do not believe it would be good for her to be seen abroad in such again."

"No, sir, that it would not!" the housekeeper averred, almost beside herself at the wayward conduct of one of those she still considered in her charge. "And what Miss Poole will say when she hears about this—"

An urgent tug at her apron strings made the woman stop suddenly and turn bright red. Mr. Markham smiled quizzically.

"I imagine you mean you don't know what Miss Poole would have said," he corrected gently. She hurried to agree.

Katherine, fading but game, said in a voice that was little more than a croak that she knew. All eyes turned toward her expectantly.

"Hit him with the broom, Mrs. Goodsley," she repeated, eyes closing once again. "Hit him with the broom."

Markham's soft laugh was the only reply as he made his way from the room and left her to the tender ministrations of her sisters and their faithful family friend.

Supper that night was a quiet meal. Katherine, confined to her room with hot tea and gruel, alternately slept and fretted, sometimes even fretting as she slept, her dreams disturbed by a large man who looked remarkably like Nicholas Markham and who kept staring down at her with the sardonic smile that made her want to kick his shins, just to get his attention. But every time she started to do so, his face took on the look of tenderness she'd seen when he'd lifted Chloe onto his lap, and she awoke, confused and uncomfortable, to find Mrs. Goodsley at her side, saying soothingly, "There, there, Miss Katherine. Go back to sleep, do."

In the dining room they were halfway through their meal when Edward Farthington noted that one of their party was missing. Since nothing had been said for quite some time, everyone seeming, now that he came to think of it, absorbed in thoughts of their own, he decided to play the host and commented on the absence.

"Well, Elizabeth," he said jovially, claiming his niece's attention from her barely-touched plate, "this is a nice rack of lamb you've got for us tonight."

"Thank you, Uncle," she said automatically; with Katherine in bed there had been no one to ruin the evening meal. Neither Elizabeth nor Mrs. Goodsley had the heart to treat good meat so. She lapsed back into abstraction, and Edward cleared his throat again.

"Your sister is not eating with us, tonight," he remarked, as if no one else might have noticed. "I trust she is not unwell?"

Elizabeth focused on his face again. "I beg your pardon?"

"Your sister," Edward repeated. "She is not eating with us. I trust she is not unwell?"

He meant it only as conversation; he was not prepared for what happened next. Elizabeth, the calmest and politest of the Farthington sisters, one moment sitting at the table smiling sweetly at him, turned into a termagent before his eyes. She pushed back her chair and stood, her eyes sparkling in such a way that made the duke's glaze over in admiration—to Markham's unexpressed amusement—and said, as she shook her napkin at him, "You trust—you trust—you *trust* Katherine is not unwell, Uncle? How can you even *speak* to me of trust— you who have not given a moment's thought to any of us in the past seven years? You who bring unknown strangers to our home with the information that you hope to sell it to them, regardless of *our* feelings in the matter!"

Across the table from her Markham said, "Ahhh!" as another piece fell into place, but no one heard him as Elizabeth continued.

"You should be *ashamed* of yourself, Uncle Edward!" she cried, starting to shake. "You haven't cared one fig for my sisters or myself in all this time, and now you have the temerity to say that you hope my sister is not *unwell?* Well, she *is* unwell, Uncle! She is *very* unwell! And what's more, it is all *your fault!*"

The duke, seeing tears sparkling on Elizabeth's eyelashes, rose instinctively to put a protective arm around her shoulders. He, too, glared at Farthington, but at his touch Elizabeth once more became aware of her setting and her sudden and completely unexpected breech of good manners. With a gasped, "*Oh!* If you will excuse me!" she fled the room.

Edward Farthington sat gaping after her. "But—but—what

did I *say?*" he asked plaintively, slewing his body around toward his companions.

"You, sir, are a cur!" The duke ground the words out, throwing his napkin down as he, too, quit the room. Farthington gaped after him, too.

Mr. Markham continued to chew.

"Has everyone in this house gone *mad?*" Farthington demanded, turning back toward his final dining companion. Markham gave him that saturnine smile that never failed to make him uncomfortable and went on eating.

When the silence had lengthened between them, Farthington asked again, this time belligerently, "Well, sir? Are you not going to answer me? What do you think?"

Markham sighed and dabbed the corners of his mouth delicately, regretting that he, too, was about to quit the first truly excellent meal he'd had since coming to the Hall. He rose and gazed down at his host, seated uneasily at the head of the table.

"I think," Markham said in a tone he might use to comment on the weather, "that it would be extremely interesting to see an accounting of your care of the Farthington sisters' estate in the past seven years."

Farthington blanched noticeably and seemed to shrink in his chair.

"I also think," Markham no longer was looking at his host as he strolled to the door that Horton, his face impassive, was waiting to open for him, "that unless you are very, very careful, someone might just take enough interest to look into that care."

A strangling sound came from the table and Markham met Horton's eyes. The former smiled, and Horton, feeling younger than he had in some time, so far forgot himself as to smile back—a situation he rectified immediately, to Markham's silent amusement.

Chapter
Seventeen

FOR THREE DAYS Katherine was unaware of the insidious shifting of loyalties occurring within her household; for three days she sneezed and coughed and slept, lulled in dream-filled slumbers by the dark brown liquid left for her by Dr. Brownley, who knitted his thick brows at her and said sternly that she was to take her medicine and make no to-do.

Since that statement was followed by an equally stern request to be told just what mischief she had been up to this time that had so landed her in the basket, Katherine, about to balk at the smell emanating from the cloudy liquid, thought better of her intentions. With a face that made the doctor smile, she gulped the medicine and turned over on her side, feigning sleep. Beside her the doctor chuckled.

"She'll do," he said to Elizabeth, who watched anxiously from the foot of the bed. "Always was a strong little thing. Just keep her in bed two days past when the fever breaks; I'll stop in day after tomorrow to see how she's doing. If you need me before then, you need only to send word."

Katherine heard Elizabeth thank him profusely for coming, which made her grimace. She'd seen no reason to call the doctor and thought her sister should not have done so. She'd tell Elizabeth so, just as soon as Dr. Brownley quit the room—if she wasn't asleep already. The medicine was making her so drowsy. . . .

That feeling, however, was dispelled by the good doctor's next words.

"Well, it would have been most difficult not to come," he confided to the eldest of the Farthington sisters with another of his dry chuckles. "The gentleman who came for me was most insistent. In fact," Dr. Brownley rubbed his chin in reflection, although Katherine could not see it, and lowered his voice confidingly, "I think he would have dragged me out against my will, if I'd said I wouldn't come. Not that I would have refused, of course!"

Elizabeth accepted his hasty disclaimer with a smile and said, her soft words stiffening Katherine's spine, "Yes, I am very grateful to Mr. Markham for his prompt actions."

Markham, Katherine thought. Of all the interfering, overbearing . . . She stopped her own mutterings as the doctor continued the conversation.

"He said he was staying here," Dr. Brownley continued, his alert old eyes focused sharply on Elizabeth's face. She explained that he was a guest of their guardian and uncle, Edward Farthington, and the doctor snorted.

"Edward, eh?" Disgust was apparent in both voice and posture. "How a man like your father ever had a brother like your Uncle Edward is beyond me—and everyone else in the neighborhood. Well, I suppose he's up to no good here."

Dr. Brownley waited expectantly but Elizabeth said nothing. After a few moments he said that yes, well, she needn't tell him, it was none of his business, but he hoped she realized that if he could ever be of service to her and her sisters . . .

Impulsively Elizabeth placed her hand on his arm. "You have been such a good friend to us all our lives, doctor!" she said. "We appreciate your concern, believe me. And we treasure your friendship."

The old man harumphed, but he was visibly pleased as he opened the door to escort her out. The last thing Katherine heard before the door shut behind them and she drifted into slumber was, "These two friends of your uncle, they're not—importuning—you in any way?" and Elizabeth's tranquil response that her uncle's guests were most gentlemanly.

That statement made Katherine frown heavily as she fell into an uneasy sleep.

She awoke from it once to find the room darkened and lit only by the fire and a candle that burned on the dresser. Mr. Markham stood over her, a pillow in hand, and she gasped as he grinned down at her.

"Good evening, Miss Farthington," he said, his voice pleasant. Katherine stared suspiciously up at him through sleep-drugged eyes.

"Am I dreaming?" she demanded.

His smile deepened. "Do you often encounter me in your dreams, Miss Farthington? Your sweetest dreams, perhaps?"

"Nightmares!" Katherine started, then had to pause to cough as he chuckled. She glared up at him. "You, sir, are the stuff nightmares are made of!" Another thought occurred to her. "And what are you doing here?"

He smiled again, a most attractive smile, Katherine thought, which made her realize she was delirious. She frowned up at him once more.

"Your sister was sitting with you," he said, "but she has gone to fetch her embroidery so that she will have something to busy herself with during the night. She feared to leave you alone in case you should awaken, so I volunteered to stay the few moments she was gone."

Katherine's frown grew. "But what were you doing here in the first place?" she demanded, trying to infuse some authority into the thread of a voice her cough had left her. Markham grinned and held the pillow in his hands out toward her.

"It occurred to me," he said, "that you might need another pillow." Katherine could not stop herself from glancing to the left, where her second pillow used to lay. In spite of herself, her cheeks grew as red as her nose.

"I don't know what you mean," she sniffed. He leaned down and without so much as a by-your-leave lifted her slightly to slip the second pillow beneath her head. Katherine felt a wave of warmth sweep through her and firmly blamed it on fever.

"Is that more comfortable?"

He was standing quite close to her, smiling that devastatingly disturbing smile that once again reminded her of how warm the room had grown. Katherine ignored his question as she told him he shouldn't be there.

Markham grinned. "I believe, Miss Farthington," he said, "that you have made that clear from the moment we arrived."

She, trying to understand that through the buzzing in her head, lifted her chin at him. "No, no," she said, "that wasn't what I meant. I meant you shouldn't be here. Now. In my bedchamber."

"Oh."

Katherine thought a moment. "Although you shouldn't be at Farthington Hall, either."

Mr. Markham smiled and strolled over to warm his hands by the fire. Katherine glared at him.

"Well?" she demanded when he said nothing.

He lifted his head, and his eyes regarded her inquiringly.

"Well?" he asked.

Katherine sneezed. "Get out!" In vain she searched the bedstand and the bed for a handkerchief. She had, at last, to accept the one he held out to her after watching her in amusement for several moments.

"Thank you!" Katherine said in far from grateful tones. Markham grinned.

"Do you know, Miss Farthington," he told her, once again returning to his place by the fire, "I do not believe I have ever met anyone like you."

One eye appeared from the handkerchief to try to read his face. Unable to do so, she asked with foreboding just what he meant by that. Markham had to work not to laugh.

"Just what I said," he told her. "That I've never met anyone like you before in my life."

Katherine sneezed, and a muffled voice told him that that was too bad.

"Yes," he said, an odd little smile playing around his lips, "I rather think it is."

The eye emerged from the face full of handkerchief to regard him again in suspicion.

"And just what does *that* mean?" Katherine demanded as Elizabeth came back into the room, a soft "thank you" for Markham interrupted when she saw that her sister was awake and regarding the gentleman with hostility.

"Oh!" Elizabeth said, dropping her embroidery. Obligingly the gentleman bent to retrieve it for her; this time she managed to stammer out her thanks as he placed it in her hands. He smiled down at her as he started toward the door.

"Well?" Katherine croaked from the bed, torn between her relief that he was leaving and her frustration that he was ignoring her question. Markham turned and smiled down at her again.

"When you are well, Miss Farthington," he promised, "we will discuss it!"

Had she been standing, Katherine surely would have stamped her foot. The thought made him grin even as his hand closed on the doorknob.

"I am not a child!" she called after him, the words fading in and out in her throat. "And I will not be treated like one!"

He turned back to her and once again that enigmatic smile that both intrigued her and made her long to hit him was on his lips. "No, Miss Farthington," he said softly as he started to close the door, "you are not a child, and I thank goodness for it. And believe me—" There was a look in his eye that made Elizabeth gaze speculatively from one to the other as her sister lay glaring and the gentleman stood, smiling at her anger. " I have no intention of treating you as one."

"Well!" Katherine huffed as the door shut quietly behind him. She picked up the pillow he had so thoughtfully brought her and threw it at the door where it landed with a harmless thud. Exhausted, she fell back on her remaining pillow and closed her eyes as Elizabeth quietly put down her embroidery and set to work straightening the room. When she returned the pillow to Katherine's side, her sister opened her eyes and smiled weakly at her.

"Thank you, Lizzie," she said drowsily. Elizabeth smiled as she brushed the hair out of Katherine's eyes.

"Go to sleep now, dear," Elizabeth whispered, wetting a cloth with violet water and wiping it across Katherine's brow.

Kate smiled again. "That feels good," she said.

"Go to sleep."

"The last time I went to sleep," Katherine informed her, a frown creasing her brow, "I woke up to find that—that—that impossible man standing above me!"

Elizabeth said she was sorry; she'd just stepped out for a moment; she hadn't thought Katherine would awaken, or she never would have left her. . . .

"It's bad enough he invades my dreams," Kate muttered, starting to slip over the border into unconsciousness. "But when he invades my room, too . . . It's the outside of enough, isn't it, Lizzie?"

Smiling, Elizabeth agreed that it was.

"But it was very nice of Mr. Markham to be so concerned for you," Elizabeth added. "Especially after you'd tried to smoke him out of the library like that. . . ."

That brought to mind something Katherine had been wondering about earlier but had forgotten, and she dragged her eyes open to stare at her sister in puzzlement.

"That reminds me," she said, "why wasn't Markham in the library? And what was Tom doing here, and with him?"

Elizabeth rinsed the cloth in the violet water again and once more applied it to her sister's face as she said gently that Tom had called to invite the gentlemen to go out hunting with him. While he and Mr. Markham were talking, he'd grown so enthusiastic about his Charger that the other gentleman had walked down to the stable to go over the horse with him. Katherine snorted, an action that set her to coughing.

"Charger!" she scoffed. "He can't hold a candle to my Thunderer."

"No, dear, of course not," Elizabeth agreed, lifting her sister's head slightly so she could sip water from a glass Elizabeth held to her lips.

"Not that Mr. Markham would know—"

Seriously Elizabeth said that Mr. Markham had been much taken with Charger, but she understood he had told Tom that the horse he'd ridden the night before to the Small Swan Inn probably was the better.

"Oh." Katherine appeared absurdly gratified as she lay back on the pillow, her eyes half closed. "Well, perhaps he does know, a little. . . ."

Smiling, Elizabeth said she also understood that Mr. Markham had said he'd give much to see Thunderer put through his paces.

Katherine shook her head. "Well, he won't," she whispered, her voice almost gone as once again sleep came to claim her. "Because he won't be here long enough. And that's a very good thing, isn't it, Lizzie?"

Katherine's quiet breathing kept her sister from answering, and Elizabeth couldn't help but be glad. Tiptoeing over to the small rocker by the fireplace, she picked up her embroidery and set quietly to work, but she hadn't placed many stitches before her hands were stilled, and the material lay unnoticed in her lap. Her lovely forehead was furrowed as she gave deep consideration to Katherine's last question.

Despite what the middle Farthington sister said, Miss Elizabeth Farthington, at least, was not so sure.

Chapter
Eighteen

IT WAS ON the fourth day, when Katherine's fever broke, that Chloe was allowed to sit with her for a time. She was there partly to entertain Kate, who wanted to get up but was detained from doing so by a firm Elizabeth and a scolding Mrs. Goodsley. Both said the doctor had ordered bedrest for another two days. Chloe was also there to reassure herself that Kate was indeed much better, and not, as the child still obviously worried, in imminent danger of shuffling off this mortal coil.

Kate, propped on her pillows, smiled at the picture made by her smallest sister. The child sat comfortably at the foot of Katherine's bed, her back propped against the tall bedpost, her feet curled under her, and her hair falling forward as she bent over the calico cat purring happily in her lap.

"Calico is happy you're feeling better, too," Chloe informed her sister. Kate gravely thanked the cat for her good wishes.

Calico, sitting with eyes closed and tail twitching as her young mistress caressed her, showed no sign of hearing, and Kate laughed.

"She hides her concern well," Kate teased. Chloe, looking up, said seriously that she thought the cat was just worn out from worry. Instantly Kate's laughter vanished, and she held out a hand to the child who took it immediately, shifting her body so that Calico was disturbed from the comfortable nest she'd made in her mistress's lap. The cat opened her eyes, gave a huge yawn, and jumped down from the bed to find a non-moving place in which she might sleep as Kate told Chloe that she was sorry the child had worried so about her. Chloe, snuggling up to her sister, said that she hadn't meant to worry; Elizabeth and Mrs. Goodsley and Horton and Matthew and Johns and the duke and Mr. Markham had all told her Kate would be all right, but still . . . If anything *had* happened to her . . .

"My darling, it was just a silly cold!" Kate cried, hugging the child close. Chloe said that the doctor was not usually called for silly colds.

"Well, that was that man Markham's fault," Kate said, thinking aloud. "Of all the foolish starts—"

Chloe wiggled around until she could see Kate's face clearly as she asked with some anxiety if her sister did not like Mr. Markham.

Unable to lie under that innocent gaze, Kate hedged and said that it really didn't matter if she liked him or didn't like him; what mattered was that he and the duke and Uncle Edward leave as quickly as possible, before either of Uncle Edward's friends decided to buy the Hall.

Chloe sighed and settled into the crook of Kate's arm again. "Well, I like him," she said, "and I don't really think he and the duke are Uncle Edward's friends. I heard them talking when they thought no one was around, and . . ."

Her voice trailed off as she realized she'd just confessed to a crime that would surely earn her a scold from Elizabeth. Katherine, knowing she, too, should chastise the child for eavesdropping, was torn between her duty as Chloe's elder and her curiosity to know what the men had said. Curiosity won.

"And what did they say, Chloe?" Katherine asked, trying to keep her voice light. The little girl, glad no scold was coming, heaved a sigh of relief and said that it hadn't been much, really; it was just the way they said it.

"And what did they say?" Katherine prompted again. Chloe's forehead wrinkled.

"That Uncle Edward had been grossly der—der—" She thought deeply for a moment before pulling the word triumphantly from memory. "—derelict in his duty, that he was a prosy old bore, and perhaps they should buy the Hall, if things are that bad. I didn't hear any more, because they'd moved away by then, and I didn't think I should follow them." There was silence at the end of her speech, and she wiggled around to see her sister's face again. Katherine looked shocked, and Chloe regarded her doubtfully.

"Should I?" the little girl asked. Again there was silence, and she tweaked the sleeve of her sister's nightgown to attract her attention. "Should I have, Kate?"

Katherine's gaze transferred to her sister's face, but it took her several moments to realize what the child was asking her. Still ringing in her head were the words, "So perhaps they should buy the Hall, if things are that bad." With real determination, she dragged her mind back to what Chloe had just asked her, and when she'd assimilated the words, said, "Oh? What? Why no, dear, of course not! You did just right!"

Chloe, reassured, settled herself comfortably against Kate again, one hand absently picking at the coverlet as Kate asked if Chloe was *sure* that the gentlemen had said they still might buy the Hall. Absorbed in her task, Chloe nodded, and Kate heaved a long sigh. At the sound the child looked up again to say that she was sure that if Kate just *told* them the Hall wasn't for sale . . .

Katherine shook her head, and now it was Chloe's turn to sigh. "They're really very nice," she offered. "While you were sick, the duke played at jackstraws with me every night, and he has been very kind to Elizabeth as well. Once I went into the music room and he was holding her hand—"

"Holding her hand?" Kate asked with foreboding. Chloe nodded.

"I asked Elizabeth why, and the duke said that it was because Elizabeth's hand was cold, which I thought was very nice of him, don't you?"

Katherine muttered, "Very nice indeed!" and Chloe continued.

"And Mr. Markham took me riding with him, and we rode over to the squire's stables to visit my pony."

Kate gulped. "You went—to the squire's—to visit—your pony?" she repeated.

Chloe nodded. "And Tom saddled him up, and we all three went riding, and I had the most wonderful time." She thought a moment. "When are the horses coming home, Kate? I miss them."

Katherine patted her shoulder and said, "Soon," and Chloe went back to her absorption in the heavily patterned coverlet.

After a moment Chloe remembered another bit of information she thought her sister might enjoy—since she had, after all, been given what Elizabeth said was the very important task of entertaining Katherine. She looked up to say, "Oh! And while we were out riding, we encountered Mrs. Baggington and giggly old Margaret, and Tom introduced them to Mr. Markham, and Mrs. Baggington's eyes got very big, and Margaret's mouth fell open, and she even forgot to giggle, and since then they've been to inquire about you. Twice."

Kate groaned, knowing, even if Chloe did not, that Mrs. Baggington and her daughter had not come to inquire about her health, but to encounter the gentlemen staying under her roof. She knew also that she should censure her sister's reference to Margaret Baggington—even though, she thought ruefully, Chloe had probably heard it from her own lips. Chloe gazed anxiously at her.

"Are you feeling all right, Kate?" the child asked. "Would you like me to fetch Elizabeth? Are you tired? Elizabeth said I mustn't stay if you're tired. . . ."

Needing time to think, Kate smiled and said that she *was* rather sleepy; instantly Chloe climbed off the bed and considerably touched her sister's heart by tucking the covers in around Kate's shoulders before quitting the room after repeated inquiries as to whether there was anything at all Kate might need.

Assured that there was nothing, Chloe said that she would be back later to see her sister; she was almost out the door when she remembered Calico, asleep near the hearth, and tiptoed back to pick up the slumbering cat.

Calico, finding it very difficult to find a place in which she might sleep undisturbed this day, gave a meow that showed she considered life very hard. Kate, watching the cat's disgusted face as her young mistress carried her out the door, could not but agree.

*   *   *

Katherine's next visitor was Elizabeth, who slipped into the room to make sure the fire burned warmly. Surprised to find Kate wide awake, Elizabeth eyed her speculatively. "Chloe told me you were sleeping," she explained, "and I thought I'd just come up and make sure everything was all right in your room."

Katherine went straight to the point. "Chloe told *me* you were holding hands with the duke," she said. "In the music room."

"Oh!" Elizabeth's cheeks turned crimson, and it was apparent she would have preferred to be elsewhere. "It wasn't what it seemed. . . ." Her voice trailed off, and Katherine, watching her for several moments, said that that was a very good thing, because it seemed quite odd.

Elizabeth sighed and sank into the chair near her sister's bed without thinking. "It was the night you were taken ill," Elizabeth said. "I became very upset with Uncle Edward during supper—"

Instantly Katherine fired up on behalf of her sister. "That old makebait!" she snapped, oblivious of her language. "What did he do to upset you? So help me, I'll—I'll—"

What she would do went unsaid as Elizabeth said that what Uncle Edward had done was to inquire after Katherine. Kate blinked, cocked her head to one side, and considered deeply. Try as she might, she could find nothing untoward in that, and said so—cautiously.

Katherine watched her sister's fingers lace and unlace in her lap.

"That's just it, Kate," Elizabeth said, her fair head hanging. "There was nothing untoward in it at all, but somehow, when he said he trusted you weren't ill—as if he cared a rap about any of us, or had for seven years—and used the word 'trust'—I just couldn't contain myself."

In spite of her best intentions, Kate giggled. She said that she wished she'd been there to see it, and Elizabeth shook her head at her.

"I shouldn't have done it," she said.

A surprised Kate asked why not.

"Because Uncle Edward is still our uncle, and a guest in

our home. And to behave so before Geo—I mean, the duke, and Mr. Markham—it was unforgivable!''

Katherine said handsomely that *she* forgave her, adding again that she wished she'd been there to see it. Elizabeth smiled.

"It's certainly not something I wouldn't do!" Katherine continued, trying to comfort her sister. Elizabeth, seeing how well meant it was, could not then say just how little comfort there was in that thought. Some of that must have shown in her eyes, however, because a rueful twinkle came into Katherine's. She said that it was very kind of her sister not to say that that certainly was no standard to go by.

Elizabeth smiled again. "You see the trouble I get into when you're not nearby!" she teased.

"But it still doesn't explain why the duke was holding your hand!" Kate grinned, but returned them firmly to the point.

Elizabeth, who had hoped they wouldn't find themselves there again, looked away and said that, yes, well, you see . . .

She took a deep breath and said that the duke had followed her after her outburst, and had been most kind, and had taken her hand in comfort just as Chloe tripped into the room. . . .

Kate, watching her closely, was worried. "You like him very much, don't you, Lizzie?"

Elizabeth raised her head, and her eyes shone. "He is so kind, Kate. And such a gentleman! And he makes me feel so very—I don't know—precious—when I'm with him.''

Saying stoutly that her sister *was* precious and *should* feel that way, Kate felt her worries grow. "But Lizzie—" She tried to find the right words. "He won't be here very long, after all, and he is—oh, my dear, he *is* a *duke*—"

Kate was floundering for words, and some of the light went out of Elizabeth's eyes as she sighed. "I know," Elizabeth said quietly. "I know I am no match for him—"

That look of sadness made Katherine say that Elizabeth was a match for anyone, but her sister shook her head even as she smiled.

"Not in the eyes of the world, Kate," Elizabeth said. "We may live very retired here, but even I know that."

Wanting to shout that the world was often wrong, Katherine could not help but acknowledge Lizzie's statement. It was what she'd meant when she'd started this conversation.

"But," Elizabeth smiled bravely, "I intend to enjoy his company while he's here. It will give me something to remember—" She seemed to feel she had said too much and stood, ready to leave the room.

Katherine, watching her, thought that for her sister's peace of mind—and heart—it would be better if the duke left. Soon.

Chapter
Nineteen

AFTER HER DISCUSSIONS with her sisters, Katherine thought long and hard. Not only was there still the danger that the duke or Mr. Markham might make an offer for the Hall (as Chloe had told her), there was now the added danger that Elizabeth's tender heart would be injured by the duke's eventual departure. It was apparent that his leaving would cause her sister a pang or two now, but Katherine reasoned that added time would allow the attachment to grow stronger. Wishing to spare Elizabeth additional pain, it seemed more important than ever that the gentlemen be made to quit the Hall as quickly as possible. But how?

Kate really had thought that the conditions that greeted them upon their arrival long since would have sent them off again, but they'd remained. And if she didn't have enough to worry about with Elizabeth and the Hall, there was that Markham man, poking his nose into everything. Taken Chloe to see her pony, indeed! If she wasn't careful, he was going to upset all her plans by discovering just exactly what they were about, and if he told her uncle—well! It was apparent from Uncle Edward's conversation that he was looking for a way to make some money. If he thought the Hall was fit enough to sell . . .

Something Uncle Edward told Horton while in his cups made Katherine believe that because the duke and Markham hadn't yet posted back to London, Farthington still harbored the hope that one of them must have some interest in the place and might yet be convinced to buy it. He'd also said that he thought if they didn't, no one else would, because anyone with a half a mind could see that the place was falling down. . . .

Katherine believed that her uncle *had* only half a mind. She took his words to mean that if the duke and Markham didn't make an offer on the Hall, Uncle Edward wouldn't soon be back with other prospective buyers. She thought that she and her sisters and their beloved home then would be safe until Elizabeth reached the age where the estate would come into her hands, to be later divided with her sisters when they, too, reached the specified ages.

That made it even more important that their unwanted guests be sent packing before Uncle Edward discovered the truth, or Markham told him.

But how?

That question returned to plague her. She was so deep in contemplation of it that when a large and furry object suddenly leaped onto her bed and over her ankles, she gasped and kicked. It was all she could do not to scream at the sudden attack.

An indignant Calico, unused to such treatment, hissed and arched her back, regarding Katherine with grave censure. Recognizing her attacker a moment after she kicked at it, Katherine laughed and held out a hand to the cat, saying coaxingly, "My goodness, Calico, I thought you left with Chloe! You scared me half to death!"

It took her only a moment to realize that the cat, who now was sniffing her hand as if trying to decide if she really did want to make up—and if Kate really *should* be forgiven— must have slipped back into the room either when Elizabeth entered or left, probably in search of that warm place by the fire. Kate waggled her fingers and after hesitating a moment more, the cat slipped her head under them and began to purr, rubbing her body along Kate's legs in a way that showed just what a large-minded, forgiving cat she was.

Eventually she settled herself on Katherine's hip, and Kate, intent on making up with the animal, rubbed her ears and laughed as Calico, eyes closed, twitched her whiskers and kneeded the coverlet with her front paws.

"You really did scare me, you know," Kate said conversationally. The cat did not open her eyes. "I thought you were a ghost!"

A moment later she sat straight up, again disturbing the cat. Calico, stiff-legged, yawned and stretched and jumped to the floor to sit with her back to the errant human being. Had she been paying attention, Kate might have laughed, but she was not. Instead she was thinking deeply. Finally she said aloud, "Calico, you're an inspiration! A genius!"

The way Calico twisted an ear showed that it was too late for that now, but Kate still was oblivious.

"If only—" Her eyes narrowed, and she was mapping her plan when her door opened cautiously, and Chloe's face appeared around it.

Seeing her sister awake, Chloe started, "Kate, have you seen Cal—?" Her eyes fell upon the animal in question. Coming forward, Chloe said solicitously that she hoped her cat had not been a bother. Kate, distracted, said that no, Calico was a wonderful cat! An inspiration.

Gazing down at the feline who sat, nose in the air and head turned pointedly away from the woman praising her, Chloe was doubtful as she asked just what Calico had inspired Kate to.

"Oh, Chloe, the most fun!" Despite her sister's protests, Kate threw aside the covers and crossed to her wardrobe to survey its contents.

"I don't think you should be out of bed—" Chloe said; when that failed to elicit a response, she eased toward the door saying she would just get Elizabeth. That *did* bring Kate's head up, and she hurried to intercept her little sister, closing the door firmly before she took Chloe by the hand and led her back to sit beside Kate on the bed. Calico, disgusted, jumped from her small mistress's arms and stalked to the open wardrobe, into which she disappeared.

"Chloe," Kate said, thinking fast, "how would you like to help me play a trick on Uncle Edward?"

Chloe eyed her consideringly. "Does Elizabeth know about it?"

Kate bit her lip and said that no, it was to be a secret trick; one only she and Chloe would know about. Chloe's consideration grew.

"Would Elizabeth like this trick?" the child asked, watching Katherine closely. Kate crossed her fingers behind her back and nodded. Unfortunately she chose that moment to gaze straight into her sister's trusting eyes, and after a moment she sighed.

"Well," Kate said, "the truth is, Chloe, I'm not sure if Elizabeth would like it or not." She paused, met her sister's gaze again and heaved another sigh. "Well, actually, Chloe, chances are very good she would not."

Thinking aloud, Chloe said that Mr. Markham had said that in matters of how to behave, it would be best if she took the lead from Elizabeth, not Katherine. . . . Chloe flushed as her sister started up with an "Oh he did, did he?" and wished the words unsaid as Kate glowered at something Chloe could not see. Hastily Chloe asked just why Katherine wanted to play a trick on Uncle Edward. Her attention recalled, Kate gazed down at the child.

"You don't like Uncle Edward, do you, Chloe?" he asked.

Chloe shook her head.

"I don't like him either."

Chloe, who knew that, said that she didn't think Elizabeth or Horton or Matthew or Mrs. Goodsley liked him, either.

"Yes, well." Katherine, hoping to avoid a catalogue of all the people who did not like Uncle Edward, made a hasty interruption. "He is not a very—likable—person."

"He's a gudgeon," Chloe said with relish. Katherine patted her hand and nodded.

"You would like to see him leave, wouldn't you, Chloe?" Katherine asked.

Chloe's head moved up and down with vigor.

"So would I!" Katherine told her. "That's why I want to trick him. To make him leave. Wouldn't that be fun?"

Chloe's eyes lit up, and excitement showed in her face. "Could we, Katherine?"

Now it was Katherine's head that moved up and down, and Chloe said that she would like that. She would like that a lot. Then she thought. "But—why wouldn't Elizabeth like that, Katherine?" she objected.

Hastily Kate said that Elizabeth would like the end result

very much. It was just that she might not approve of the—
method—of attaining that end.

"Oh." Chloe thought, and her head tilted to the side as her
wide eyes surveyed Katherine's. "Why?"

"Because—" Too late, Katherine wished she'd involved
Matthew in her plan and not her little sister. Still . . . it *was*
too late. . . . "Because, Chloe, tonight Uncle Edward is
going to see a ghost!"

If she had thought to shock the child, she succeeded,
Chloe's eyes grew larger, and her mouth formed a perfect
"O." With a quick glance over her shoulder to see if the
poltergeist was already in the room with them, Chloe breathed,
"He is?"

Katherine nodded, and her own eyes sparkled. "He is,
Chloe."

"A *real* one?" The little girl looked over her shoulder
again, and Kate assured her that no, the ghost wasn't going to
be real. The ghost was going to be Katherine, dressed up in a
sheet and moaning. She gave a delicious shiver, and her sister
joined her.

"Really, Katherine?"

Kate nodded. "If," she said, watching the child closely,
"you'll help me."

Chloe, thrilled that she, too, would have a part in what she
now could see—despite what Elizabeth might say—was a
wonderful trick to play on Uncle Edward, asked hopefully if
she got to be a ghost, too.

Regretfully Kate shook her head, and Chloe's face fell.

"But Kate—" she protested; hastily her sister assured her
that her part was even more important. It was up to Chloe to
set the stage.

"Set the stage?" the girl repeated.

Kate nodded. "First, Chloe, you must make sure that the
drawing room windows that face the east lawn are unlatched.
Can you do that?"

Chloe, listening intently, nodded, and Kate went on.

"Then—and you may get Matthew to help you if you like, but
make sure that the two of you tell no one—try to get as many
of the room's candles in line with that window, so that a sudden
gust of wind through it might put them out. Do you understand?"

Again Chloe's head went up and down; she might not understand why she was to do so, but she understood what she was to do.

"Then, when everyone is gathered in the drawing room after dinner—and *everyone* must be there, Chloe, especially Uncle Edward—although if Mr. Markham were absent, I wouldn't mind—you must slip up here and tell me, and I will do the rest."

Noting the look of determination on her sister's face, Chloe had no doubt that that was true. Still, she could not resist asking what "the rest" might be.

Kate gave the smile that Tom always said reminded him of a cat that got itself locked in the pantry with the cream. "I shall be dressed in white, Chloe, and I shall open those windows—it's to be a dark night, thank heavens, and we'll hope the wind doesn't go down—and the candles will blow out, and I shall point at Uncle Edward, and moan, 'Youuuuuuu! Youuuuuuu'!"

Chloe gave another delicious shiver, and Kate grinned down at her. "Then I shall vanish. If that doesn't put him in a coach back to London in the morning, I don't know what will!"

Chloe, wishing she might play a bigger part in the scheme, suggested that she herself add to the scene by screaming. Instantly Kate approved her plan.

"Oh, it will be such fun!" Chloe said, jumping off the bed and dancing about the room to the apparent disgust of Calico, whose nap once again was disturbed. "I can't wait to see Uncle Edward's face. Do you suppose that he'll faint dead away? Oh, I hope so! Wouldn't that be grand?"

Katherine, sure that Elizabeth would tell her she shouldn't encourage the child to wish her uncle would faint dead away, thought it would be rather grand herself and grinned again. And if a certain other person—who could remain nameless—in the room also was jolted out of his usual superior demeanor by the sight of the Farthington Hall ghost, so much the better!

Chapter
Twenty

THE FIRST PART of Katherine's plan could not have gone better. Shortly after 8:30 P.M., Chloe, her eyes sparkling with hard-to-conceal excitement, slipped into her sister's room to find Katherine dressed all in white. A sheet was thrown over her head and shoulders to conceal her hair, and one of Pooley's old umbrellas rested in her hand.

"Oh, Katherine!" Chloe whispered, dancing around her sister in delight and surveying every detail of her ghostly costume. "You look wonderful! But—" She eyed her sister thoughtfully and found one flaw. "Won't they know it's you when they see your face?"

Katherine giggled like a child herself and demonstrated how she meant to pull the sheet now over the top of her head down over her face at the last minute. Chloe's eyes grew big as her sister's laughing countenance disappeared, replaced by a mask of white. She assured Kate that she was sure Kate would scare Uncle Edward half to death.

Katherine put the sheet back up and said that she sincerely hoped so. Then, eyeing Chloe with great expectation, she asked if everyone was gathered in the drawing room.

Chloe nodded. "The duke and Elizabeth are there, and Uncle Edward is sitting right in the chair that faces the east windows—" Katherine said that that couldn't be better and asked about Markham. Chloe grinned with delight.

"Mr. Markham has strolled down to the stables to see his

horse," she reported importantly. Remembering her sister's earlier words about how it might be better if Markham wasn't present, she was sure this would please Katherine.

She wasn't sure it had, however, for a look at Kate's face showed that a struggle was going on there. Katherine, regretting that she wouldn't have a chance to scare the odious gentleman, decided after a moment that it probably was better he wouldn't be there. She never could depend on him to behave in the appropriate manner. Only half-listening as she thought, it took her several moments to assimilate Chloe's next words.

"And Tom is there and the Reverend Woodsley—"

"*What?*" Katherine asked.

Chloe nodded. "They arrived a little over a half hour ago, and Elizabeth invited them to join the gentlemen for port. And I'm to have cakes!" She paused then, glancing at her elder sister out of the corner of her eye as she said that she knew she shouldn't say it, but . . .

The child hesitated, and Katherine prompted her. "Yes, Chloe?"

"Oh, Kate!" the child pleaded. "Please, please scare Reverend Woodsley, too! He's prosing on forever, and asking me about those sermons Elizabeth made me read, and then he's—he's—"

Words seemed to fail her, and again Kate prodded.

"He's *informing* me about them!"

"He is?" Kate's eyes twinkled, and Chloe nodded.

"And Mr. Markham—who went to the stables shortly after the reverend arrived—said that I might go with him, but Reverend Woodsley said to Elizabeth that he was sure I would rather stay and improve my mind, and then Elizabeth said—"

Katherine, who could guess what Elizabeth said, promised to do her best to frighten the reverend, too. In great accord the sisters left the room, Chloe asking doubtfully if Katherine was sure that ghosts carried umbrellas.

Actually, Katherine assured her, she was very sure they didn't. With it coming on to rain, however, she didn't want to be out in the bushes without some protection. She had no desire to spend even more days in a sickroom, and she

planned to drop the umbrella just before she threw open the
windows to haunt Uncle Edward and guests.

Chloe, seeing nothing wrong with the plan, nodded. She
made her way back to the drawing room, down the front
stairs as Katherine slipped down the back stairs to await her
moment. Kate made her way to the window and looked
inside, and that moment came when Matthew and Horton
entered the room bearing a tray carrying port and glasses and
a tray of other refreshments. Remembering that Chloe had told
her she hadn't asked Matthew's help in preparing for tonight's scene, Katherine giggled, drew the sheet over her
head, and pushed the window open just as an obligingly large
gust of wind swept by her and into the room, dousing almost
all the candles there.

The port tray clattered out of Matthew's suddenly nerveless
fingers as he turned toward the window and the sight there,
and the tray in Horton's charge was saved from a similar fate
only by his happening to have set it on a small table before he
turned. It did not, however, save it from being knocked to the
floor when Matthew stumbled back and into the table as, eyes
gaping, he pointed toward the apparition.

The noise woke Uncle Edward, who was to Matthew's left.
Farthington sat up with a testy, "Eh? What?" and looked up
straight at the white-clad shadow as Chloe, enjoying herself
immensely, screamed.

"*What?*" Edward Farthington repeated, pressing himself
farther back into the chair, his eyes staring.

Katherine, who'd forgotten at the last minute to drop her
umbrella, used it to good effect as she pointed it at the
startled gentleman and utter her most ghostly, "Yooooouuuu-
uuuuuuuu!"

Edward leaped from the chair and hid behind it. Off to her
right Katherine saw Elizabeth, who had turned white when
the windows blew open and Katherine's small figure appeared
there, sink into a graceful faint—right into the arms of the
duke.

Sorry for that, Kate concentrated on Edward again.
"Yoooooooouuuuuuuuuuuuuuuu. Yoooouuuuuuuuu. Yoooooou-
uuuuuuuu!"

She would have gone on, but she noticed that Tom, whose

mouth had hung open at first sight of her, now was edging around the room, adjuring the duke to hand Elizabeth to the Rev. Woodsley who stood as if he'd—well—seen a ghost, and help him catch this blasted thing.

"Drat!" thought Kate. She stepped back from the window and turned to speed around the corner and off toward the stables, knowing Tom's and the duke's hot pursuit would cut off her escape route to the back of the house and up the back stairs.

She was halfway across the lawn when her pursuers rounded the corner (for it had taken the duke some time to gently lay Miss Elizabeth on the sofa and leave her to the tender ministrations of Chloe and Mrs. Goodsley, who had come huffing up from the kitchen as soon as she'd heard Chloe scream), but she was hampered by her skirts and the sheet she'd wrapped about her. With their long legs, she knew she could never outrun them. She could feel the men gaining on her as she turned a corner into the stable and raced toward the back of the building to the old wooden manger where she'd often hidden in games of hide and seek as a child. Diving into it, she stuck her head up for a moment and discovered the astonished face of Mr. Markham, who had been bent over in his horse's stall to inspect the animal's front leg when she'd run past but had straightened at the sound, and seen her land in the manger. Katherine groaned, dropped down into the manger box, and pulled a convenient handful of hay over her.

A moment later Bellingham and Tom, breathing heavily as they, too, rounded the stable corner, skidded to a halt.

"Nicholas!" the duke cried.

Mr. Markham looked at him.

"Sir!" Thomas said.

Both the new arrivals were looking around, peering into the building's shadows, and Markham raised an eyebrow at them.

"Yes?" he asked.

Both stared at him, their mouths opening and closing as they peered around the stable again, stepping farther in, until they'd passed him, still standing in his horse's stall. They were bending now and then to peer under and over anything that attracted their attention.

"Gentlemen!" Mr. Markham said when the two seemed to be making their inevitable way toward the back manger. They looked at him.

"Did you lose something?" Markham asked.

The duke and Tom exchanged glances and stared around the building again. Tom came toward him.

"Didn't you see it?" Tom demanded.

Markham looked at him.

"You must have seen it!" the duke seconded, coming up to put his hand on Tom's shoulder as the two stared at Markham.

Markham was polite as he asked just what *it* was that he was supposed to have seen.

Tom and Bellingham glanced around the stable again and then at each other. Somehow, in the face of Markham's calm demeanor, they seemed to find it remarkably hard to tell him.

"Well, George?" Markham asked gently when he felt he'd given them enough time.

"Well . . ." the duke began. He gazed at the youngest man present. "You tell him, Tom," the duke said.

A startled Tom took a step back as he said that no, he thought it would be better if the duke told him. . . .

Wearily Markham said he wished *someone* would tell him, and Bellingham said that oh, very well, he would do so, but if his friend laughed—

Markham raised an eyebrow and waited, and the duke sighed.

"We're chasing a ghost, Nicholas," George said, his frown daring the other man to so much as smile. Ever one to take a dare, Markham did.

"It appeared up at the Hall," Tom seconded, not knowing, as the duke did, that that smile would soon be replaced by a chortle. "And we chased it down here—"

He was interrupted by laughter, and his young face grew indignant in the face of Markham's clear disbelief. "We did!" he insisted.

The duke glared at his friend in disgust. "We did," he seconded.

Markham made a show of trying to contain his merriment.

"I see," he said, pursing his lips in such a way as to show to a nicety just how much he did not. "You say this—this—"

"Ghost," the duke averred, frowning at him.

"Thing," Markham said, as if he hadn't heard him, "was up at the Hall?"

Both men nodded.

"And just—when—did you see it?"

Eager to make him believe them, Tom told him about the window being thrown open and the candles being blown out, and stared when Markham seemed to murmur, "Nice touch."

"What?" Tom asked, sure he had not heard right. Markham said it was nothing and begged him to continue.

"Then," the duke said, taking up the tale, "Miss Farthington fainted." He had to stop a moment to argue with Tom over whether Miss Farthington fainted before or after Matthew dropped the port tray and knocked the other tray over, but their discussion was interrupted by an even more appreciative comment from Mr. Markham.

"Fainted, did she?" When the duke nodded, Markham said that he hoped George had had the good sense to catch her. Bellingham said that well, of course he had, it had been his pleasure, to which Markham murmured, "I'm sure," causing the duke to blush as he hadn't done in some time.

Tom, unsure what all that was about, continued the tale.

"And then the ghost pointed its umbrella at Edward Farthington—"

"The ghost carried an umbrella?" Markham interrupted, intrigued.

Without thinking Tom said that well, it *was* coming on to rain, then continued his story. "And it said, 'Yoooouuuuuuuuu! Yoooouuuuuuuuuuuu! Yoouuuuuuuuu!' in the most affecting way—I tell you, it was enough to raise the hair on the back of a man's neck!"

"I'm sure," Mr. Markham said, wondering if he really had heard a stifled giggle from the back of the stable. "And then what happened?"

"Then the duke and I set off after the ghost, and it ran this way. . . ." Tom's words trailed off, and he looked at Markham in puzzlement. "Are you *sure* you didn't see it come in here?"

Solemnly Markham assured him that he hadn't seen a single ghost, and a dissatisfied Tom said that well, then, he supposed it was gone. . . .

"Unless it went back up to the house," Markham suggested. That caused the young man's eyes to light as he said that he'd just be off to take a look. . . .

The duke, who showed an inclination to linger, was sent on his way with the suggestion that Miss Elizabeth Farthington might be in need of some looking after.

When both were gone Markham strolled to the back of the stable and leaned over the manger to remove the loose layer of hay there.

"Well?" he asked, gazing down into the questioning eyes of the second Farthington sister.

Katherine, her nose tickled by an errant hay leaf, answered, "Achoo!"

Chapter
Twenty-one

WITHOUT ANOTHER WORD Mr. Markham bent and lifted her out of the manger, setting her on her feet and dusting her off even as Katherine protested that she did not *need* his help and could scramble out very well herself without him.

"I suppose this time you really *have* caught pneumonia, which you seem determined to do," Markham said, ignoring her protests as he voiced the thought uppermost in his mind.

For a moment Katherine stared at him, surprised at his apparent concern. She shrugged it off with, "Don't be silly! It was the hay that made me sneeze!"

To prove that she sneezed again, and Markham, making a point of picking the last piece of hay from her skirt hem, said, "Well?" in a tone that reminded Katherine forcibly of Miss Poole.

"All right," she conceded, "perhaps I am not *completely* over my cold. . . ."

In spite of herself she sniffed, and Mr. Markham handed her his handkerchief.

"Miss Farthington," he said, "we must talk."

Katherine, catching a sneeze in the piece of snowy linen, looked up cautiously. "Must we?" she questioned.

He nodded and grinned in spite of himself. "We must. But first, it seems, we must get you back into the house and into your bed, and we must hope that you haven't further injured your health with this newest escapade."

About to protest that she hadn't been hurt a bit by her recent adventure, Katherine felt another sneeze coming on and swallowed the words. Hard on the heels of the sneeze was the realization that if she were back in her bed, she couldn't be part of the meeting Mr. Markham was proposing. In a voice that she hoped was appropriately faint, Katherine agreed that perhaps he was right; she *was* feeling a bit fatigued. . . .

She glanced up to find a great deal of amusement—and comprehension—in the gentlemen's gaze, and his "Doing it up a bit too brown, Miss Farthington," made her blush.

"I don't know what you mean," Katherine said, looking away.

His hand cupped her chin as he gently turned her head back toward him. "Don't you, Katherine?" he asked, something in his eyes making her gulp even as she moved back to break the contact. He shrugged and remarked conversationally that it seemed she had made quite a stir.

In spite of herself, Katherine giggled.

"I can see you are truly repentant." Markham's voice was dry, and Katherine giggled again.

"If only you could have seen Uncle Edward," she excused.

He raised an eyebrow. "I understand your sister fainted."

At once Katherine's face sobered, and she gnawed on her lower lip. "I am sorry about that," she said. "Poor Lizzie! I should go to her—"

"Oh, I imagine she'll come to you," Markham said, catching her hand as she started toward the door. "After all, she'll want to tell you about it, and see how you're feeling—"

Katherine's eyes widened, and she tried to pull away from him as she said, "That's right! What if someone already is looking for me, and they know I'm not in my room? Oh, dear! What will I do?"

She would have run out of the stable and toward the Hall, except for Markham's firm grip on her hand. His voice was cool as he told her he doubted they were aware of her absence yet, because he doubted the stir she'd made had as yet subsided.

"If you go rushing up there now, and someone sees you,

your secret will be out, Miss Farthington. Unless you want that?''

He already knew that she didn't and nodded when she gazed questioningly at him.

"But—what shall I do?" she asked. "I've got to get back into the Hall!"

"Follow me," he said and, her hand still in his, poked his head out first to make sure no one was around. Then he motioned her to follow him and, staying in the shadows, got them safely to the back door, where he released her hand (something she had told him repeatedly that he might do) and stepped back to look down at her. "I trust you can make your way safely from here?" he asked.

Katherine nodded and, about to open the door, stopped to look up into his face. "You won't tell anyone, will you?" she asked. In spite of herself, her voice carried a pleading note.

Markham smiled. "I will not—" Her look of relief made him add, "—*if* you agree to meet me tomorrow for that talk I mentioned earlier."

Katherine gazed down at the ground. "I am not allowed out of my room," she said.

"What?"

"The doctor." She glanced up into his face and then away, embarrassed. "The doctor said I must keep to my room one more day."

"Ah, yes." Mr. Markham smiled. "And you are so good at following doctor's orders."

In light of her recent actions, Katherine turned crimson. She said that, well, it might be harder to get out of her room during the day, with so many people about, and Chloe and Elizabeth and Mrs. Goodsley popping in every so often to see if she might need anything. . . .

"Miss Farthington," Markham said with a deep bow, "I have complete faith in you."

Katherine's gaze was doubtful. "You do?"

"I do." He bowed again. "I have no doubt that such an ingenious young lady as yourself will find a way to meet me in the library—at oh, shall we say, 3 P.M., at which time I am

sure I can persuade my friend, the duke, to take your sister
walking in the gardens—for our little talk."

"You don't?" The tone in which the words were uttered
was more doubtful still, and again Markham smiled.

"No," he assured her, "I don't. For if you don't appear, I
can't help but feel that something I've seen tonight but forgotten will suddenly recur to me at 3:15 P.M.—something that
would interest your family and friends amazingly."

"It will?" Katherine echoed, her hand clenching and un-
clenching on the door handle. Markham, seeing that, took the
small hand and, with another bow, placed a soft kiss upon it,
pausing as he straightened to look full into Katherine's eyes.

"It will," he promised. "And now, Miss Farthington, I
must stroll around to the front door to hear the story of the
Farthington Hall ghost as told by those players who have not
yet revealed their roles to me. Good night."

"Good night," Katherine replied, her response automatic.
She stood watching until he had turned the corner of the
house, then let herself in the door. Cautiously she made her
way up the back stairs, the hollow feeling in her stomach
making her think that perhaps—if she had *any* luck at *all*—
she *was* on the way to pneumonia, after all.

When Markham strolled into the drawing room a few moments later, it was all he could do to control the twitching of
his lips occasioned by the sights there.

To his right Matthew was sweeping up the glasses and
decanter that had shattered when he dropped his tray. Horton
alternately supervised and read him a lecture on the proper
ways of footmen. From what Markham could hear, it suggested that not even when he has been run through with a
sword and is *dying,* does a good footman do any more than
deposit his tray and—being careful not to bleed on the carpet—
take himself off to a quiet place to expire, so as not to upset
the ladies.

Farther to his right the Reverend Woodsley, Chloe, and
Thomas were huddled around Edward Farthington, who was
babbling, "It was her, I tell you! Her! That Poole woman,
come back to haunt me from the grave! She came to see me

once, early on, in London, carrying that same umbrella. She pointed it at me then, too, and said, 'You, you, you—' "

"But this time she said, 'Yoooouuuuuu, yoooouuuuuuu, yooouuuuuuuu,' " interjected Chloe, who was enjoying herself immensely.

Farthington goggled at her as the reverend, in a voice of grave censure, said that children should not be allowed in the drawing room at this time of night. Tom, firing up on behalf of his young friend, asked just who Woodsley thought he was to be telling Chloe how she should go on in her own house, and it was only Markham's intervention that stayed a thirty-minute homily by the reverend (who was little more than eight years older than Tom) on the impertinence of youth.

"My goodness," Markham drawled, gazing down at his host, "you look as if you've seen a ghost, Farthington! What happened here?" Out of the corner of his eye, he saw the duke comforting the still-shaken Miss Farthington by the simple expedient of putting one arm possessively around her shoulders and holding both of her hands in one of his own. He smiled.

Glad of a new audience—for his old one was starting to pale on him—Farthington started up out of the chair and even went so far as to grab Markham's lapels—which Farthington hastily let go of as Markham, eyebrows raised almost to his hairline, gazed down at him. "But I did see a ghost, Markham!" Farthington told him. "I did! Everyone saw her! Right here. In this very room. The window opened, the candles blew out, and she—she—"

"She?" Markham repeated, removing a speck of lint from his coat sleeve as he listened. "Who might 'she' be, Farthington?"

"Why, that Poole woman, of course!" the other man cried. "I tell you, it was her—even down to the blasted umbrella—"

"Umbrella?" Markham was more polite still, and the reverend, who felt he had been too long left out of the conversation and who also felt that the newcomer was much too calm about what they'd seen, said, beetling his brows, that one might almost think Mr. Markham did not believe them.

Markham smiled faintly and inspected the other side of his coat for lint. "Might one?" he asked.

The reverend bristled and said, "Now see here—"

At that Markham looked up, and there was something in his gaze that made Woodsley hesitate. "Quite right," Markham approved, causing the other man to start. Markham looked around. "I *am* seeing," he said. "And I must tell you, I see nothing that looks like a ghost."

"But it was here!" Farthington protested. "It was here, I tell you! That Poole woman! Come to haunt me about—"

He broke off suddenly, aware that the whole room waited to hear what a ghost might come to haunt him about.

"Yes, well," Farthington said, "she was quite mad, you know!"

"She was not!" Chloe cried. "You can't say such things about Pooley—"

Testily her uncle said that he could say what he liked, and an angry Chloe, carried away by the events of the evening, essayed a quick kick to his shins. Without thinking Farthington raised his hand to find it gripped, hard, by Markham. All amusement was wiped from the latter's face as he breathed, "You dare!" to the smaller man.

"Chloe!" Elizabeth called, her voice urgent as the frightened child, aghast at what she'd done, gazed up at the men around her. "Chloe, my dear, it's time you were in bed—" Elizabeth moved forward as if to snatch the child from them, but Markham stayed her with a movement of his hand.

"Yes, Chloe," he said, smiling down at the child, the kindness in his face sending some of the fear in her own away, "I'm sure it is far past your bedtime. But first—" His voice stopped her as she made to scurry away, "—I believe you owe your uncle an apology."

Chloe stopped, gulped, and gazed up into her uncle's angry face as he continued to glare down at her. "I am very sorry, Uncle Edward," she faltered, looking toward Tom for encouragement when her uncle said nothing. Her long-time friend nodded encouragingly, and she continued. "I should not have—kicked you—"

"No, you should not have," Farthington blustered. "And

let me tell you that had I kicked *my* father, it would have been
a quick beating for me—''

"You are not my father!" Chloe cried even as Markham,
in a low voice that only Edward could hear, said, "And it's
too bad, apparently, that your father didn't discipline you,
Farthington. I, however, could rectify that situation."

Looking round so that he could fully see Markham's face,
Farthington gulped and said that oh, very well, it was forgiven; he was sure she hadn't meant it; it had been the heat of
the moment. . . .

Chloe, incurably honest, opened her mouth to say that she
had meant it but was still sorry. Tom, seeing that coming,
clamped a hand over her mouth and dragged her across the
room to Elizabeth, who wrapped her arms protectively around
the child and said that they would leave the gentlemen to their
conversation. Head high, she wished them all a good night.

Bellingham, a darkling look in his eye for his host, moved
to open the door for the ladies and held it as Chloe, Elizabeth,
and Mrs. Goodsley, who could not resist a "hmmph!" toward
Edward Farthington as she followed her charges, stiff-backed,
passed through.

"Really, Farthington!" the duke exploded as soon as the
door was shut. He was interrupted by the Reverend Woodsley,
who said that *he* was a great believer in discipline for children
and that he thought that to spare the rod was to spoil the child.

"Oh, who cares what you think?" Tom so far forgot
himself as to snap. The reverend, after one incredulous look
at this recalcitrant parishioner, said that he would bid them
all adieu and that he would that night—and here he looked
pointedly toward Tom—*pray* for all of their immortal souls.

Markham, grinning, said that they didn't wish to detain
him, a statement that added even more iron to Woodsley's
backbone as he departed.

"Well!" Edward Farthington said as he gazed uneasily
toward the three grim-faced men who were left regarding him
after his only ally departed. "I believe I'll just be turning in,
too. Had quite a shock, you know. Gave me such a turn . . .''

His words fell off as no one answered, and he sidled
toward the door, opening it with obvious relief and bolting
through it as soon as he was able. A collective release of

breath seemed to fill the room at his departure, and Mr. Markham turned toward the almost forgotten Matthew and Horton, who had faded into the woodwork during the past scene.

"Horton!" Mr. Markham said with his most attractive smile. "What have you got in your cellars that's particularly good?"

Horton, collecting himself, promised to go immediately and see.

Chapter
Twenty-two

BY THE TIME Katherine had climbed the stairs to her room, hidden her costume in the bottom of her wardrobe and crawled into her nightgown and then into bed, she was as tired as Mr. Markham had prophesied she would be, and even a little tireder. It occurred to her that she really *might* have overdone that night.

She hadn't been in bed long when she heard her door softly open. Pretending sleep, she believed the visitor would take one look at her slumbering pose and go away again. She was wrong.

A persistent, "Katherine, Katherine!" and the shaking of her shoulder made her open her eyes and stare up into the face of her elder sister, who was frowning down at her in a way that made that hollow feeling return to Katherine's stomach.

"Lizzie?" she questioned, rubbing her eyes as if she'd just been awakened from deep repose. "What is it?" She sat up and gazed in feigned puzzlement toward the window. "Is it morning? What is wrong?"

"You know very well it isn't morning!" Elizabeth scolded as she settled herself on the edge of Katherine's bed. "So you might as well quit pretending. And there is a great deal wrong—*also*, as you know!"

Vainly Katherine tried to maintain her pose. "Why, I don't know what you mean—" she started. Elizabeth whipped a wet umbrella from behind her back and shook it in her sister's face.

"Yours, I presume?" Elizabeth asked, her voice so very dry that it occurred to Katherine that the eldest Miss Farthington had been taking lessons from Markham.

"Why, I believe that is one of Pooley's," Katherine said, as if she hadn't seen the umbrella in ages. Elizabeth, disgusted, said that she knew very well it was Pooley's umbrella, just as she knew that Katherine had used it that night and, in her haste, left it outside the window from which place Elizabeth had retrieved it. And, Elizabeth threatened, if her sister didn't quit pretending, Elizabeth thought she might very well use the umbrella to do Kate a violence.

Katherine sighed. "Oh, very well," she grumbled, not looking at the other woman. "If you've figured it out, I don't suppose there's any use in denying—"

Elizabeth agreed there was not, and Katherine was repentant as she gazed at her frowning sister. "I'm sorry, Lizzie," she mumbled, watching to see if her words had any effect on the angry Elizabeth. "I didn't mean to make you faint—"

"Make me faint?" Elizabeth interrupted, pardonably disgusted. "As if I wouldn't *scorn* to do such a paltry thing! I fainted—actually, *pretended* to faint, my dear—when it appeared to me that dear George and Tom, without something to slow them down, might catch and unmask you. *Then* how would you explain your actions?"

At the end of her speech, Katherine, who had ignored the "dear George" portion of her sister's words, exclaimed, eyes shining, "Oh, Lizzie, well done!"

Elizabeth frowned at her again. "It was *not* well done, not at all! You ought to be ashamed of yourself, Katherine!"

"You mean for not telling you?" Thinking she understood, Katherine started to apologize. "If I'd known you'd be such a Trojan about it—"

"No, I do *not* mean for not telling me!" It didn't take Elizabeth long to correct her, and Kate watched as her sister rose from the bed and walked to the fireplace to stoke the flames burning there before returning to the bed again. "Ghosts, indeed!" Elizabeth said, shaking her head. "A fine way for a Farthington of Farthington Hall to be carrying on!"

In spite of herself, Kate giggled. "Uncle Edward Farthington certainly carried on, didn't he?"

For a moment Elizabeth's brow lightened, then heavy censure settled there again. "He certainly did," she agreed, knowing that she held the trump card. "In fact, he carried on so much that had Mr. Markham not been there, I believe he would have struck Chloe—"

"*What?*" She got no farther for at her last words Kate, all amusement wiped from her face, had bounded from the bed and grasped her shoulders.

Elizabeth explained what had occurred in the drawing room after Katherine's appearance. She watched as her sister's eyes took on a dangerous glint and her jaw tightened.

"That—that—" Katherine started. She turned from Elizabeth and walked purposefully toward her wardrobe. Watching, an uneasy Elizabeth asked what she was about.

"I am about to get dressed," Katherine said, each word coming tight from her throat, "and then I am about to give Uncle Edward the door."

Hurriedly Elizabeth crossed to her and took her arm. "He has already been chastised, Kate," she said. "You needn't worry."

Her sister's eyes still held that dangerous gleam. "If he ever lays a hand on Chloe—" she started.

Elizabeth said she had no doubt he would not; it was apparent he did not want to face the wrath of either of his London guests.

"Well, he'd be wise to worry about my wrath, too!" Katherine said, allowing herself to be led back to bed. Elizabeth agreed that he would.

"Oh, Lizzie, I'm so sorry!" Kate cried, gazing up at her sister as the latter tucked her warmly up in bed. "I had no idea it would come to that. Whatever do you suppose possessed Chloe to kick him?"

Elizabeth smiled as she said that it was nothing Kate wouldn't have done herself.

"Yes, but—that's different!" Katherine cried, when she realized she couldn't deny what her sister said.

Elizabeth cocked her head and asked why.

"Because if I'd done it, Chloe wouldn't have been in danger of being hurt!"

"But you would have been."

Kate hunched an impatient shoulder as she said that didn't matter, and Elizabeth reached out a hand to smooth the hair back from her sister's forehead. "What a gallant spirit, you are, my dear," she marveled. Kate gave her a puzzled look.

"You mean a foolish spirit, don't you?" Katherine said, remembering her sister's earlier words.

Elizabeth said it might be a foolish, gallant spirit, but she was glad her sister possessed it.

"You are?"

The doubt in Kate's voice made Elizabeth smile, even as she nodded. Then, seeing that Katherine still was shaken by the fix into which Chloe had gotten herself, she changed the subject by saying that dear Kate would have much to answer for when Mrs. Goodsley figured out who the ghostly figure had been, because Matthew had dropped and broke several of the best glasses and a prized decanter.

A small smile on Katherine's face answered the one on Elizabeth's, and the eldest Miss Farthington continued, "Personally, I don't mind the loss of the decanter at all, because at least when Matthew dropped his tray, he had the good sense to spill most of it toward Uncle Edward."

Kate looked at her hopefully. "You mean—"

Elizabeth nodded. "The port landed 'splat!' in his lap!"

"No!"

Elizabeth nodded again.

"I didn't see that!"

"It was so dark you probably couldn't," Elizabeth said. "And then, of course, Uncle Edward was so quick to hide behind his chair—" She could not stop the giggle that rose in her throat at the remembered sight, and Katherine joined her.

"And then—after you left—" Elizabeth said, starting to choke again, "Reverend Woodsley was so busy giving excuses as to why he couldn't join Tom and Geo—I mean, the duke!—in the ghostly chase—"

"Oh, I wish I'd heard that!" Katherine said wistfully.

"It was wonderful! First he said he'd hurt his knee—and then he said he didn't believe the Church believes in ghosts, so he couldn't go chasing after what he officially didn't believe in—and then it was that he couldn't leave Chloe and me undefended, in case—or, I think, unless!—the—the—*thing*—came back. . . ."

"How brave of him!" Katherine deadpanned, and Elizabeth was off again, enjoying a hearty laugh. Finally sobering, she was reminded that she'd come to chastise her sister, not to praise her, and her face grew serious again.

"Well, yes, I guess it was a little bit funny. . . ." Elizabeth said, patting her hair and smoothing the worn muslin of the faded gown in which she still managed to look quite beautiful. "But you had agreed, Katherine, not to bring the ghost up—"

"I said I wouldn't unless it was an emergency," Katherine objected. "And Uncle Edward's continued presence certainly strikes me as an emergency!"

"Yes, well, I still say you shouldn't have. . . ."

"You aren't going to tell Mrs. Goodsley it was me, are you, Lizzie?" Katherine coaxed, reaching for her sister's hand and squeezing the fingers there. "Because I'm sure if you do, I'll never hear the end of it! She hasn't forgotten the time I was six and dropped the silver platter down the well. . . ."

Elizabeth giggled at that memory, too, and Katherine knew she would remain silent even before she said so.

"But I *should* tell her, if only to see that you get a sufficient scold, Kate!" Elizabeth said. "For this conversation just proves I'm no good at it—"

A glum Katherine said that her sister need not worry; Kate had no doubt that she would get a sufficient scold on the morrow. . . . As her voice trailed off, Elizabeth looked at her curiously; after a moment a reluctant Kate told her about the encounter with Mr. Markham in the stable. Elizabeth's eyes were wide by the time Katherine finished, and the former stared at her sister for several moments before asking, "And you mean he really *didn't tell* Tom and the duke it was you?"

Katherine said he had not, and a suddenly thoughtful Elizabeth gazed for several moments into the fire. "Well!" she said.

With a testy, "It isn't well at all!" Katherine asked just

what she meant by that. Elizabeth would not say. Instead she
rose from the bed and bade her sister good night, dropping a
soft kiss on Katherine's cheek before exiting the room, shaking her head and saying, "Well, well, well!"

Katherine, watching her go, was determined to understand
her sister's cryptic utterances. She set her mind to the task,
only to have it go wandering repeatedly to what a certain
gentleman had said, and how he'd looked when he said it,
and how his hands had felt when he lifted her—as if she
weighed no more than a feather—from the manger.

Pounding her pillow, she turned to her other side determined once again to ponder Elizabeth's remarks. She would
have, too, had not the sleep of the suddenly exhausted claimed
her.

Chapter
Twenty-three

DESPITE KATHERINE'S FERVENT hopes, there were no acts of divine intervention to prevent her from meeting Mr. Markham at the appointed hour the next day.

Although she awoke with a scratchy throat, it had disappeared by the time the doctor arrived near noon; and while he told her that she was to keep to her room for two days more after this one, he could not be brought to tell her that she looked on the verge of a relapse. In fact he so far dismayed her as to pronounce, in the most jovial of tones, that she was well on the mend.

"I think my nose looks redder this morning," Katherine told him, gazing hopefully into the long mirror that stood near her bed.

Elizabeth, also there during the doctor's visit, assured her it was no such thing.

"And I have a cough—" Katherine said. The doctor asked her to demonstrate, and when she did it sounded minor even to her own ears.

"No, Miss Katherine, you'll do," the doctor reassured her, surprised to find this Miss Farthington, usually the most rambunctious of patients, fretting so about her illness. "No need to worry. You'll be up and about in no time!"

"But I shouldn't get up today?" Katherine questioned. The doctor, mistaking the pleading note in her voice, said in his fatherly way that oh, very well, he supposed it wouldn't hurt her to get up for just a little bit. . . .

Behind him Elizabeth, watching her sister's face, giggled, and the doctor turned toward the eldest Miss Farthington. "Yes, she always can work a person around her little finger, can't she?" he asked, also mistaking the meaning behind the giggle.

"She'd certainly better hope so!" Elizabeth said, leading the way toward the door. There the doctor turned and told Katherine that while he supposed it did no good to tell her so, she was not to overdo, and she was to keep to her room for the next several days.

"That means I shouldn't venture downstairs, doesn't it?" Katherine asked, still trying to find a reason to avoid her meeting with Mr. Markham.

The doctor laughed. "Oh, very well!" he said. "You might sit quietly for a time in the library, if you feel like it! But quit your cajoling, now, for I'm *not* giving you permission to go outside. The weather has turned, and there's a cold wind blowing."

"Oh, Katherine wouldn't *dream* of going outside on a day like this," Elizabeth assured the doctor, her lips prim, her eyes alight with remembrances of her sister's nighttime escapade.

"I would hope not!" the doctor agreed. "That would be foolish beyond permission."

"Beyond permission," echoed Elizabeth, while Kate frowned glumly at her.

When Elizabeth had seen the doctor out and returned to her sister's room, it was to find Katherine sitting up in bed, a pleading light in her eyes.

"Lizzie," Katherine began, smiling in the coaxing way that almost always brought her what she wanted. "Do you suppose—"

"No," Elizabeth said.

Katherine blinked at her in surprise. "But I didn't even get to ask you anything!"

"You needn't," Elizabeth told her, "because the answer will still be 'no.' "

"Well!" Taken aback, Katherine could only stare at her sister before trying again. "I bet you misunderstood me!" she said, starting to smile again. "You don't really know what I was going to say—"

Elizabeth raised one of her delicate eyebrows as she sank gracefully into the high-backed chair nearest her sister's bed. "Don't I?" Elizabeth said. "Well then, let me guess. You are wondering if you can convince me to tell Mr. Markham that the doctor said you've taken a turn for the worse and really must remain in bed today. Am I right?"

An embarrassed Katherine did not meet her eyes as she said that well, yes . . . it was *something* like that . . . only not quite. . . .

"Oh?" Interested, Elizabeth asked how her sister's plan differed. Katherine traced the figures of the coverlet with one finger as she muttered that, well, she'd rather thought they might say she had to remain in bed for the next week. . . .

"Katherine!" The tone was remonstrative, but there was laughter in Elizabeth's eyes. "As if Mr. Markham would believe that!"

"He would if you told him!" Katherine looked up eagerly. "I know he wouldn't believe me, but if you were to say—"

"As if I would!"

"I would for you," Katherine sighed, returning her attention to the coverlet. Elizabeth said that they both knew there would be no need to tell such stories for Elizabeth.

"I know." It was the heartfelt sigh again. "It is really very bad of you, Elizabeth—to be so good."

Her sister giggled. "Now you *are* being silly," she said. "As if I am!"

"No, really!" Katherine's eyes were serious as she looked up. "You always do the right thing and say the right thing and act the right way, and you're so polite to such idiots as the Reverend Woodsley and the Blabbingtons. It is most lowering, believe me."

"Well, I wasn't very nice to Uncle Edward the night you took sick," Elizabeth reminded her, causing her sister's face to brighten slightly as Kate said she'd forgotten. "And the next time the Reverend Woodsley stops by—if he is foolish enough ever to do so again—I intend to send him off with a flea in his ear for *his* remarks on Chloe's upbringing, let me tell you!'' Her cheeks were delicately flushed by the end of her speech, and her eyes sparkled.

Katherine, surprised, could only stammer, "You will?''

Elizabeth, recalled to this place and time, nodded firmly. "I will.''

"Oh.''

"So,'' Elizabeth smiled encouragingly at her, "don't you think that if I can do that, you can meet Mr. Markham this afternoon?''

Katherine said it was not the same thing. She added hopefully that perhaps Mrs. Goodsley would drop by to sit with her that afternoon, which would preclude Katherine's leaving the room. With only the tiniest twinkle in her eye, Elizabeth informed her that Mrs. Goodsley already had promised Chloe that the two of them would bake gingerbread and crumb cakes after luncheon was served.

"Oh.'' Deflated, Katherine picked at the coverlet again until it occurred to her to ask if that was that odious Markham's idea.

"No, dear.'' Elizabeth's face was tranquil. "It was mine.''

"Lizzie!''

Her sister smiled and rose from the chair. "Now, Katherine,'' she said, walking toward the door, "you're the one who is always saying a rider must get over rough ground as lightly as she can. Although—'' Elizabeth's forehead puckered as she stopped, one hand on the doorknob, to look back at her sister, "I have never really understood what that means.'' She brightened. "Until now!''

Katherine left her room at five minutes to three with a resounding slam of her door. Peering hopefully around, she saw no one and sighed. Descending the stairs, she made as much noise as she could, thinking that perhaps Matthew, or Horton, or the duke, or even her Uncle Edward might come to investigate and, finding her there, keep her in conversation—or suggest she return to her room because of doctor's orders—thus preventing her meeting Mr. Markham. Although she believed his threat that he would tell the others it had been she under that sheet if she did not *try* to meet him, she also guessed that if something that could be considered legitimate prohibited her from keeping their appointment, he would not tell and would wait several days until they might meet again. She didn't want to meet him in several days, either, but she had the optimistic hope that something would occur to her between now and then to avoid such a meeting altogether or to better prepare her for it.

Alas, she met no one in the hall.

Horton had been invited by Chloe and Mrs. Goodsley to be the first—well, the first behind Chloe—to sample their baking, and Matthew was on his way to the village on an errand of Mr. Markham's. The duke and Elizabeth were indeed strolling in the gardens, despite the chill wind, but that had been Elizabeth's idea, and the duke—although cold—was much too much a gentleman to protest. Uncle Edward was in the morning room, napping.

When she reached the library door, Katherine took one last despairing look to the left and the right. Seeing no one, she took a deep breath, threw back her shoulders, and turned the knob. Inside the library a fire burned cheerily in the grate and Mr. Markham, who had been seated beside it in the chair long ago occupied by her father, rose at once, looking toward the clock.

"You are very prompt, Miss Farthington," he said with a smile.

"Yes, well," Katherine sighed as she came forward and sank into the chair opposite his, "I guess we might as well get it over with."

Markham almost laughed. Instead he said, "And I am very glad to see you, too."

Her quick glance up made it clear Katherine had caught his meaning. She colored, saying, "Well, it wasn't that—it was just that—that—"

"That you'd rather be almost anyplace but here," Markham supplied for her. She blushed again.

"You seem to make a habit of putting the most uncomplimentary words in my mouth," she complained.

He grinned. "Come now, Miss Farthington," he said, "deny to me, if you can, that that isn't *just exactly* what you were thinking."

Unable to do so, Katherine frowned at him. "And that's another thing," she added. "You have this odious habit of seeming to read my mind!"

Markham's grin grew. "It is, my dear, most interesting reading!"

"Don't call me that!"

Markham raised an eyebrow in inquiry, and Katherine's frown grew.

"I am *not* your dear!"

"Ahhhh." He waited a moment, meeting her frosty look with a measured one of his own. "No, you are not. You are the ghost of Miss Poole, and the person who stuffs pillows down chimneys, and, unless I very much miss my guess, the creator of pepper soup, and the one who has glass panes removed from windows and shingles removed from roofs and cold baths sent up to unsuspecting guests—"

Despite her best intentions, Katherine giggled. Mr. Markham gazed questioningly toward her.

'I wish I could have seen that!" Katherine said, recalling Matthew's highly-colored account of the look on Mr. Markham's face when he first stepped into the cold water.

"Why, Miss Farthington!" The teasing note behind his feigned astonishment made her blush crimson as she realized, too late, what she'd said. "My dear, if I'd known!"

"You know very well that isn't what I meant!" Katherine sputtered furiously. "As if I would!"

"Would what?" he asked promptly, further discomfitting her. After several more moments of sputtering, Katherine pressed her lips firmly together and held her chin up, frowning at him.

"Mr. Markham," she said, "I do not believe this conversation is going anywhere."

"Don't you?" It was that whimsical smile again, the one that made her regard him with even greater suspicion. "Now I—I thought it was progressing in the most interesting fashion."

"Hmmmph!" sniffed Miss Farthington. She reached for the handkerchief tucked into her left sleeve and gave her nose a defiant blow before raising her chin at him again. "If you have nothing further to say to me, sir—" She started to rise, but was pressed gently back into her chair by her companion, who informed her that he had a great deal—oh, yes, a *great deal*—more to say.

Katherine's face fell, and it was apparent that she'd been afraid of that. Again, Markham had to struggle not to laugh. Instead he said, "Now, Miss Farthington, if you please—I would like an accounting of just what is going on here."

Katherine jerked her ill-used handkerchief from one hand to the other as, not looking at him, she said that she had no idea what he was talking about. Markham smiled.

"No?" he said. "Well then, perhaps *I* should tell *you* what I believe has been happening ever since your uncle, my friend, and I arrived."

Inclining her head politely, Katherine made it apparent that he was welcome to do so if he wished, and Markham grinned.

"All right," he said, "correct me if I'm wrong. But I believe that ever since we arrived, you've been trying your best to get us to leave again. The thing I could not figure out was—why?" Although Katherine ostensibly was directing her face to the fire, Markham knew he had her complete attention as he continued. "Then I realized—although your uncle is in favor of selling Farthington Hall, you and your sisters are not. Am I right?"

Reluctantly Katherine turned to face him. Almost of its own volition, her head moved slowly up and down.

"Then, my dear Miss Farthington, why didn't you just tell us?" Markham asked. "Neither the duke nor I would buy a home away from three young ladies who did not wish to sell it!"

He stopped, aware that she was regarding him in startled surprise. "You wouldn't?" she breathed.

"Of course not!" He rose and took a hasty step around his chair, pausing to lean upon its back as he gazed down at her. "What kind of men do you think we are?"

The quick rush of color to her cheeks answered that, and his sardonic, "I see," made her turn even brighter crimson.

"You see—" she said, thinking aloud, "—Lizzie and Chloe said we should ask you—but I thought—I thought—"

Mr. Markham was heard to say that he did not believe she had thought at all, and Katherine glared up at him.

"Yes, well, a lot you know!" she sniffed, her brows

drawn together as she met his eyes. "Because if Uncle Edward is so in debt that he thinks now of selling our home, it really wouldn't matter if you or the duke bought it, would it? He'd be back soon enough with someone else. So we decided—"

"Who decided?" The question was dry, and Katherine frowned at the interruption.

"All right—*I* decided—that we would make the Hall appear so dilapidated that you all would leave, and Uncle Edward wouldn't be back. And then, when Lizzie comes of age, we'll all be safe. And it was a *good* plan, whatever Tom and Lizzie might say, and it would have worked, too, except for you!"

Markham smiled at the reference to Katherine's friend and sister even as he considerably stunned her by asking in the most disinterested voice possible, "My dear Miss Farthington, what makes you think your plan may not yet work?"

Katherine blinked at him. "I beg your par—*what?*"

Again Markham suppressed his laughter. "I said, what makes you think that your plan may not yet work?"

"Well, I suppose now that you know, you'll tell Uncle Edward—" she began.

He remarked somewhat acidly that he avoided conversation with Edward Farthington whenever possible, and the arrested look on Katherine's face was replaced almost immediately by one of great hope.

"By all that's famous!" she crowed. "Does this mean you're leaving?"

Markham *did* laugh at the pleasure that thought so obviously brought her, even as he told her that no, he had no plans to cut his visit short. The sparkle in Katherine's eyes dimmed slightly.

"Why not?" she asked.

Markham said that while he had no desire to buy the Hall—and would see that the duke did not, either—he had found that both enjoyed the view there enormously and had no desire to leave it so soon.

Katherine's gaze was one of acute suspicion. "And what do you mean by that?"

Markham told her he meant what he said, adding, when

she continued to watch him with that speculative gaze, that they intended to stay the full length of their visit.

"Oh." Katherine digested that. "Well, as long as you don't tell Uncle Edward . . ."

"Miss Farthington," he promised, "I will do everything in my power to see that your uncle does not bother you again."

"You will?" Surprise was back in her face, and he grinned. "I will."

"Oh." Another thought came to Katherine, and she looked away as she said, with some difficulty, that she wanted to thank him for his actions last night on behalf of Chloe. . . .

"It was my pleasure."

"I don't know what possessed her—" she said, embarrassed, and was startled when his next words echoed Elizabeth's.

"It was nothing you wouldn't have done." His shrug dismissed the topic and he held his hand out to her, waiting until she put her small one into his.

"Let us be friends, Miss Farthington," he said. "Now that you know you have nothing to fear from me, perhaps you might even find that I can help you."

Wondering with half her mind why her fingers felt as if they were tingling, Katherine had to work to make the other half of her mind follow the conversation.

"Well . . ." She was tired and felt a sneeze coming on. Reaching for her handkerchief, she applied it vigorously to her nose before looking him straight in the eye and replying, "Very well, Mr. Markham. Friends."

Chapter
Twenty-four

IT WAS REALLY quite funny what a difference it made when she and Mr. Markham declared a truce, Katherine thought nearly a week later as she slanted a glance toward her riding companion whose attention at that moment was diverted by the approach of Tom and his father. She'd been confined to the house by her lingering sniffles, and this was the first day she'd been allowed to ride. Mrs. Goodsley and Elizabeth were adamant that she wasn't to go out until the doctor approved it and Katherine, who usually could talk them around anything, found herself frustrated on the issue by the implacable gentleman to her left, who stood firmly with them. Yet her enforced confinement had not proved nearly as irksome as it always had before. She knew, although she wouldn't say it out loud, that it was the gentleman with whom she now rode who had brightened her convalescence.

There had been games of chess that truly tested her skill. Before her partners had been limited to the Reverend Woodsley, who, each time he lost, treated her to a sermonette on the vanity of winning; Elizabeth, who never concentrated on the game; Tom, who played as he rode, always taking impetuous chances; and Pooley, who was a good player but seldom available. Mr. Markham could be depended upon to take advantage of each mistake she made and, each time she thought she had him, to execute some move heretofore unknown to her. Katherine, who liked to learn, found their games exhilarating and was not above crowing when she bested him.

Under the duke's aegis, she'd undertaken the rudiments of piquet and was looking forward to the day she could challenge Markham with her skills in that game, too.

Then there had been afternoons spent comfortably reading aloud in the library. She and Markham were usually joined by Elizabeth and the duke and, sometimes, when they were enjoying a book she did not regard with suspicion, Chloe. The discussions that arose out of their readings fed Katherine's eager soul, for neither Markham nor Bellingham seemed to find it odd that the ladies had opinions on the subjects under discussion. Even more surprising to Katherine, who had more than once tried to intelligently discuss something with Reverend Woodsley, only to be patronized until she was in danger of tearing out her—or his—hair, the gentlemen listened without the least sign of superiority. Any teasing that was done was done because their views differed, not because they felt one's idea was superior to another's on the basis of gender.

Evenings often were spent in the music room with Elizabeth at the piano, sometimes joined by the duke as they sang duets. Markham, who disclaimed any musical ability, was one night persuaded by his friend to add a fine baritone to some of Lizzie's favorite songs. Then it had seemed only fair—at least, that's what Elizabeth said—that Katherine perform, too, and her harp, long relegated to a corner because of lack of time to practice it, was pulled out to the middle of the room. Once tuned, it was accompanied by Elizabeth on the piano and put through its paces as Kate recalled pieces she had not played in months—even years.

Something of her love of the music and the instrument must have come through her fingers and showed on her face. After that, her performances became a part of their convivial little evenings, which were curtailed only by the appearance of Uncle Edward (who, most often, was still in the dining room with the brandy and unaware of their entertainments), or a neighbor come to call.

Since the weather had taken a nasty turn, and the feel of snow was in the air, the latter were scarcer than they might have been. That afforded all of those who liked to gather in the music room much more pleasure than any one of them was likely to admit.

Now, as the squire and Tom approached, Katherine tried to stifle the pang of disappointment that seemed to fill her chest each time she realized Mr. Markham, who was becoming a much too familiar part of her world, soon would be leaving. Although he and the duke, by tacit agreement, seemed ready to stay as long as Uncle Edward remained at the Hall, believing that one or the other of them still might buy it, Katherine could not depend on her uncle's hopes remaining staunch on that point. She knew that once he realized the gentlemen had no intention of buying, he would be off. She could not count the times he already had said how much he missed London and couldn't imagine why anyone resided in the forsaken north. Even though dinners at the Hall had improved tremendously following Mr. Markham's discovery, no one there thought it necessary to repair the windows in Edward Farthington's room (as they had been in the duke's and Mr. Markham's) or to fix the leak in his roof (as the roof over the other two rooms had been fixed), or to increase the amount of fuel to burn on the hearth, or to dust, or to do any of the other things that had been done to make the other gentlemen more comfortable.

"Kate!" Tom called as soon as he was within shouting distance. "So they couldn't keep you inside any longer!"

"No," Mr. Markham agreed, turning to smile at her in a way that always seemed to tilt her stomach a trifle sideways, "we couldn't."

"And I see Thunderer is back where he belongs," the squire added, smiling at Katherine with fatherly affection. "I didn't think I could keep him in my stables much longer!"

Katherine's smile was for Markham as well as the new arrivals. She had been quite touched that morning to find that he'd ridden over to the squire's the day before to bring her horse back for her, so that she might ride with him.

The moment almost had been ruined when her uncle, who never appeared at the breakfast table, walked in in the middle of their discussion to demand, in the voice of one whose head hurt him after an evening of over-imbibing, what Katherine was to ride.

She herself had been so surprised by his appearance that she could only stutter for an answer, and Elizabeth had grown white at the question.

Markham, however, had only said, with perfect truth, "A horse out of the squire's stables," an answer that made Chloe giggle and the duke turn a laugh into a cough as Uncle Edward stared suspiciously at them.

"Oh," was all Farthington said before slumping into a chair and demanding a cup of coffee. Matthew, poker-faced, placed a cup in front of him, and Markham, who had a pretty good idea of the temperature of that liquid, suggested that if Katherine was done with her breakfast, they should be off.

The duke, following his friend's lead, suggested a stroll to Elizabeth and Chloe, and in no time Edward Farthington was left alone in the breakfast room to grumble about his cold and runny eggs.

"Your uncle certainly can clear a room," Markham had grinned at Kate as they made their way to the stable. She, light-hearted, said that it was a trait that ran in the family.

"I will remember that," Markham promised, a faint glimmer in his eye making her catch her breath even as she strove to understand his meaning.

"You will?" The question was tentative as he threw her into the saddle and she sat, watching as he swung easily up onto his own horse.

"Of course," he assured her, and his eyes twinkled. "In case I ever need a room cleared, you know."

"Oh." It seemed a most unsatisfactory answer and gave Katherine much to think about as they set off in the direction of the squire's land.

Now Katherine, firmly recalling her mind from this wandering it was so prone to these days, heard Tom eagerly inviting Markham and the duke to go out shooting with him the next day. He promised it would be a rare thing if they didn't return with a brace of birds for dinner.

Markham said he was sure the duke would be as delighted as he was to accept the invitation. But he caused Tom's face to fall somewhat when he suggested that it would be impolite for them not to include their host in the invitation as well.

"Oh, very well," Tom agreed, his sulky tone bringing

down his father's immediate chastisement, "but that prosy old bore will probably scare everything we come upon."

The squire, while telling his son severely that he should not speak so of his elders, could not help adding that the boy was right, of course. Years earlier, when Edward Farthington had visited his brother, Katherine's father, and the squire had gone out hunting with them, Edward had ruined every chance at a bird they'd had, and had finished the day by ill-judgedly loosing his gun and raining shot down upon one of the groom's boys who was with them, several pieces of which had landed in the boy's leg.

"Oh, was he hurt?" Katherine cried, appalled.

The squire, remembering, smiled and said that the boy mended quickly, but he rather thought Katherine's father had had a great deal to say to his brother, and that Edward's pride might have taken a good deal longer to heal. "At any rate," the squire said, thinking aloud, "your uncle left the next day, which was considered good by the entire neighborhood—"

Tom's hoot and demand to know just who was being tactless now brought the squire up short and, glowering at his son, he said that, well, while it was very good to see the two from the Hall, he couldn't be sitting there all day chatting. . . .

He cantered off, followed by a grinning Tom, who paused only to call back that he'd be over for the gentlemen bright and early the next morning. After promising to be ready Markham, aware that they'd been out for over an hour now, cast an appraising glance toward Kate and turned his horse back in the direction from which they'd come. A short time later the two of them were ensconced in the library, drinking the hot tea an anxious Mrs. Goodsley had been brewing for her middle lamb.

When Tom's projected treat was proposed to the duke and Farthington that night at dinner, Bellingham agreed to it with his usual good nature, saying that it was very kind of young Mannerling to go to the trouble of offering them a bit of sport.

It was her Uncle Edward's actions that surprised Katherine. He'd sat throughout most of the meal in a fit of abstraction, shoveling whatever appeared on his plate into his mouth as if he had no idea what he was eating. His brow remained beetled, as if he wrestled with some heavy problem, and from time to time he frowned at each of his guests in a way that the gentlemen seemed to ignore, but which had Katherine and Elizabeth exchanging puzzled glances and slight shrugs whenever no one else was watching.

When Markham issued Tom's invitation, however, Farthington snapped his fingers and with a "That's it!" seemed to come alive, saying jovially that once the gentlemen saw what good hunting there was to be had in the north, he'd have to be beating them off, so eager would they be to buy the Hall.

That statement was followed by an awkward silence as his four dinner companions (Chloe having elected to eat with Mrs. Goodsley as often as possible to avoid her uncle) exchanged glances. Uncle Edward didn't seem to notice. Instead, he lapsed into reminiscences of the fine hunting to be had around Farthington Hall, recounting exploits Katherine was very sure he'd never taken part in, and ending with, "Why, I remember the last time I was out hunting here—"

Katherine, who had had more than she could stomach of his bragging, giggled. When he directed a frowning glance toward her, she said that yes, the squire had remembered that last hunting trip himself earlier that day.

Reddening, Edward's frown grew as, in blustery tones, he asked her just what there was to laugh about in that.

About to tell him, Katherine opened her mouth just as she encountered another frown, this one from Mr. Markham, who shook his head slightly. Kate considerably shocked her sister, who had been waiting with quiet fortitude for what she expected was a coming clash between Katherine and their uncle, by closing her mouth again.

"I believe," Mr. Markham put in, drawing Edward's attention to his elegantly clad form, "that the squire told us you had abysmal luck that day—that not a bird was taken."

"Well, I don't know what's funny in that!" Farthington snapped, directing his gaze back toward his niece. Again it was Markham who spoke.

"Oh, come now, Farthington," he said, amused. "Surely you must know that in the case of hunting, your niece's sympathies always lie with the birds!"

"Eh?" Uncle Edward puzzled over that statement for some moments before he thought he understood its meaning. "Oh." He smiled patronizingly at his niece. "Squeamish about shooting things, are you, my dear?"

Katherine, with a frown apiece for her uncle and Markham, said clearly, "Not *all* things, Uncle."

The duke, taking a sip of his wine, choked and started to cough, creating a diversion as Markham smiled at Katherine.

"Touché, Miss Farthington," he said, raising his glass in acknowledgment. That brought Farthington's attention back to his other dinner companions, and he was suspicious as he asked just what that meant.

"I believe," Markham said, sipping his wine as Katherine, eyes smoldering, directed her attention strictly to her plate, "that Miss Farthington was making it clear that while she has a sympathy for birds, it does not extend to—er—bird-brains."

The duke, once more caught in the act of swallowing, started to cough again. This time his host rose to pound him on the back, and the conversation was lost, to Elizabeth's relief, and to Katherine and Markham's unacknowledged amusement.

Chapter
Twenty-five

THOMAS LED THE gentlemen off that morning with numerous admonishments to the Farthington sisters not to expect them back until dusk, so Katherine and Elizabeth, seated companionably in the library about 3 P.M. where Kate worked on the Hall's books while Elizabeth sewed, were surprised by a vigorous pounding on the Hall's front door that was soon followed by the sound of raised voices.

Easily recognizing Tom's excited tones and the commanding voice of Mr. Markham calling for calm, they exchanged startled glances before hurrying to the door and down the hall. There a rare sight confronted them.

Horton, his face aghast, was standing as if turned to stone. His hand still held open the front door, and he stared at the vociferous party that had just invaded the hall. Matthew, trying his best to be helpful, darted here and there, sent in one direction by a call for bandages and in another by a demand that someone take the gentlemen's coats immediately, and in a third by the suggestion that brandy was needed—at once!

"Yes, brandy!" Katherine heard her uncle second as she and Elizabeth arrived on the scene. "The very thing."

An angry Markham turned toward his host. "It is for the duke, you idiot!" he said.

Farthington, coloring, said that yes, yes, of course, but he imagined there might be a dram or two left for—others—

Markham turned his back on the older man. Elizabeth,

turning pale, clutched her sister's arm and repeated, "The duke?" in faint but terrified tones.

Matthew, who happened to have darted their way for the moment, heard her and shook his head gloomily. "Yes, Miss Elizabeth," he said, his own eyes starting, "your uncle has gone and shot the duke, and they've carried him in, looking fit to die—"

"No such thing," said a weak but testy voice; Matthew's ears had not been the only ones tuned to Elizabeth's cry of fright. "It will take more than a little buckshot to do in the Duke of Bellingham, let me tell you."

At the sound of that voice, Elizabeth loosed her hold on Katherine's arm and flew the few remaining feet across the hall. She shouldered her way through the tall forms that surrounded Bellingham until she could kneel beside him as he still sat in the rough chair of arms Tom and his groom had formed to carry the injured man back to the Hall.

"Oh, George!" she cried, large tears welling up and over her lower eyelids as she stared at his pale face and the blood oozing from his leg. She turned toward her uncle, eyes flashing. "Murderer!" she breathed. "You—you—*you!*"

Hastily Farthington said that it was all a mistake, he hadn't meant to shoot his guest, in fact . . . His voice trailed off as the duke leaned forward to pat Elizabeth weakly on the shoulder. "No, no, Lizzie," he told her, "it was an accident. The veriest scratch, I assure you! I'll be up and about in—in—"

His eyes seemed to roll in their sockets and his head lolled to one side, stopping when it hit the arm of the groom who, with Thomas, still held him. Markham, long since tired of what in his mind, at least, came dangerously close to histrionics, said acidly that if they were all done being hysterical, he'd suggest they carry Bellingham into the morning room and lay him down and tend to his wound before he bled to death. Instantly he regretted the last words as Elizabeth turned even whiter. Rolling his eyes, he told her that it was his cursed tongue; the duke wasn't going to die—

"You should learn to mind your tongue!" Katherine informed him righteously as she leaned down to lift her sister to her feet.

In spite of himself Markham felt his brow lightening.

"Perhaps you will give me lessons, Miss Farthington," he said, his polite words not at all hiding the fact that he knew, as well as Katherine, that she was in no position to do so. With a "hmph," Kate lifted Elizabeth and hurried with her to the morning room, calling to Mrs. Goodsley, who, with Chloe, had just appeared. She told the housekeeper they would need hot water and clean bandages, and that good lady, nodding, disappeared back in the direction from which she'd come.

Horton, recovering, closed the door and dispatched Matthew for the brandy. Then he directed Thomas and the groom to carry the duke into the morning room and put him on the sofa—at once. Since they were already headed that way, his direction might have been thought unnecessary. Thomas, however, was much too easygoing a young man to say so, and his groom stood too much in awe of the normally contained butler to consider uttering a cheeky word.

Having deposited their burden on the sofa, both men stepped back with a sigh of relief. The groom touched Tom's shoulder and said that he'd just be running along now, if the young master had no more need of him. . . .

Tom nodded and the groom prepared to depart. He was stopped by Katherine, who told him that there was one more service he must yet do. Surprised, both groom and Tom stared at her.

"You will have to ride for the doctor," Kate said briskly, propping a pillow under the duke's injured leg as her sister tenderly placed one behind his head.

"No, no—" The duke, who had come round again, tried to deter her. "There is no need, Miss Farthington! It is the veriest scratch, I'm sure. . . ."

Well, that might be, Katherine told him, but she certainly didn't want him dying through any action of a Farthington, nor did she want him invalided there for weeks, unable to return to London. . . .

"Katherine!" Elizabeth gasped, frowning at her sister as Mr. Markham turned his laughter into a very unconvincing cough.

"Oh." The duke, abashed, begged pardon. "I didn't think—of course I don't want to be a bother to you—"

"You are not a bother to us!" Elizabeth assured him, adding another pillow to the ones she'd already placed behind his head. "Katherine, on the other hand . . ."

Her sister, who had heard Mr. Markham's sotto voce suggestion that they take tongue-minding lessons together, blushed and said that she had not meant to be rude. It was just that—just that—

"Just that you'll feel better if the doctor sees to George," Markham ended for her. She threw him a grateful smile as she nodded. "Well, so will I!"

This unexpected concern from one who had bound up far worse wounds for him so surprised the duke that he could only goggle at his friend for several moments. "You—will?" Bellingham managed to gulp out. His question was met by an enigmatic look and a decided nod, and not for the first time did the duke wish he knew what thoughts lurked inside Nicholas's mind.

"So will I!" Elizabeth seconded Markham, her hand gently brushing the hair back from the duke's brow as she gazed worriedly down at him.

"Oh." The duke thought. "Well, then . . ."

Thomas said he'd see his groom off, and the two departed as Matthew entered the room with a full bottle of brandy. Farthington, his eyes brightening, came forward from the corner into which he'd scurried, believing—correctly—that with Mr. Markham in his present mood, it might be to the host's advantage to play least in sight. Waving Matthew away, Uncle Edward poured a glass out and was raising it to his lips. Before he could drink it was removed from his hand, and he looked indignantly up into Markham's scornful face.

"Always the perfect host, Farthington," Markham drawled as he crossed to the couch and lifted his friend's shoulders, placing the glass to the duke's lips. George sipped the brandy gratefully and sighed as Markham laid him back down.

"Oh—of course—" Farthington stuttered. "I forgot myself—in the heat of the moment—"

"It would seem," Markham remarked to the room at large, his eyes roving everywhere but toward the older man, "that you often do." He sighed. "If only others could forget you, as well."

Uncle Edward, a freshly poured glass at his lips, choked and sputtered angrily. Katherine giggled. "And what are you laughing at, Miss?" he blustered, glaring at her.

She did not have time to answer as Markham placed himself firmly between her uncle and Katherine. "The same thing I am," he said, surveying his host with a sneer. Grumbling, Farthington retreated to the corner, thoughtfully taking the brandy with him. The duke, observing the distress on Elizabeth Farthington's face, said that they mustn't fight on his account.

Markham strolled back to the sofa to stand over him and said, "Why, George, I don't believe we were," in such a tone of mild surprise that his friend had to grin.

"Now, Nicholas," the duke said, "don't go getting yourself in trouble when I'm laid on my back unable to stop you."

Markham smiled but was saved from replying by the entrance of Mrs. Goodsley, who came bearing a tray containing a bowl of steaming water and a pile of clean white bandages.

"Now then, sir," Mrs. Goodsley said kindly as Horton drew up a small table for her to set her tray on, and she turned toward the duke. "I believe we should just be having a look at your wound—"

Chloe, who had been standing in the background watching everything with interest and keeping quiet so her sisters wouldn't notice her presence and send her from the room, crept forward at the housekeeper's words and stared with interest at the duke's bleeding leg.

"How were you shot?" she asked.

"Accident," grunted an all-but-ignored voice from the corner.

"It's nothing, really—" the duke started for what seemed like the hundredth time. Mr. Markham interrupted.

"You see, Chloe," Markham said, smiling at the little girl. "There are gentlemen who never should be allowed to consider themselves marksmen or to handle guns." He seemed to consider something, then went on. "Of course, there are 'gentlemen' who should never be allowed to consider themselves gentlemen. . . ."

"Nicholas, for goodness sakes!" the duke implored as a small roar came from the corner.

"Sir, you are insulting!" Farthington's words were slurred slightly by the serious inroads he'd made on the brandy, and Markham ignored him.

Seating himself beside the duke's leg, Markham said, "Now, George," as he took a knife from the tray and held it consideringly in his hand. All eyes focused on him. "I'm going to have to slit your boot to look at your wound—"

"Ladies present!" his friend warned, vivid color rushing to his face as he tried to struggle to a sitting position.

Markham glanced around. "Ladies," he said, "I believe my friend would be more comfortable if you were to leave us."

"Would!" the duke agreed, his head nodding vigorously. He cradled a pillow in preparation for his friend's exploration.

"Well, I wouldn't!" Elizabeth surprised everyone—including herself—by saying. She blushed as all eyes turned toward her, but stood her ground. "I wouldn't be at all comfortable—not knowing—how serious your wound—"

The way her words trailed off and the convenience of her hand resting on the back of the sofa made it seem incumbent that the duke give that hand a squeeze and say that, very well, if she really wished to . . .

Markham interrupted to ask—in a superior tone that raised Katherine's temper immediately—if either of them was squeamish.

"Squeamish?" Elizabeth repeated. Katherine frowned at their questioner.

"Not going to faint on me, are you?" Markham asked. "Because one patient is more than enough!"

"As if we would!" Katherine told him, moving to her sister's side so that she might support Elizabeth who had been known, on occasion, to grow decidedly green at the sight of blood. "*I* am *never* 'squeamish'!"

"Me either!" Chloe said happily. Elizabeth bit her lip. Everyone turned toward the youngest Farthington sister, who realized at once that speaking had been a mistake.

"Mrs. Goodsley," Markham suggested, "perhaps you and Chloe would be good enough to make us some tea. . . ."

"Tea!" the little girl cried. "I don't want tea! I want to stay and watch—Katherine—Elizabeth—please!" The resolute shakes of both of her sisters' heads seemed about to send her into tears when Markham hit upon the happy thought of saving all the pieces of buckshot for her.

"If you don't mind, George?" he asked, turning toward the duke.

Ever polite, George said, "Not at all," and Chloe's face brightened slightly.

"And will you tell me about it later?" she demanded.

"Detail by detail," Markham promised. Bellingham, suppressing a shudder, told him he didn't have to be so deucedly cheerful about it. Markham grinned as a clucking Mrs. Goodsley led her youngest chick from the room.

"Now, then—" Markham said purposefully. The duke braced himself as the sound of ripping cloth and leather gave way to growing pain as Markham, as carefully as he could, removed buckshot from his friend's leg. Matthew held the leg while Markham worked, Horton held the basin, and Katherine held Elizabeth. They were almost done when the sound of knocking was heard at the front door.

"Probably the doctor," Markham said, intent on his task. The knocking continued, and he glanced around.

"Farthington, get that, will you?" he asked, when it was apparent everyone else's hands were engaged. Grumbling, Uncle Edward heaved himself out of his chair and stumbled to the door, muttering that he hadn't come there to be a servant, you know. Under her breath Katherine said they wondered why he *had* come, and Markham smiled as he assured the duke that there seemed to be just one more piece of shot left in his leg. That piece had landed in the basin with a satisfying "clink" when the sound of the front door opening was followed a moment later by a terrified scream.

"*Aiiiyyyyeeeeee!*" they heard, sending shivers up and down everyone's spine. "*Aiiiyeeeeee!*"

Katherine, whose eyes had grown large at the sound, let go of Elizabeth's hands and started toward the door, only to be forcibly stopped by Mr. Markham.

"But—" she said, gazing up at him.

"Stay here," he said. "I'll see."

He started toward the door, pausing only when he realized she was right behind him.

"Katherine, please," he said. "In case there should be something wrong—any danger—"

"I want to be there with you," she said. Something in her large eyes tugged at his heart, and a rather lopsided grin appeared on his face.

"I tell you what," he said. "Let me go look. If I find myself overpowered, I shall call out, and you must come to the rescue."

"I could, you know," she said. He smiled at the now-familiar tilt of her chin.

"Yes," he agreed, "I imagine you could. And would." With difficulty he raised his eyes from her face to her sister's. "Miss Farthington," he said, "if you would just keep Katherine company—"

Understanding at once, Elizabeth came forward to take Katherine's arm. The two sisters stood in the middle of the room, watching Markham's broad back as it disappeared through the door that he shut firmly behind him.

Chapter
Twenty-six

IN THE HALL a strange sight met Markham's eyes. Edward Farthington, his once florid face now drained of color, his eyes protruding, was crouched against the wall, his gaze fixed on the doorway. At Markham's entrance Farthington swung wildly about, teeth chattering.

"It's—it's—" he hissed, swinging back toward the un-moving figure who regarded him with beetled brows. His eyes rolled up in his head, and he dropped like a stone to the floor. Markham gazed from the downed man to the visitor and back again. Gradually he began to smile.

"How do you do?" Markham asked politely, stepping over Farthington's inert form to come forward and execute his best bow. "Unless I very much miss my guess, you must be Miss Poole."

The visitor nodded slowly and stepped across the threshold, dropping her valise with a soft "whump" on the floor. She stuck her umbrella into the coatrack as one long accustomed to doing so.

"I must," she acknowledged. She untied the strings of her cloak in a no-nonsense way that reminded Mr. Markham of one of her charges and made him smile. "But then, who must you be? And what—" Her nose wrinkled in distaste as she gazed toward the unmoving Edward Farthington on the floor, "—is that old makebait doing here?" A thought occurred, and she fixed Markham with a steady stare. "Friend of yours, is he?"

Hastily Markham disclaimed. He was saved from further conversation by the opening of the morning room door, and a moment later Katherine's determined face appeared. She was followed in short order by Elizabeth, Matthew, and Horton, all of them wanting Mr. Markham to know that they had done their best to detain her.

Their chorus was quieted immediately at sight of Markham's companion. Then, with what could only be described as whoops of excitement, the morning room's occupants erupted into the hall, the Misses Farthingtons' shouts of, "Pooley! Pooley!" joined by the deeper accents of their companions, who took it upon themselves to tell Miss Poole, if they might be so bold, just how happy they were to have her with them again.

The first rapturous delights had not yet died when a small whirlwind blew out of the kitchen shrieking, "Pooley, Pooley!" with such joy that Miss Poole's face, already pink with satisfaction, turned absolutely crimson. She braced herself to withstand the fervent hug that followed as Chloe threw herself upon her mentor.

"Oh, Pooley, I *missed* you!" Chloe said, gazing up at her, teary-eyed.

"Well, did you now?" her governess returned mildly, one hand going out to brush the hair out of the girl's face as she gazed down at her with fondness.

"And we have *needed* you," Chloe continued, still clinging to the spare-framed woman in a way that brought an odd lump to Mr. Markham's throat.

"Well, that I do believe," the governess said. She looked from Edward Farthington to Mr. Markham and back again. Chloe, following her gaze, told her that Uncle Edward had come to visit. Her tone made it apparent that that was no great treat, and Miss Poole frowned.

"Been bothering you, has he?" she asked, ready to do battle on her charges' behalf.

"Oh, yes," Chloe nodded.

Miss Poole's frown grew, and her gaze shifted to Markham. "Anybody else been bothering you?" she asked.

For all his vaunted savoir faire, Markham felt as if he were six and in charge of his own strict governess. He shifted uneasily from one foot to the other, and his comfort was not

increased when Katherine Farthington, a mischievous smile
on her face, breathed an "Oh, yes!" of her own.

"Now see here—" he started, but was interrupted by the
entrance of Mrs. Goodsley. The housekeeper had puffed her
way up the stairs and now emerged on the scene like a ship in
full sail, her glad cries at sight of her longtime friend shifting
Miss Poole's attention. But only for a moment.

"Edith," Miss Poole said, her gaze transferring back to
Mr. Markham, "we have to talk."

Yes, indeed they did, Mrs. Goodsley seconded warmly;
and wasn't it a good thing she'd just made a fresh pot of tea
for the injured duke—

"Duke?" Miss Poole repeated.

Mrs. Goodsley nodded. "And there's enough left for us,
too, I'm sure. So come along, and we'll have a good chat—"

Chloe's loud and vociferous protests that she had much to
tell Pooley, too, were dealt with gently but firmly. Miss
Poole was eager to hear what had been going on at the Hall
from someone who had common sense and the ability to tell a
story with no bark on it. She promised Chloe that if that
young lady would go with Matthew to put Miss Poole's
valise and trunk in Miss Poole's room, she might wait there
for Miss Poole to unveil the surprise she'd brought her from
Scotland.

"A surprise?" Chloe was delighted at the thought and
danced ahead of Matthew to pick up Pooley's valise and to
supervise Matthew's disposition of Miss Poole's trunk. Elizabeth and Katherine might have been harder to get rid of
except for the timely arrival of the doctor and Tom, who
confided in an aside to Markham that he wasn't much good in
the sick room and so he decided to ride for the physician
himself.

The doctor paused at Edward Farthington's silent form, but
he was waved into the morning room by a chorus of voices
informing him that the real patient was in there. Shrugging,
he stopped only to tell Miss Poole that it was good to see her
again before he turned his attention to the duke.

"You should go look after the duke, too," Mrs. Goodsley
urged Katherine and Elizabeth, both of whom agreed that was
the thing to do. "And I'll send the tea up shortly." The

sisters disappeared, and were about to be followed by Tom and Markham, when Mrs. Goodsley detained them for a moment to introduce Mr. Markham to her newly arrived friend.

"We did meet," Markham said, smiling as he bowed over Miss Poole's hand in a way that made her regard him with suspicion. "But I believe I had the advantage."

Miss Poole's shoulders shook slightly as her keen eyes rested on his face. He had the feeling all his thoughts were readily apparent to her, and it was not a feeling he liked in the least. "I would not be surprised, sir," she said, her tone quite dry, "if you often do." She further confounded him by saying, in a take-charge tone, that if he and Tom wished to be useful, they could clear the hall.

"Clear the hall?" Tom echoed, gazing down at her.

"Yes, Thomas," Miss Poole said. "Please. If that—that—" She gestured toward Edward Farthington and sniffed in a way that made Mr. Markham grin, "—person has been here for some time, I would imagine that he has a bedchamber. Please remove him to it."

"But—" Thomas protested, gazing at Farthington's bulk. "Dash it, Miss Poole, the fellow's bedchamber is on the third floor!"

"Oh?" The politeness of her tone made him push farther.

"In the old wing!"

"Ahhhhh." Miss Poole considered.

"It would take us ages to get him there, when he's like this!"

Miss Poole nodded and smiled sympathetically at him as she reached out to pat his arm. "Quite right, Thomas," she told him. "You really are quite right. So—I suggest that you get started."

Turning, she linked her arm through Mrs. Goodsley's, and the two disappeared through the door leading down to the kitchen. Tom's further inarticulate protests were ignored, and when the door shut softly behind the two, he turned a dismayed face toward Mr. Markham, who shrugged.

"Well, Thomas," the gentleman said. "Perhaps we'd better. Get started."

It took them some time to heave Farthington's bulk up the

two flights of stairs and down two halls, helped not at all by their burden's occasional lapses into consciousness, at which times he tried fervently to convince them that he had seen a ghost.

"You saw her, didn't you?" Edward said, his head lolling toward Mr. Markham. The latter recoiled from his host's less-than-fragrant breath.

"Saw who, Farthington?" Markham parried, even as he adjured the man to move his feet.

"The ghost!"

"I saw no ghost." Behind Farthington's back, Markham nodded away Tom's efforts to explain that Farthington had seen not spirit but flesh. Tom, surprised by the command in Markham's eyes, subsided.

"It was that Poole woman." Farthington's head slewed toward Thomas, who countered with, "It was?"

Farthington groaned. "She's come to get me, she has. Back from the dead."

"Or Scotland," Tom muttered. He was hit a moment later by Markham, who shook his head warningly at him.

"What?" Farthington demanded, fixing his bleary gaze on Tom.

"I said I thought all ghosts went to Scotland," Tom supplied, thinking fast. "That's what my nanny used to tell me. . . ."

His words trailed off as Farthington regarded him in puzzlement for several moments. "Strange thing to tell a child," Edward decided, looking toward Markham for confirmation.

"Perhaps it depended on how strange the child," Markham said, frowning at Tom. Farthington giggled.

"That's good," Edward approved. "Very good." There was a pause as he lapsed into oblivion again, only to come out of it somewhat as the two men, grunting, finally lowered him onto his bed.

"It's cold in here," Thomas said, rubbing his hands as he looked around.

Farthington groaned. "It's always cold in here," he said. "Ever since I got here."

Markham told the room at large that he understood that haunted rooms were always cold. Farthington, who had lain down with both eyes closed, opened one of them.

"What?" Edward said.

"Oh, you know, Farthington," Markham shrugged. "They say it's always cold in the area surrounding ghosts. I'm sure you've heard that before."

Glancing around with great uneasiness, Edward assured him he had not.

"Oh. Well." Markham shrugged again. "I daresay it's all humbug anyway. I mean—ghosts!"

He laughed, and after a moment Farthington laughed with him. It was a forced, weak sound that ran off badly. Starting toward the door with Thomas after him, Markham only stopped when his host asked anxiously where he was going.

"Why, back to the morning room, of course!" Markham raised one eyebrow in surprise. "To see how the real invalid is doing." Farthington's face flushed slightly. "Besides, a little sleep will do you good."

Already the shadows were lengthening in the bedroom, and Farthington glanced uneasily about as Markham said they would see him at dinner.

Edward nodded. "Send that man—Matthew, I think his name is—to wake me, will you?"

Markham agreed he would.

"And tell him to bring a candle! No, tell him to bring several candles. It's dark in here!"

Markham shrugged and turned toward the door again as his host said, "I've heard that ghosts don't like light. Have you heard that, Markham?"

Markham turned an innocent face back toward the bed. "Why, no," he said. "I don't believe I've heard that at all."

"You haven't?"

Markham opened the door and ushered Tom through it. The last words Farthington heard them say were Markham's, "Have you heard that, Thomas?" and Tom's quick and hearty, "No!"

Shivering, Edward pulled the covers up over his head and lay, eyes wide, until the brandy he'd so recently consumed once again took effect.

Chapter
Twenty-seven

It was, at least for Edward Farthington, unfortunate that as he followed Matthew down the stairs to the dining room that evening, the two of them encountered Miss Poole just coming out of Chloe's room.

The excellent governess, by this time having been apprised of all that had happened at Farthington Hall since her absence, could not resist, as Farthington stood, eyes starting from his head as his color drained and he started to sweat, hissing "Boo!" at him as she glided by. Matthew, standing wooden-faced and unsure of how to proceed—for Miss Katherine had not yet had time to tell him how they were to explain Miss Poole's reappearance at the Hall—touched Farthington's shoulder with a solicitous, "Sir?" when Miss Poole disappeared down the back steps. Farthington gazed wildly up at him.

"If you would just follow me, sir—" Matthew suggested, turning toward the main stairway. Farthington grabbed desperately at his arm.

"You saw her!" the older man stuttered. "Dash it, man! You had to see her!"

Matthew almost gave in to the pleading in Farthington's eyes before the admonishment of his mentor, Horton, was heard in his ears. "A good servant," Horton often intoned, "sees and hears nothing. At least, nothing to talk about. To certain people."

Certain that Edward Farthington was one of those "certain people," Matthew shook his head. "Saw—who, sir?" he asked cautiously.

Farthington groaned and waved him ahead. "And I used to think my brother kept such very good brandy," Matthew heard a voice mourn behind him. He grinned, but his grin was quickly erased by the sight of Horton, already holding the dining room door open for the last guest.

Conversation at dinner that night could be called random at best, and extremely desultory if one took a more realistic view. Markham's thoughts were on his recent interview with Miss Poole; Elizabeth could hardly chew for worry over the duke, eating that night in his bedchamber, at the insistence of the doctor and any number of his nurses; and Katherine was pondering what could be making Markham frown so. Farthington, sure that if he stayed any longer at the Hall his demise would be imminent, so lost his appetite as to be able to eat no more than three helpings of the chicken and two pieces of Mrs. Goodsley's apple pie, along with single helpings of all the other dishes that graced the table.

It was when his nieces rose to leave the gentlemen to their port that Edward cleared his throat and, his mind made up, told the ladies that he would be departing the Hall on the morrow.

"You will?" Elizabeth said in polite surprise.

"You will?" echoed Katherine, her voice carrying joy.

"You can't!" came from Markham. The force behind his words made all three turn toward him in surprise.

"I can't?" Now it was Edward's turn to echo.

"He can't?" Elizabeth was even more surprised.

"What do you mean, he can't?" Katherine was jerking her head toward her uncle in a most meaningful way as her eyes flashed fire at this man she had come to think of as her ally. Markham ignored her.

"I mean—" Markham started. "That is—" He paused and thought rapidly. "We haven't concluded our business here, Farthington!"

Edward shook his head mournfully. "Thought of that," he said, his head continuing to move from side to side as his fingers drummed on the table. "Thought of it a lot. If you and Bellingham haven't come up to scratch yet, you never will. Hate to think it, but there it is.''

Katherine, watching Markham with wrinkled forehead, was even further puzzled by the effect the words "up to scratch" had on him. He colored slightly, and pressed on.

"Oh, you never know, Farthington," he said easily. "Perhaps another week or two in the country . . ."

Edward's shudder was visible as he pondered the thought. "Not for anything," he said, and Markham thought it a shame that it was at this particular point in their relationship that his host developed a certain backbone. "Miserable, crumbly old place. Besides." He sighed heavily, and whisked his handkerchief across his forehead. "Haunted, you know."

Markham grinned. "Come now, Farthington. There are no ghosts!"

"Easy for you to say," his host countered. "The dratted woman doesn't bother you. You don't see her."

A solemn Markham agreed that he had yet to see a ghost at Farthington Hall. That statement brought him a fine glare from Katherine as well as her uncle.

"It could yet be arranged," Katherine suggested, the words coming out hard through gritted teeth. Markham grinned, but Edward Farthington could not repress another shudder.

"No, no," her uncle said, "you mustn't say such things, Katherine—not even in jest." He lowered his voice and looked around uneasily. "You never know who might be listening."

At that moment Matthew, who was listening outside the dining room door, let the silver tray he was holding in his hands slip. It hit the floor with a resounding crash, causing Edward to jump violently.

"What was that?" Farthington demanded as the other three exchanged glances.

"What was what?" Markham's tone was bland as he intercepted whatever soothing thing Elizabeth had meant to say. She raised her eyebrows at him, but remained silent. Edward shuddered again.

"You see?" Farthington said, his body rising with his voice as he gazed wildly about the room. "You don't see her—and you don't hear her—"

He jumped as Matthew entered the room, the slightly
dented tray in hand, and asked if there was anything he could
be getting them. . . . Horton frowned majestically at him,
and the footman disappeared again.

"I leave tomorrow," Farthington said with conviction,
sagging back into his chair and taking recourse to his handkerchief to wipe his perspiring face yet again. Kindly Katherine offered to help him pack.

"You can't pack and you can't leave," Markham said from
the other end of the table, drawing all eyes toward him again.

"Why not?" demanded Edward and Katherine as both
glared at him.

"Because," Markham's voice was calm, his nose in the
air, "my friend Bellingham is unable to travel because of his
wound, and it would be most irregular if he and I were to stay
here without our host."

The words "most irregular" were Miss Poole's, and had
been applied to the whole visit. Markham had little doubt
about what she would say if he and his friend's host hied off
on them.

"Oh." A small frown puckered Katherine's forehead as
she considered. Elizabeth looked quite worried, and even
Farthington paused.

"Perhaps if we traveled by easy stages—" Edward suggested.
Markham shook his head.

Edward thought. "Perhaps you two could repair to the
nearest inn—"

"Uncle Edward!" Elizabeth was shocked at this breach of
hospitality and shook her head reproachfully at him.

"Now don't 'Uncle Edward' me," he countered testily.
"I'm trying to think—"

"With what?" Katherine muttered under her breath, causing Mr. Markham's lips to twitch. Her uncle glared at her.

"What was that, Katherine?" he asked.

"I believe Miss Farthington was asking what other alterna-
tives are available," Markham said smoothly, making Katherine both grateful and irritated. "I do not believe there are
any."

"But there must be—" Farthington began. He was interrupted by the entrance of Tom, who had come, he said, to see

how the duke was getting on. Edward's face brightened at sight of his young guest.

"Of course!" Edward rose in delight; he hurried forward to take Tom's hand and pump it vigorously. Surprised, the young man looked from one to the other of the room's inhabitants for enlightenment. It was not long in coming.

"The very thing!" Farthington continued. "You can repair to the squire's! After all, it was this young man's fault the duke was injured—"

A general chorus of disagreement greeted that statement, and Farthington said that oh, very well, if they must carry on so, he would admit that it was indeed he who had pulled the trigger. . . .

"Most gracious of you." Markham's voice was dry, and Farthington gazed at him in dislike.

"Really, Uncle!" Again Elizabeth's voice carried that note of chastisement. "How can you even try to blame Tom—"

"Well, it was his idea we go hunting, wasn't it?" Edward countered, his face turning florid as he tried to justify himself before their extremely skeptical gazes. "Foolish idea, anyway!"

Katherine, firing up on behalf of her friend, who was looking as if he half believed Edward Farthington, said that if her uncle cared to follow that line of "logic," the blame must in the end come back to him again, since it could be reasoned that the duke would never had been shot if Edward hadn't brought him to Farthington Hall. . . .

"Yes, well—" Farthington had a look of dislike for Katherine, too, as he said that he was sure he wasn't one to assign blame; it was just that—just that—

He couldn't seem to think what it was that was just that. Thomas, his head in the air like that of a buck sniffing danger, asked with caution if something was amiss.

"Ghosts!" Farthington told him instantly, before the others could speak. "Ghosts are amiss!"

"Oh." Tom grinned. "Miss Poole been visiting again, has she?"

Tom was the third inhabitant in the room to encounter Farthington's dark gaze as Edward muttered that they could all joke, but when they found him lying in his bed with his throat slit . . .

"Oh, come now!" Markham was, Farthington considered, far too jovial. "More likely Miss Poole would beat you to death with her umbrella, so you needn't worry she'll slit your throat—"

Thomas and Katherine gurgled at the thought, and even Elizabeth smiled. Farthington, backing away, waved his arms at them in disgust and said they might as well all get out and leave him to his misery. Since the four were only too willing to oblige, they were soon ensconced in the nursery where a fire burned cozily and Miss Poole entertained Chloe with a story of Scotland ghosts before putting her youngest charge to bed. Listening, Markham asked with a twinkle if that was where she'd learned to say "Boo!" so convincingly (for Matthew had told him about the chance meeting in the hall), and was delighted to see her turn pink.

"I couldn't resist," Miss Poole apologized, looking self-conscious as the others clamored to know to what Markham referred. "It was most improper of me."

The acknowledgment that Miss Poole had been "improper" only increased the clamor, and soon all the inhabitants of the room were giggling at the word pictures Markham drew of Uncle Edward's encounter with the undauntable Miss Poole.

"Oh, I wish I could have seen it!" Chloe said wistfully, gazing up at her heroine wide-eyed.

"Well, perhaps you'll get a chance tomorrow, love!" Katherine comforted her as she led her small sister off to bed, dropping a soft kiss on her forehead as the child, heavy-eyed, fell asleep as soon as her head touched the pillow.

Alas, there was to be no chance on the morrow.

When Uncle Edward did not appear at the breakfast table, no one was surprised; he often had not joined them for breakfast, having, as Matthew so eloquently put it, "Made a batch of it" the night before.

Luncheon did not bring the family together, for Elizabeth, visiting the duke in his room, was persuaded to join him in a meal there. Katherine and Markham, out for one of their morning rides, stopped at the squire's and were persuaded to join that gentleman and his wife and son for a light meal, and Miss Poole and Chloe ate in the nursery. Horton and Mat-

thew, pleased not to be bothered by any of Farthington's
peevish demands, decided between the two of them that if he
cared to sleep all day, they certainly weren't going to wake
him.

It was only when Elizabeth, Katherine, and Markham sat
down to dinner that night that Edward's continued absence
was remarked upon. Elizabeth asked Matthew if he would
kindly go up and tell their uncle that they awaited his presence before beginning the evening meal. Matthew had not been
gone long when he returned not with Uncle Edward, but with
a distinctly bemused expression and a note addressed to
Farthington's eldest niece.

"Oh, dear!" Elizabeth's hand flew to her cheek with foreboding as she opened the message.

"Read it aloud, Lizzie!" her sister urged. Automatically,
Elizabeth began:

My Dear Niece,

*A Most Important Engagement in London that I had
heretofore Forgotten was remembered by Me last Night
after You and your Sister had gone to bed. Not wishing
to Wake you, I leave you this Note instead to tell you
that I have Gone. I know you would not Wish me to
ignore this Matter of Grave Importance, so ask that you
will convey my Apologies to my Guests, the Duke of
Bellingham and that Markham Fellow* (here Mr. Markham was seen to smile) *and tell them—tell them—*
(inspiration seemed to have failed Uncle Edward, Elizabeth thought, for in the end he decided on)—*oh, tell
them Something Polite! You'll know how to do that,
because you have a lot of your Father's Kindness and
your Mother's Gentle Beauty in you—I've seen it these
past few weeks. Your sisters, on the other hand, take
after our Great-Aunt Agatha, for a more Tart-Tongued
Old Lady never lived*—(Mr. Markham guffawed at the
look of chagrin that crossed Katherine's face, and she
turned her full glare upon him as Elizabeth hastily continued) *but there; That's another Story.*

*At any rate, I am Sure that the Duke will be Well in
no time, and Eager to return to London, as I am.*

(Markham noted with interest that Elizabeth frowned at the thought, and smiled.) *That's a devilish place you girls live in—Cold and Draughty and Dirty and Dull, except for the Ghost. Don't imagine I'll be able to get anyone to buy it. Pity.*

> *Regards, your Affectionate Uncle,*
> *Edward Farthington*

"Well!" By the time she was finished reading the note, Elizabeth's cheeks were pink and her eyes sparkled. She balled the offending piece of paper up in her hand. "Of all the—*affectionate uncle*, indeed! That old—old—"

"Makebait," Katherine supplied, when her sister seemed in danger of exploding without the proper word.

"Yes!"

"Worm," Katherine tried.

"Yes!"

"Gudgeon!" Katherine was warming to the task, but Elizabeth, suddenly recalling herself, shook her head at her sister.

"Really, Katherine," Elizabeth said.

"Well, he is!" Katherine insisted.

"I do not believe," Elizabeth used her best big-sister voice, which never failed to irritate Katherine completely, "that what Uncle Edward is—or isn't—is of any interest to Mr. Markham."

"Not at all," Markham said politely, his lips showing only a slight twitch. "I beg you, do not discontinue your discussion on my account!"

Katherine showed no intention of doing so, but Elizabeth, frowning deeply, ignored her as she once again addressed their guest. "I believe, Mr. Markham, that my uncle has placed you and George—I mean, Bellingham—I mean, the duke—in a very awkward position."

Markham inclined his head in agreement. Katherine, her mind still filled with all the epithets she'd reserved for years for her uncle, gazed from one to the other in surprise. "What do you mean?" she asked.

Elizabeth tried to explain. "Well, you see, Kate," she

said, her words for her sister, her worried gaze on Markham, "the gentlemen came here as Uncle Edward's guests—"

"Yes, well." Katherine shrugged. "I imagine they'd rather stay as our guests. Wouldn't you?"

She was gazing at Markham with such happy expectation that he could not disappoint her. Yes, he said, that might be what he would rather; but the world being what it was . . .

"Pooh!" Kate snapped her fingers and laughed at their concern. "As if the world cares at all what happens at Farthington Hall!"

Markham, who knew just how much the world might care, regarded her thoughtfully as he sat, rubbing his chin and thinking deeply. At last he turned toward Elizabeth.

"Of course, with Miss Poole here . . ." he suggested.

Elizabeth nodded.

"And no one would expect you to turn an injured man from your door—"

Again Elizabeth nodded. Katherine said comfortably that they could all be glad that the duke wouldn't be injured for so very long, after all. . . .

At that Markham turned his thoughtful gaze toward her.

"Oh, no, Miss Farthington," he said, once again rubbing his chin in that considering way. "I believe you are mistaken. A wound such as old George suffered—well, who knows?"

Surprised, Katherine said that she had understood it was only a minor wound, the veriest scratch. . . . She paused and watched the silent message being exchanged between her sister and their guest before Markham once again addressed her.

"You never know, Miss Farthington," he said. "You just never know."

Chapter
Twenty-eight

ONLY TWO PEOPLE in the house were more surprised than Katherine to hear that what had been described to her as a scratch might develop into a more serious injury. The first was Miss Poole, and the second, the duke himself.

Knowing very well that that was how it would be, after dinner Markham went in search of both people.

He found Miss Poole in the library, and after ascertaining politely that she could be interrupted without damaging her schedule or her work, he gave her his most attractive smile as he informed her of their host's defection. Miss Poole put down the quill she had been holding and said, "I see."

Picking it up again, she favored him with her most direct stare as she said, "Then I imagine you have come to tell me that you and the duke will be leaving tomorrow. Most kind of you, I'm sure."

No, no; hastily he disclaimed. She had misunderstood. He only wanted her to understand that Farthington was gone, but he and the duke must linger on until his friend's wound was quite healed.

"Pish," said Miss Poole.

"I beg your pardon?" He thought he heard wrong. No one ever said "pish" to Mr. Markham.

"I believe, sir, that I was told your friend's injury is minor," Miss Poole said.

"Yes, but sometimes these things are worse than they first appear," he countered.

"Posh," said Miss Poole.

Mr. Markham goggled at her before a slow smile crept across his lips and ascended to his eyes.

"I believe, Miss Poole," he said with a deep bow, "that you and I should talk."

The governess rose from behind the desk and motioned him to the largest of the two chairs placed comfortably beside the fire. "In that case—" she said, and took the other chair, sitting straight-backed in it as she regarded him with composure, "—talk."

It was odd, Markham mused, that once issued that open invitation he should find it so very hard to do so. "You see—" he began, then stopped and thought. "The thing is—" he tried again.

Miss Poole, after giving him several chances, decided to take the conversation into her own capable hands.

"Mr. Markham," she said, her eyes fixed on his own, "what are your intentions here?"

"My—" Startled, he leaned back into the chair before that slow smile once again creased his face. "Miss Poole," he said, his tone solemn, "you are a remarkable woman."

"Pish posh," said the remarkable Miss Poole, and waited. As he continued to grin at her, she prodded him again. "Your intentions?"

"Completely honorable."

Miss Poole humphed. "Over the years, Mr. Markham, I have found that 'honorable' means different things to different people."

He laughed. "It means what it says, to me."

Miss Poole nodded. "Well, yes," she said, surprising him as she continued to regard him thoughtfully. "And if you mean by that word that I have no need to fear for my charges' virtue, I do believe you. But for their affections—"

Her voice trailed off as Markham leaned forward in his chair.

"Their affections?" he asked. Miss Poole pursed her lips.

"Miss Poole," Markham said, "let me ask *you* a question."

She raised her eyebrows, cocked her head, then nodded.

"What do you consider an appropriate time for a couple to know each other before becoming betrothed?"

Miss Poole's eyebrows rose farther, and her eyes drifted to the left as she thought. "I have always," she said at last, "thought that a year is a very good length of time."

"*A year?*"

Mr. Markham looked so discomfitted that the governess was hard put not to laugh. Instead she discomfitted him further by saying, "I take it, Mr. Markham, that we are talking here about yourself and Katherine."

"Well, yes, but—" Markham rose and took a hasty turn around the room before returning to lean on the back of the chair he had so recently vacated. "A *year?*"

Miss Poole pursed her lips. "I was talking, Mr. Markham, in generalities. If we are talking in particulars—say, you and Katherine—" She looked at him for confirmation and he nodded, leaning forward eagerly, "—then I would say—a month."

"A month!" He came round the chair to take her hand and shake it warmly. "That's what I thought—a month. Of course, if Katherine will think so . . ." Some of the joy went out of his face. "She is very unpredictable, your Katherine. And I don't even know if she returns my feelings—although I have hopes—"

He looked at her for confirmation, but Miss Poole, who had made a very accurate assessment of her second charge's emotions, only gazed back at him, believing that a little unsureness might be a very good thing for this normally in-charge man.

"And your friend?" she asked, changing the subject.

"What?" Markham's thoughts were still on his own problems, and he had little time for the duke.

"Your friend? What are his intentions?"

"Oh. George." He waved his best friend's own nuptial plans away. "He loves Elizabeth, of course. It was love at first sight, in fact. Always a romantic soul, old George."

"Yes. Well." Miss Poole frowned. "Elizabeth has told me that there was a woman in London—"

With difficulty Markham focused on his friend's romance, seeing by her face that Miss Poole was more than a little concerned. "Oh. That. She didn't hold a candle to Elizabeth. He's very well out of it."

"That may very well be." Miss Poole's tone was tart, and now Markham gave her his full attention. "But would Elizabeth be very well out of it if you and your friend were to leave tomorrow and never be heard from again?"

Hastily he assured her that that was not the case. "George is a good man, Miss Poole," he told her. "The best I've ever known. He has a kind heart, and I've always thought that if he could find someone who could love him as he himself loved—"

Miss Poole held up her hand and gave a nod of satisfaction. She said that that was rather how she, herself, had read the situation, but she wanted to be sure before allowing something that might hurt her charges and friends. . . .

"Don't you mean your children, Miss Poole?" He asked the question gently and was touched by the arrested look in her eye.

"Well, yes," she said, her voice gruff as she gave a little sniff. "They are the children of my heart, to be sure."

"And they love you." She looked gratified, and Mr. Markham was moved to add, "I can see why."

"Pish," Miss Poole said and rose, indicating the end to their interview.

Markham had expected that to be his most difficult interview, so he was surprised when he found that, after informing the duke that he was much more badly hurt than he'd first thought, George proved inclined to argue.

"Dash it, Nicholas," his normally good-natured friend said, frowning at him from his place in the bed where he sat, propped up by pillows and resplendent in a green dressing gown. "I don't want to be invalided here forever! What will Elizabeth think?"

At mention of Elizabeth, Markham pointed out that the duke would receive a great deal of sympathy. The duke's frown grew.

"I don't want her to feel sorry for me!" he snapped. "I want her to—" He stopped suddenly and looked away. Markham finished the sentence for him.

"Love you, George?"

The duke continued to look away from him, and Markham smiled as he sank down onto his friend's bed. "Well, I think she already does."

"You do?" The eager words proved he now had Bellingham's full attention, and Markham grinned.

"I do. But—" He raised a hand to prevent his friend pelting him with the questions that rose quickly to his mind, "—what good will it do, if we have to remove from here before you can press your suit?"

Much struck, the duke said that he would ask Elizabeth to marry him tomorrow. Markham looked at the bedpost and said Miss Poole considered a year a very good amount of time for a couple to know each other before proposing marriage. . . .

"A *year?*" His friend's reaction was much like Markham's, except that the duke so far forgot himself as to try to stand, wincing at once as his injured leg hit the floor.

"There," Markham said, helping Bellingham get the leg comfortably back onto the bed again. "You see. You *are* hurt more than you thought."

"No, no," George started to protest, "it was just a foolish, clumsy thing to do—" He met his friend's eyes, read the message there, and sighed. "Think a moment, Nick," he said tiredly, "I can't pretend to be laid up by this scratch for a year!"

"No, but a few more weeks—"

"A few weeks isn't a year!"

"No, but they'd take us past a month of being here, and Miss Poole says that in our cases, a month ought to be enough!" Markham was grinning at him, and the duke found himself torn between the relief he felt at hearing he wouldn't be expected to wait a year to press his suit and an urgent desire to box his friend's ears for even for a moment putting him through the trauma of believing that he might. He compromised on threatening the latter, and Markham's grin grew.

"Dash it, Nick, it's going to be mighty boring, lying up here by myself!"

"I imagine Elizabeth Farthington might be cajoled into relieving your boredom," Markham soothed.

The duke frowned. "And what will you be doing while I'm playing the invalid?"

Markham said that he had a great deal to keep himself busy.

"I hope she leads you a merry chase," George said. "And I wish old Farthington had peppered your leg, instead of mine." He paused, and in spite of himself, his frown lifted. "You know, Nicholas, I just realized—peppered soup, peppered leg, and now—" He gazed in speculation at his friend. "With any luck at all, peppered you!"

A laughing Markham bade him good-night and was almost to the door when the duke raised another objection.

"You know, Nicholas," Bellingham said. Markham, looking up, was surprised to see the laughter had quite disappeared from the other man's face. "It's getting on toward Christmas."

"Yes?" Markham's eyebrows rose. Rarely was the duke one to remark on the calendar.

"My Grandmother—your esteemed Godmama—is expecting us at Christmas."

"So she is." The tone was noncommittal, but the duke noted the arrested gleam that had crept into Markham's eyes. He had not been thinking of the dowager duchess.

"In fact, she is expecting us early."

"She is?"

George grinned. "She always expects us early. Every year! You know that as well as I!"

"Well . . ." Markham thought deeply. After several moments he snapped his fingers, and the duke waited in expectation. "I tell you what, George!" Markham said. "You must write her a letter. Tell her we'll be a little late arriving this year."

It was apparent Markham thought the problem solved, but Bellingham was appalled. Protesting that he never wrote letters, he said he wouldn't know how to begin; he wouldn't know what to say; the dowager duchess would be displeased; no matter what he said, it would make the old lady suspicious. . . .

A burst of sudden inspiration struck, and his brow lightened as he suggested that Nicholas should write her instead.

"Oh, no," Markham said, shaking his head as he took a couple of backward steps toward the door. "No, no, no!"

"Yes," the duke pleaded. "Yes, yes, yes!"

"She's your Grandmother—"

"She's your Godmama—"

"She'll believe you. You never lie to her."

"She'll believe you, because you do it so well!"

Markham, aware that this argument could go on forever without getting them anywhere, looked into his friend's determined face and tried to effect a compromise. "I tell you what," he said, watching the duke closely. "What say we both write her?"

George, his head tilted to the left, was suspicious as he considered the question. "Does that mean that you'll write her?"

"Of course," Markham said. "And you?"

"I will if you will." The duke continued to give his friend his complete attention.

"Good." Markham's head bobbed up and down, glad that was settled. "Good."

"You'll write her tomorrow?" the duke pressed.

"If you will."

"Oh, I will!" Bellingham raised one hand into the air, as if taking an oath. "Of course. And you?"

"Of course! Well then," Markham beamed, "good-night, George."

"Good-night, Nicholas. Don't forget. You'll write tomorrow."

"Of course."

"Of course."

Chapter
Twenty-nine

MR. MARKHAM WAS right in one thing, at least—the Duke of Bellingham was not destined to spend his convalescence alone in his room. In fact, so solicitous was Elizabeth of "poor George's" health and well-being that the duke was moved, after the first few days, to protest that she must have other things to do. He told her that while he liked nothing better than having her with him, he did not want to take her away from her duties, or have her slaving over them late at night, when he slept. . . .

The latter thought seemed to have such a powerful effect on him that Elizabeth could only smile, and blush, and assure him it was no such thing; he was her first concern, and—and—

"Really, Elizabeth?" the duke questioned. The happiness leaping into his eyes caused her to turn away as she said, with only the barest catch in her voice, that of course; at least, until he went away. . . .

Bellingham almost pressed his suit then, but Miss Poole was present. Remembering his friend's caution that Miss Poole felt he had not known Miss Farthington long enough to propose to her, the duke held his tongue, merely saying that well, yes, that wouldn't be for some time, he was sure. . . .

"Really, George? I mean—your grace?" Elizabeth replied, acting for all the world as if he hadn't caught hold of her hand several moments ago, and still retained it.

Miss Poole, watching them with a tolerant eye, grinned,

and took herself off to watch the more interesting of her charges. She was not disappointed.

If Katherine and Mr. Markham were not arguing over her Thunderer's ability to best his horse in a *fair*—and it was Katherine who, a martial light in her eye, always stressed *fair*, for, as she was willing to tell anyone willing to listen, she had been bested by Markham in an earlier race only because he got off to a head start—race, they were absorbed in a grudge match of chess, or a hand of piquet, which Katherine was determined to conquer to the point where she could beat her skilled partner. Since Markham often teased her that no really wise instructor could be expected to teach his pupil *everything* he knew, she did on occasion repair to the duke's room, to seek his advice. She soon found, however, that while the duke, himself a capable player, was perfectly willing to help her, his mind seemed to wander too often to do her any good.

Katherine and Markham were out riding when Kate, her mind on Bellingham and her sister, assumed an air of disinterest and, not looking directly at her companion, remarked that there seemed to be the scent of orange blossoms in the air.

Since it was December and the air only smelled cold—and decidedly cold, at that—to her companion, he looked at her in surprise.

"Miss Farthington," he asked, leaning forward, "are you feeling quite the thing?"

Katherine regarded him with disgust. "Of course, I'm feeling quite the thing!" she countered. "I was referring to your friend."

"To George?" Markham's surprise increased. He thought. "George is—smelling of orange blossoms?" he tried. "My goodness! He must be more critical than I thought!"

Katherine's disgust grew. "No, no!" she said. "I am not really talking about orange blossoms at all! I am talking about—you know—April and May—"

"Miss Farthington," Markham informed her, "it is December."

"Oh, for goodness sakes!" Katherine gave an impatient jerk on her reins and her horse started. Soothing the animal with one hand, she glared at Markham as she said, "If you are so very dense, I suppose I will have to explain—"

"I wish you would," Markham agreed. Katherine's glare increased.

"I am talking," she said, "about your friend and my sister. About the way they are always holding hands, when they think no one will see, and giggling, and saying those silly, inane things, and about—about—about being in love!"

Glad it was out, Katherine looked away. Markham, continuing to regard her in surprise, said at last, "Tell me, Miss Farthington—is that what you think love is? Holding hands and saying silly things?"

Katherine glanced back, read the question in his eyes and jerked her reins again. This time her horse reared, and a strong fist shot out to bring it down. Katherine's fury was evident as she brought the horse under control again.

"How dare you!" she said.

Mr. Markham's hand had returned to his side, and his stare was enigmatic. "I doubt, Miss Farthington," he said, the words coming slow as he continued to regard her, "that there is very little I would not dare—for you."

Katherine gulped, and her eyes widened in surprise as he grinned. "Now," he teased, "who is saying silly and inane things?"

Katherine averted her head. "If you are not going to be serious—" she began. Instantly his face changed, and his hand reached out to turn her chin toward him.

"Katherine," he told her, "I have never been more serious."

"Oh." She gulped again, and a new thought struck her. "You used my name!"

"Ah, yes, 'Kate of my consolation,' " he sighed, and well-read Katherine knew at once where the quote was from.

"I am _not_ a shrew!" she challenged.

He laughed. "You recognize the Shakespeare."

"Nor," she said, her nose in the air, "am I an idiot."

"Oh, no my dear," he laughed again. "That you are not. At least," he amended, as she began to look appeased, "not in most things!"

"Oh!" said Katherine, and applied her heels to her horse's sides, leading Markham—as the duke had wished—a merry chase all the way home. And Markham, who had hoped to finish his references to Shakespeare's work with, "Will you, nil you, I will marry you," found when he followed her into the Hall yard that the time was past for romantic declarations. His lady now was crowing over their recent race which, she could not help pointing out to him and the duke and Elizabeth and Johns and Matthew and Horton and Chloe and Miss Poole and Mrs. Goodsley and Tom—who just happened to stop by—*she* had won.

"Serves you right," George roasted him, enjoying Katherine's triumph almost as much as she. Markham, nodding, supposed it did.

It was six weeks after the gentlemen had arrived, and only ten days before Christmas, when a carriage pulled up outside Farthington Hall one blustery day and an imposing figure stepped down, ably aided by two footmen and a lady's maid, as the coachman looked helpfully on.

"So!" said the figure as she surveyed the Hall, one hand going up to right her bonnet as a twist of December wind scurrying around the side of the house did its best to rip the hat from her head. "*This* is Farthington Hall."

"Yes, my lady," dutifully answered the coachman, even though the woman had uttered the sentence for effect. She ignored her driver as she instructed one of her footmen to announce her. The servant leaped forward and beat a heavy tattoo on the door as the lady followed him up the shallow steps at a far more leisurely pace. Even then she was forced to wait several moments before the door swung open, and a young face peered out at her with interest.

"The Dowager Duchess of Bellingham," the footman intoned. Chloe, impressed by his lofty accents, gaped at the visitors in wonder.

"There, there now, child," a voice from behind the woman in the giant bonnet said with authority. "Stand aside and let my lady in, before she catches her death of cold." Chloe, finding the authority in the voice matched that of Miss Poole's, did as she was told. The dowager duchess sailed into the Hall, followed by her attendants.

"I," the white-haired woman said, gazing down at Chloe

from her imposing height, "am the Dowager Duchess of Bellingham. And you are—" She held out a hand and Chloe touched it gingerly, making a truly credible curtsy for one with so little experience. She breathed her name and the dowager duchess's face softened.

"So, Chloe Farthington," she said, gazing around the Hall again, "are you any relation to that odious Edward Farthington who has been hanging on the coatskirts of society forever?"

"He is our uncle and guardian," Chloe said, committing the word 'odious' to memory. The duchess's nose wrinkled in distaste.

"Is he now?" Her arched eyebrows rose.

"We don't like him either," Chloe confided, unknowingly disarming the lady, who smiled.

"And does your uncle not give you enough money to hire servants to open the doors and take people's cloaks?" the duchess demanded, at which her footmen hurried to divest her of her outer garments. When her cloak and gloves were removed, her hat tenderly placed in the care of her second footman, and her maid had assured her that her hair was not mussed—not a might—she was better able to hear Chloe's explanation. Horton was in the kitchen shelling walnuts for Mrs. Goodsley's Christmas breads, Matthew had been sent to the village, and Miss Poole had gone up to the squire's—

"Yes, well, my dear, that's all very interesting," the duchess said, walking by the little girl and giving her a friendly pat on the shoulder, "although who those people are I have no idea—"

Chloe started to explain, and the duchess patted her shoulder again. "The person I would really like to see," she said, raising her chin, "is my grandson."

"Your grandson?" Chloe's forehead wrinkled.

"The Duke of Bellingham, child!" A horrid thought struck the duchess, and her eyes grew anxious. "He *is* here, isn't he?"

Chloe assured her he was, and the relieved duchess smiled. "And where is he?" she questioned.

Chloe, glad to be able to help this imposing creature, pointed to the music room and offered to fetch him. The dowager duchess would have none of it.

"No, no, child," she said, giving Chloe's shoulder yet another pat. "Richard will announce me." Nodding to one footman, she swept down the hall. Chloe watched as the duchess gave yet another nod, and the footman threw the music room doors open, intoning once more, "The Dowager Duchess of Bellingham."

Impressed, Chloe would have been even more so had she seen the effect those five words had on the room's inhabitants. Elizabeth, who had been playing the piano, stopped suddenly, her mouth and eyes forming wide "O"'s. The duke so far forgot himself as to bound out of his chair, hastily setting down the glass of wine he'd been sipping as he limped forward with a "Grandmama!" that was so filled with guilt and foreboding that the dowager almost giggled with glee.

Instead she said, "George," in a voice that Elizabeth later said nearly made her sink, and gave him a slight nod as he kissed her cheek.

"Grandmama," George said, "I am so surprised—I didn't expect—" Under her sardonic gaze, he drew himself together and said, "That is—I'm pleased of course, but—*what are you doing here?*"

"What am I doing here, George?" the dowager duchess parried. "Why, wherever would I be? When I send word to my grandson's lodgings requesting to be told why he has not yet returned to Bellingham for the holidays, and I hear that he was injured—injured!—in the north, and has not yet returned to town. . . ." The words trailed off, and she let her gaze slowly rake her grandson, who gulped.

"My leg," he said feebly, pointing downward. The duchess's eyebrows rose for effect.

"It does not seem to unduly pain you, my love," she purred.

"Yes, well—" An anxious George found it suddenly overheated in the music room, and pulled out his handkerchief to mop his brow. "I was coming home for Christmas—really I was!—I was saying to Nick just this morning that we should be making arrangements—"

"Nicholas!" The dowager duchess snapped her fingers. "Aha! I *knew* Nicholas would be tied up in this—"

Just then the source of her "Aha!" entered the room,

accompanied by a laughing Katherine. Their arms were full
of greenery, and Katherine was calling, "Elizabeth, look
what we found—" but her words trailed off as Markham
stopped suddenly and stared, the armful of greenery he held
slipping to the floor.

"Godmama!" he said in far from welcoming tones. His
eyes found George's, and he looked ready to murder his
friend. "Didn't you write her—" he began.

George, frowning back, said he'd thought Nicholas was
going to take care of that, and when he'd thought about it, he
hadn't seen any reason for them both to write. . . .

The dowager duchess almost could forgive them for the
journey, she was enjoying their discomfiture so much. Ignoring their conversation, she said, "Nicholas, Nicholas, Nicholas. So good to see you, too." She held out a hand and
automatically he moved forward to take it, placing a kiss upon
her wrist with rare grace. Katherine, watching wistfully, wished
that she might be in the duchess's shoes. Something of her
thoughts must have shown on her face, for the duchess smiled
quite kindly at her.

"Yes," the old woman approved, enjoying center stage,
"he does that quite well, doesn't he?"

Startled, Katherine colored. Her blush increased as Markham, understanding what had passed between the two women,
grinned.

"I wouldn't know," Katherine said, her nose in the air.
She colored further as Markham, low voiced, said he would
be happy to seek her opinion.

"Hmmph!" the duchess interjected, to prevent his mind
from wandering farther and to redirect his attention to where
it belonged—with her. "I have no doubt that in time someone
will tell me what is going on here."

"Oh, I don't know—" Markham began. The duchess favored him with a rare stare, and he shrugged as the duke,
begging Nick to keep quiet, hurried forward to ask if she
wouldn't like to be seated. Regally she said that she would,
but since no one had earlier asked her—

Hastily four younger voices were raised urging her to take
this chair or that; seeing the bottle of port on the small table
next to the chair George had recently vacated, she chose that

one and poured herself out a glass before inviting them to tell their stories, if they dared.

She sat waiting expectantly as George, after several false starts, turned with real appeal toward Markham. The latter, rolling his eyes, took Katherine's hand and led her forward. "My lady," he said, "may I present Miss Katherine Farthington."

The duchess said that he could and inclined her head as Katherine essayed a curtsy not quite as impeccable as Chloe's. The duchess frowned.

"And Elizabeth!" George said, squeezing the young woman's hand for support as he helped her from the piano bench and led her toward his grandmother. "This is Elizabeth Farthington, Grandmother!"

Elizabeth's curtsy was pure grace, and the dowager duchess relaxed. Katherine sighed in envy. Markham, amused, told her there were other things she did well. Katherine frowned at him.

"I am pleased to make your acquaintance, I'm sure," the duchess said, nodding at both young women. "But I still don't understand what these two scamps are doing here. Unless your presence means that repulsive Edward Farthington is your host—although why you'd be guests of his . . ." She frowned from her grandson and his friend to the sisters and back again. "Perhaps if you'd fetch your chaperone—"

Markham cleared his throat and had started, "Well, you see, my lady," when a quiet voice from the doorway said clearly, "I am here." Miss Poole, newly arrived and having received a garbled version of what was happening from the overawed Chloe, had hurried at once to the rescue.

The dowager duchess stared hard at the woman in the doorway, at her twice-mended dress and her hair wrapped in neat braids that several times circled her head, and her forehead furrowed. "And you are?" the duchess asked.

"I am Miss Poole," the woman said, walking forward until she stood square in front of their guest. She made a curtsy that showed to a nicety that she knew her station and made no apologies for it. "I believe, my lady, that it would be good if we were to talk."

"Oh you do, do you?" the duchess retorted, staring hard at

Miss Poole. The duke, fearing his grandmother was about to get on the high ropes for which she was famous, made a slight movement that the dowager waved away in irritation.

"Oh, go away, George, and take your friends and my people with you!" she commanded, her eyes returning to Miss Poole's face. "This—lady—" The hesitation was fractional, but there was a relieved sigh as she said the word, "—and I have to talk."

It was never known what passed between Miss Poole and the dowager duchess, but when the four people waiting anxiously in the hall were readmitted to the music room nearly an hour later, it was to find both women in good humor, the duchess calling for champagne so that she might make a toast.

"A toast, Grandmama?" George said as he took the hands she held out to him.

"Of course a toast, you silly boy!" the dowager duchess chuckled. "What kind of grandmother would I be if I didn't toast the betrothals of yourself and Nicholas here?"

"*Betrothals?*" echoed four voices. The duchess grinned at them.

"You *are* going to be married, aren't you?" she asked.

"Well, yes—" started Bellingham and Markham, as "Well, no—" came from the Farthington sisters.

Elizabeth and Katherine stared at George and Nicholas in surprise. "Well, *yes?*" they asked.

"Well, *no?*" the men cried.

The dowager said with satisfaction that it was a very good thing she'd come, for it was apparent that the two men had no idea how to manage their affairs and needed her to help them along. She was interrupted in her self-congratulations by Elizabeth, who, white-faced, stepped resolutely forward to say, "I am sorry, my lady, and I mean no disrespect, but not for the world would I have you force George—into a union—he does not want. . . ." Her words trailed off, and tears spilled over her brimming eyelids as George, much moved, took her in his arms to tell her that their union was what he wanted with his whole heart, his whole being; that she was the center of his universe, and he could not imagine life without her; that—that—

He was stopped by the sight of Elizabeth's rapturous face, raised to his. "Really, George?" she breathed.

"Yes, *really*, George," his grandmother said, with quite another meaning. The duchess turned her attention to Katherine, who was standing a bit apart from Markham, not looking at him as he tried in vain to catch her eye.

"And you," the duchess said, "you're going to marry Nicholas, aren't you? Not that I would if I were you, but there never is any accounting for tastes. . . ."

Nicholas thanked her dryly as Katherine remained silent.

"Well?" the dowager duchess demanded. Katherine lifted her chin.

"I," she said, "have not been asked."

"Spunk!" The duchess gave her dry crackle of laughter. "I like spunk." With one wave of her hand, she bade Nicholas take his lady off somewhere and ask her, adding kindly that Elizabeth might like to be asked, too. When the four stood, still staring at her, she waved at them again, saying, "Oh, hurry, do! Miss Poole tells me you eat early in this forsaken place, and I wish to make my toast before dinner. Now go. Do. Shoo!" She had to wave them away with both hands before Markham, at last recognizing that she meant what she said, grabbed Katherine's hand and half-led, half-pulled her toward the library, where he took down the Farthington's copy of *The Taming of the Shrew* and, holding it toward her, said, "What it says."

Katherine raised her nose. "I," she said, knowing she had said these words before, "am not a shrew."

Markham laughed. "No, my love. You are my infuriating, baffling, entrancing, adorable—"

By now he had her in his arms, and she had to turn her face against his coat so she could crane her neck up to him. "What did you say?" she demanded.

He thought. "Entrancing?"

"No."

"Adorable?"

"No."

He thought he understood, and grinned. "Well, now,

love," he said. "You know you *can* be a tad infuriating, at times—"

"There!" Katherine crowed. "You said it again!"

A surprised Markham told her that if he'd known she enjoyed being called infuriating, he would have told her any time these past six weeks. . . . Katherine shook her head.

"No," she said, eyes closed as she snuggled contentedly against his chest. "Love. You called me your love."

He smiled, and dropped a quick kiss upon her hair. "And so you are, my dear. And so you are."

A quick look at Elizabeth's face when they rejoined the dowager duchess, Miss Poole, and Chloe in the music room a prompt half hour later convinced Katherine that her sister's time had been as pleasurably spent as her own, and she smiled.

"Ah, there you are," the duchess greeted them. "I have just been telling Miss Poole and Chloe here about how you all must come to Bellingham for Christmas. And we have been planning your weddings—"

Firmly Markham said that he and Katherine would like to plan their own wedding, thank you, and he rather imagined that George and Elizabeth would like to do the same. Taking heart from his friend's courage, the duke said that yes, they would. He was rewarded by the soft light that shone in Elizabeth's eyes. Turning back to his grandmother, he gulped, for her eyes held quite another light, but she contented herself, as Horton brought in a tray carrying the Hall's best champagne and glasses, with a compromising, "We will see."

"Yes," Markham said, lifting Katherine's hand to his lips, "we will."

"Yes," echoed the duke, busily engaged at the same task with Elizabeth, "indeed we will."

And they did.